Beulah Land

Krista McGruder

BEULAH LAND

The Toby Press

First edition, 2003

The Toby Press *LLC*
POB 8531, New Milford, CT. 06676-8531, USA
& POB 2455, London WIA 5WY, England
www.tobypress.com

ISBN 1 59264 027 3, *hardcover*

A CIP catalogue record for this title
is available from the British Library

Typeset in Garamond by Jerusalem Typesetting

Printed and bound in the United States by
Thomson-Shore Inc., Michigan

Because of Tiger John Miller

Thou shalt no more be termed Forsaken;
neither shall thy land any more
be termed Desolate: but thou shalt be called Hephzibah,
and thy land Beulah:
for the Lord delighteth in thee...

Isaiah 62:4–5

Contents

Divination

H

e never thought he would buy hay in July. Late September, sure, if he'd been too ambitious with the number of head and too generous with bales he paid the boys in exchange for their time and equipment. Late August, maybe. It had happened once, thirty-four years earlier when television transmitted images of steamy jungles and screaming planes dropping napalm. He had wondered if his crew, kids who hadn't been around to bale for him, were among those zipped into standard-issue body bags by medics who didn't look old enough to drive, much less to be collecting fingers, toes, and ears to accompany bodies into coffins. He hadn't complained when he bought a few bales, it was a small expenditure compared to what some families had paid, coaxing rabbit ear antennae into position, lips muttering as if reciting prayers.

Gerald was only into mid-July; barely past sitting up nights with a garden hose and hoping sparks from bottle rockets would not settle on the barn. A nearly empty barn, but an investment and reminder that most years he'd had enough grass for grazing and baling. Enough rain. Enough money.

The barn had survived exploding dangers from kids who also risked blowing off body parts. The season's casualties were limited to cats—an agriculture student at Vinita High School having been arrested on cruelty charges for igniting sparklers inside the creatures' rectums. The animals were owned by the granddaughter of a state senator, a skinny student at Oklahoma University. The biology student volunteered for the state wildlife department counting dead fish and turtles in the area creeks, additional victims of the drought.

Gerald watched the skinny girl in a local news segment preceding the weather. She stood outside the veterinarian clinic, an aluminum building coated by dust, and explained one cat lost a rear leg, the other its bowel control. The girl's face looked like an aged and dirty sheet. She said she hadn't slept since she found her bloody pets biting at themselves. When the news reporter asked the girl what should happen to the accused boy, her face smoothed, like a thin lacy veil falling over her head. "I'd love the honor of personally administering the same treatment to him," she replied.

The girl's face left the screen and Gerald attentively listened to the weather forecast. The meteorologist concluded with remarks about history-making records and offered a few predictions. Gerald thought about the biology girl and how different she was from girls he'd grown up knowing, with round cheeks and bottoms, all smiles and hellos waiting on him in the diner or bank. He wondered why someone in college with a politician in the family would spend summer in the mud collecting stinking carcasses, instead of going with boys and drinking spiked punch at parties. Perhaps the drought had dried up parties and punch. The newscast ended and he turned off the television. Seated at the kitchen table, he wrote a check to the girl and addressed the envelope care of her grandfather. She might use the money for her cats or the campaign she was starting for tougher animal cruelty laws. He signed his name, Gerald Richter, before noting the ledger total. Reconsidering, he braced his stub against the forefinger of his good right hand, gripping the dry paper. Then he remembered the girl's crumpled face. He felt like a desert cowboy, emptying a leaking canteen into a dead horse's mouth.

Years of familiarity with sale barns had not smoothed Gerald's distaste for air imbedded with dust, moldy hay, fecal matter. He stood inside the sale barn office, four sheets of wallboard jointed into a concrete floor. A rubber-coated electric line tacked to the wall powered the fluorescent lighting, a telephone, fax machine, computer and, depending on the season, a fan or space heater. While his eyes adjusted to the dim interior light, the sound of engaged whirring entered his ears. He imagined a swarm of grasshoppers, another plague. He blinked and sniffed, his lungs filled with musty air and he recognized Martha's box fan circulating dry air around the room.

"Too early for your spring calves, Gerald." The woman was apple-shaped, with dyed blonde hair hanging down her back like straw. She had smeared the same lipstick on her mouth for nearly thirty years and Gerald had never decided if her makeup looked more like Pepto-Bismol or pink cake batter. Either way, he liked the looks of her mouth. The pink paste reminded Gerald of how his mother kept his bedroom the same, even after he moved out to get married.

"No calves. I've got four heifers."

"You got cullers? I can put you in touch with a packer, direct. Not a lot of buyers for cullers now."

Martha was helpful to the point of the sale barn's disadvantage because her husband owned the business. She made it known she wanted to quit the cattle auction racket, quit the smelly task of shipping giant, doped beasts to feedlots and packing plants. Martha wouldn't enter the sale barn, telling everyone the office was the closest she came to eating beef.

"No. These aren't for rendering."

"Oh," Martha said. "You've got their papers?"

He produced livestock records of tagging, vaccinations, and inseminations. All were healthy, with properly sloping hindquarters and buyers should rate their frames highly. Gerald had been careful during loading, anticipating penalties buyers assessed for bruised stock. Loading had been successful, but labored, and his good arm ached. His shoulder was out of alignment, throbbing and preventing him from turning his neck. A handicap, but not the worst one he had ever dealt with.

"Jeannette with you?" Martha asked.

"No, she didn't make it."

Martha flipped through the papers. She may have wanted out of the business but she wasn't going to be closed down by the Department of Agriculture for documentation citations. She hated the government and anyone who made a career working for it. Her son, one of the boys zipped into a bag missing body parts.

"These are stockers?" Martha's nose twitched as if she were ridding it of a nuisance.

"Hope so. Never dropped underweight calves." Gerald folded his good hand over the stub.

"We've got more stockers coming in now than usual. Could depress things a bit, you know."

"Yep." Gerald thought of his dry fields, brown grass cropped so low his cattle were grazing dirt.

"How's Jeannette doing?" Martha's head tilted downward as she stamped papers to accompany the sales.

Gerald felt like he was explaining his tardiness to the school, explaining why he checked his trotlines before school. He'd never felt right letting fish hang on the hook through the afternoon. It was a hard thing for the principal to understand and Gerald had spent many hours in detention imagining gill-hooked fish, exhausted at the end of his lines.

"She's fine. She's driving for herself now."

"Tough job. White-line fever."

"She's got the cats. She keeps busy."

"She's always been a good girl. If I've told you once, I've told you a thousand times—"

He interrupted, "I know, I know." While Martha was clever enough to pass remarks with double-meanings, he did not believe she was cruel. Still, her comment always irked him. *You don't need a son with a daughter like Jeannette.*

Gerald turned toward the dusty unloading area, recalling the red circle marking the youngest heifer's forehead. He would rub that spot before she was led away. The marking ran in the line: the females had red blotches running slightly left of center on the foreheads. His wife had owned the first cow, Betty, and had named its offspring Second Betty. Gerald had tagged his cattle numerically for years but guessed he was selling the twentieth or so Betty.

"You tell Jeannette I say hello," Martha shouted after him.

"You bet," Gerald mumbled, then tripped. When he looked at the ground, he saw only the bleached shale driveway, nothing to explain why he had lost his balance.

Vinita had no shortage of mystery. Peculiarity swirled around the town carved out of old Indian Territory, like intermittent flashes of a bright and swinging skirt.

Vinita was host of the Spook light, a nocturnal incarnation rumored to represent the spirit of a white, married woman killed by her jealous Indian lover. Teenagers crowded into cars and sat out late near the abandoned army base where conscripts had taken practice before being shipped off to Normandy. The spectators drank cheap liquor and hoped to get lucky or to glimpse the ghost their parents and grandparents claimed to have seen.

A television program devoted to supernatural phenomena visited each year to update its story about the Spook light. Twice, cameras captured multicolored lights swooping over trees like bright jangling keys of invisible striding giants; once, the cameras caught shining white nodules flickering from the woods. Six other visits had produced nothing television-worthy, prompting the show host's insinuation that his viewing audience lacked sufficient faith to be granted an appearance. "It's not about whether the Spook light *exists*," he had said, facing the camera from inside a wood-paneled studio set. "It's really about the willingness of everyone to *believe*."

The television crew was scheduled to return in early August. Dry, hot weather promised clear skies and, providing the audience possessed enough faith, an appearance of the illuminated woman. To celebrate, the state senator had organized a barbecue to precede taping, inviting elected officials, ministers and farmers to fill the crowd. "To promote tourism," the senator announced during a radio interview, "We'll invite the people of this great nation to see the beauty of this mystery for themselves. What's more, I'm organizing an auction to benefit farmers so desperately in need. We'll have old-fashioned fun and fellowship and watch for the ghost." The state senator paused to clear his throat. "And of course, we'll pray."

The senator's constituents had suffered no shortage of prayer. But after four years of little rainfall, those who still prayed changed the tenor of their messages. Those who still prayed cast aside Sunday School instructions of humility, demanding proof of His divinity lest their allegiances should evaporate.

Those who still prayed crowded into churches, hoping for assurances that doubts about His grace would not push them into a dark canyon with the faithless, doubters who whispered *drought* and *forsaken* as they shuffled into mortgage companies and pool halls.

Each day without rain, each month of falling creek levels, each winter of spitting snow that did not stick—those units of time translated into thin lines on topographic charts depicting the drilling depth to water. The longer the passage without rain, the closer the lines were drawn, reflecting a steeper negative elevation, hidden water shrinking in two dimensions.

Whispers scattered. Extreme dryness called for divination, the witching work of old Indians and carneys. Those who had lost faith in prayer swelled the rumor that Granny Hopper would travel from the Ozarks to divine water. Witching water faithful produced faded photographs of divined wells on their grandparents' farms, testament to the fidelity of old ways.

Gerald heard talk in the coffee shop, listened to acquaintances he'd known for fifty years speak to the possibility.

"There's nothing to lose, far as I can see," Gerald's neighbor confessed after breakfast of eggs, bacon and glasses of whole milk. The men in the brown, cracked vinyl booth had liver-spotted hands and lines cutting their faces, erosion from sun and wind. "I hear her granddaughter handles things. They've made a business out of it."

"You've got to be out of your mind," Gerald replied, thinking of the deposit and charge per foot of drilling.

"Yep, maybe so," the neighbor placed his hand over his coffee. He waited for the waitress to refill the other men's cups then released his words quickly. "But that doesn't change the fact that old man

Beauchamp called her in and she showed him where he could drill and by God there was water. A hundred and thirty feet down. I'll take that bet and be called a crazy man."

"You would be too," Gerald spoke loudly, "if you think some shaker can find water with a tree branch. That's the most goddamned ignorant idea I've heard in a while."

"What about Beauchamp? You telling me they didn't find water on his place?"

"That water would be there whether she said so or not."

"Not saying that. Only saying it took two tries. *Two tries* out of two hundred plus acres and they got water. You can spend a lot more than that getting some Army Corps survey done up for you. What have you got against the idea?"

"Nothing," Gerald replied, then modified his declaration. "No, that's not true. What I've got against it is what I've got against anything wasting time and money. I'm against fakers."

"You against fakers in your own family, then?" Martha's husband was among the gathered men, a reedy fellow with knotty shoulders and arms. He looked at Gerald as he poured artificial sweetener in his coffee. The sale barn owner had given up sugar and drinking ten years earlier when his liver and kidneys were put on notice by his doctor. Martha's husband ate wheat toast, scraping fake butter across the bread slowly, habit formed of careful deprivation.

"What in the hell are you talking about?" Gerald splashed his coffee, felt it pool in the declivity of his stub. He wiped hot liquid from the arm he thought of as abbreviated instead of incomplete.

"Fakers in your family. You're so against them, then how do you feel about fakers in your family?"

"You better tell me what you mean."

"I've buried my parents and my son. It all hurt. It all set me back. And you know the one thing I learned?" Martha's husband leaned his head forward. Light slanted across his forehead, forming patterns from the stenciled letters on the diner's plate glass window. Patterns settled on the face of the sale barn owner, separating his eyes from his nose. His eyes were shadowed and dark and swelled with his words, a brown trickle of hardened sounds.

"Does this have anything to do with paying crazy ladies to wave a stick in your pasture?" Gerald asked.

"No. You can say I'm a hick with no education—and you'd be right. But I've learned that you can get over just about anything except being stupid."

"You haven't answered my question." Gerald choked, the words pinched inside his mouth.

"Never mind, Gerald, never mind." Martha's husband stood, waved his right hand and left with quick, jerky steps.

Gerald sat quietly, hoping the gray walls would crumble under a deluge so he could extend his legs past the collapsed barriers and look over a current of blue water washing heat and dust away.

No one talked about Jeannette Richter unless they thought she was too far away to hear it. A woman who drove her own tractor trailer rig, she was known for favorable opinions toward Democrats and organic, free-range beef. Jeannette played loud country music when she drove around the town square, acting as though she were a teenager. She attended church but never baked or helped clean up after luncheons. She joined the men outside, talking diesel fuel prices and incompetence at weigh stations.

Jeannette was built like a tall willow tree with erect posture and long arms and legs sprouting from her torso, falling sturdily toward the ground. Her eyes were dark gray and she had always resented her parents for their failure to pass along their own clear aqua eyes.

"I'm a mutant," she had announced while studying biology in junior high school. "My amino acids didn't assemble right. My chromosomes are mutated in the spot that makes eye color."

"Your amino acids didn't assemble *correctly*. Or you might say *properly*," Maeve Richter instructed.

"Didn't assemble *correctly*." Jeannette had stared at her mother before she turned away, muttering, "I wonder whose fault that was."

Jeannette came into womanhood early, developing hips and breasts before other girls and growing so tall she had to stoop to board the school bus. She attributed her physical curiosities to moral turpitude at the time of her conception. "You two must have done something really bad to get me, like this," she had asserted the night of her senior prom when Gerald presented her with a corsage. "It ain't everyone who gets the chance to drive to the prom without a date."

Gerald had not spoken as his wife would have, correcting Jeannette's grammar. He employed his good hand to pin the corsage to her pink dress, his daughter's eyes level with his own. "You had offers."

"The two boys who work for you? Not the kind of date I want."

Jeannette grinned, white teeth flashing between her lips. She had used her mother's old red lipstick, Gerald noticed, and her mother's perfume. A scent that smelled like flowers drooping with rain.

"I think you're beautiful."

"That's because you have to, Dad," she replied, leaving him to scratch scabs his stub formed from friction against baling twine. He watched his daughter leave the house and wished his wife were there to apply ointment to his flesh.

The moment Gerald met the woman who would become his wife, he imagined her death, how her skin would flake and drop in slow showers, like pushing a green sycamore through a wood chipper. Guilt, a sticky poison, ran through him—but did not stop him from courting and proposing to the elementary school teacher. Maeve had grown up surrounded by ranchers and wildcatters but had never mixed with them. The daughter of a dentist and a Welcome Wagon volunteer, Maeve was meant to live in air-conditioning, drive a new car every two years and enroll sandy-haired children in Christian day school.

There was nothing on the farm for Maeve.

Gerald married her anyway, the first girl with any prettiness who overlooked the abrupt ending to his left arm and the mortgage attached to his acreage. He had not been unattractive on their wedding day, his square face stretched by a stiff smile, his thick brown hair set in a permanent wave by drugstore hair potion. His wide-set eyes swept across guests in the church pews; compressing them into a small basket of life he planned. It was the only time he would wear a tuxedo jacket, one sleeve empty at its cuff, and his veins had pulsed with the greediness of a boy opening his birthday present.

Less than a year later, Gerald saw hay bales, bags of seed, and cloying clumps of cow manure wearing down his wife. He watched her grimace at dirt on the kitchen linoleum; saw her red eyes when she returned from a trip to her parents' three-story brick home; watched how the birth of their daughter brought only fatigue and money worries.

Rescuing Maeve would have been like relocating deep tree roots to the shifting ocean floor. Gerald could not have spared her for a return to life where fish swam in tanks and not in the live well, waiting to be filleted for dinner. So Maeve had ushered their daughter through the bleeding ritual of womanhood and then acquired colon cancer and a colostomy bag. Gerald believed if anyone had ever contracted cancer because of wishing, it was his wife. Maeve was of rigid Protestant stock for whom the only acceptable way of quitting on a family was dying.

"We consume too much flesh. That is the reason I'm sick." In her last week, Maeve reclined against bed pillows and sipped a puree of carrots a visiting nurse had prepared. "I believe it's a curse haunting us. The way we live rots in us. Oh, we deserve this."

Gerald covered his stub with his good hand. The wicker chair was uncomfortable, unwrapping straws were prickly indicators of household neglect. He would repair the chair when Maeve did not require tending, when time was free to rectify broken fixtures. Guilt settled within him, borne from anticipation of the end of their marital mistake.

"It was eating all that meat." Maeve had moaned and thrown her dish against the painted silver wall, a color she had chosen because she believed other colors showed too much dirt. "It's a judgment on this whole used-up land. You should eat and eat of everything you do and then you can feel like I'm feeling."

Maeve's arms folded across her breasts, two flaps of skin Gerald helped her wash. She excluded her daughter from the business of dying, Gerald believed, because Jeannette was a disappointment.

Maeve had decided her daughter should be denied any comfort of conscience.

Gerald's mind turned the same thought, hundreds of revolutions in a single setting. He could gain nothing by intervening between his wife and daughter. Their burden was a smooth and deep pool that should remain untouched, lest it spill and drown all of them. He sat under the single exposed bedroom light bulb, wishing the room was large enough to accommodate two beds.

Until Maeve's illness they had shared the bed. Afterward, he slept on the couch to avoid disturbing her. Each night, after she drifted to chemically induced unconsciousness, he walked the fifteen feet of hallway to the living room. He drank two or three beers before pulling the quilt his mother had stitched for him across his body, reminding himself to doze lightly in the way children slept the night before Christmas, listening for noises in the house.

They developed a system for night emergencies. Maeve would place her hand on the cowbell resting on a nightstand. If she was too weak to shake the clapper, she was to shove the copper casing. Her husband would run, summoned by the sound of the herder's tool falling against the floor planks, his thudding footfalls overpowering noises of crying regrets.

As Gerald drove home from the diner, the late July sun was gathering strength. Driving over bumpy county roads made him thankful for being born on a farm and being allowed to obtain his full license at fifteen, only a few months before the baling accident. Since then, he'd had only to pass the eyesight exam to renew his driver's license. Every three years he waited in line at the DMV to have his picture made with the empty cuff hanging, the office workers ignoring or overlooking his impairment.

Gerald followed his long gravel driveway, past the short house and stopped in front of the stone well house. He filled five-gallon buckets with the garden hose drawing from the well, taking care not to overfill them. Grasping the handles with his good hand and bracing the bottoms of the receptacles with his stub, he shoved the buckets on the truck bed, four wide, five deep.

The old truck handled smoothly in the packed dirt pasture tracks. Gerald closed the first aluminum gate behind him but left other gates separating his network of pastures open. He had no fields closed for growing because he needed the entire acreage for grazing. Driving past the three empty ponds, he saw cracked bottom mud, the water long evaporated. If rain returned, he would dredge the ponds to deepen capacity. If rain returned, he would dump loamy loads of soil and seed the banks with fescue and clover, inviting growth of blackberries. He would recreate lush grounds, the pretty property that had convinced his wife to take a chance on pastoral life.

Thirty-three head followed the truck, conditioned to understand the results of a passing engine: water filling the troughs, hay filling the feeders, salt and mineral blocks falling under the hickory stand. Early in the summer, Gerald had hauled watering troughs to the south pasture where the stock could rest under hickory shade. Despite the drought, the hickory trees were leafing. The oldest drew enough water to support a full presentation; the youngest sprouted more sparsely, supporting fewer branches.

Gerald stood on the tailgate, pouring water into the tanks. Cows ushered their calves to the troughs slowly, imbued with trust that each would receive sufficient watering. Located on the small stretch of ground between the trees and the south pasture fence, the troughs were shallow and long so even the smallest calves could drink. The mother of the recently sold spotted heifer dipped her head, was the first to shake and clear her nostrils. The Betty looked poor, lacking green grass and fresh rainwater. Still, she had dropped a healthy male in late spring and nursed him nearly to normal weight, her udder's bounty, no doubt, stealing flesh from her chest and haunches. When Gerald remembered, he brought carrots and scattered them, as Jeannette had done as a girl. The heifer sniffed and rolled orange vegetables into her pink lips, eyes blinking, watching him, as though Gerald might take her treats as he had always taken her male offspring.

After he watered the stock, Gerald started digging postholes for his south pasture fence. He thought of boys hired to take Jeannette's place, teenagers who asked for breaks from tasks she had performed without fatigue. Digging fence postholes was the hardest part of the business. At twelve, Jeannette had been strong enough to break the ground alone. She drove the open steel jaws downward and closed the clamp grabbing rocks, weedy roots, and red earth. Lifting the digger, she emptied its contents into the wheelbarrow and dumped the rocks into a pile, insisting someday: she would build a stone fence.

But Jeannette had announced a boycott of all farm activities, even bottle-feeding calves, before Maeve took to her sick bed.

"I don't think it's right to send them away to get killed. Raising them here is certain death." Pushing away the white plate with yellow flowers painted in the center, Jeannette pointed to the dinner meatloaf. "This here is the product of death."

"*This here*," Maeve uttered, flatly. "It's a disgrace that my educated, fourteen-year-old daughter talks like an illiterate cracker."

"Whatever. You know what I meant. The disgrace is eating animals we raise like pets. We should give them a good kick every day, so they understand that we don't love them, that we *hate them*. That way, they won't leave this farm thinking they've been betrayed. They'll get shipped to the slaughterhouse *happy*."

"You're the only beast that deserves to be kicked." Maeve dragged the platter of meatloaf away from her daughter. "You forage for your own food from now on, or eat hay if you've got so much of a better idea about what I should make this family for dinner."

Gerald had not intervened. He understood his failings as a blind person understands imperfections of his lover's skin, palpable markers connecting unknowable flesh tones, notions of shade and color buried inside the consciousness of a man who can only trace distances between shapes of distress. He had sat silently, estimating the cost to hire someone to help him, estimating the working hours to compensate for Jeannette's lost labor.

Jeannette had borne blisters ripping her skin, seed ticks settling in private places, chiggers crawling up her legs. But she had not been able to adopt the farm ethic to nurture calves for slaughter. She quit working for Gerald and took a clerk's job in the feed store. She had ridden her bicycle eight miles each way, pedaling past her pile of stones and Gerald, who would not stop working to wave.

Gerald picked through the remains of his daughter's old stone pile and tossed rocks to shore up the new posts, finished for the day. The sun's low rays angled into his eyes. The day's heat was passing, but he would sweat through the night. He drank hot water from his jug but took no comfort from the liquid.

The dark was creeping from east to west when Gerald drove to the house. Lights shone through the kitchen windows, meaning Jeannette had returned from a trip. Likely, he would find a hot supper inside. Jeannette was a decent cook but only prepared food she enjoyed: roasted vegetables and pastas, simmering fish stews, rice flavored with tiny portions of meat.

Gerald did not complain or ask for fried chicken, mashed potatoes and corn bread. He knew he was thinner than he'd been in the thirty years since his wife died—mostly Jeannette's doing. Even when she went on the road she left healthy, frozen casseroles with non-fat cheeses for her father. They consumed without commentary, never acknowledging deviation from Maeve's kitchen habits.

Jeannette's rig was parked to the side of the gravel driveway, leaving enough space for Gerald's truck to pass. Radio music hit his ears first, then he saw her through the open driver side door. She wore a straw cowboy hat and red tennis shoes, like those she had worn as a child, when she had washed his truck and squirted him with water from the hose.

"What's that music? Anything good?" Her music was a curiosity to him, a sad undertaking, as if she had emptied her feelings on a river, floating for anyone to retrieve.

"It's good," Jeannette grunted, then seemed to relent. "It's Hank."

"Doesn't sound like Hank." Gerald listened closely for a lonesome twang in the noisy competition between the singer and the instruments.

"It's Hank iii. Grandson of Hank. He covers some of his granddaddy's stuff."

"Never heard of him."

"That's the way he likes it. He's a rockabilly, kick-Nashville-in-its-teeth kind of guy." Jeannette brought a cigarette to her lips, drew inward and exhaled. Smoke seeped from her mouth to join an invisible river.

A faint ammonia odor of cat urine emanated from under the bench seat that could be converted to a bed. Jeannette traveled with three cats, maybe more. The cats ate from a pink ceramic dish Maeve had used to set out fruit on a table, fruit that no one ever ate and was always discarded. Gerald imagined the cats curled in balls on Jeannette's chest when she pulled off the road to sleep.

"Since when do you smoke?" he asked.

"I'm forty-five Dad. I'm allowed to smoke."

"Didn't say you weren't."

"You didn't have to say anything."

"Any reason why you started now?"

"I've been started for a while and I only smoke one a day. It's my indulgence. I won't get cancer."

"They're your lungs."

"Don't I know it."

Night smells mixed with cigarette smoke and cat litter. His daughter was wearing perfume. The scent glided past Gerald, a familiar scent with a name he could not remember or may have never known. Air and silence between them, like dark layered earth disguising pockets of water.

"I'm going to call an outfit in here to dig a well in the south forty. I can't keep hauling water. House pump isn't strong enough and it's running dry."

"I know somebody." Jeannette snuffed her cigarette in the ashtray and slid the metal door closed. "I can make a call."

"Who?"

"Outfit about ten miles south. They'll give us a rate. I handle long runs for the owner. They'll probably do it on installment if you need."

"I sold four heifers, I'm not too old to manage my money."

"I'm not saying that. I'm just saying the owner will cut us a rate." Jeannette stretched her arms in front of her.

"What's this guy's name?"

"It's not a guy. It's a woman."

Gerald hesitated. "What's this woman's name?"

"Sheila Lundy."

"Can you give her a call for me? Sooner the better."

"Sure thing." Jeannette yawned and snapped fingers on both hands. "Kitty, kitty. Time to go to bed."

A cat's tail appeared from under Jeannette's seat, switching.

"How many have you got now?"

"Just four."

"*Just* four?"

"I like being the crazy cat lady, Dad. It's one of those clichés."

"You hear about the girl on the news and what happened to her cats?"

"Sure."

"You ever worry about things out on the road? You know, a lot of those guys don't like cats—or women."

"I should know Dad. I'm the one who's been driving."

"Well, aren't you worried?"

"Why do you care now? My career is not a new development. Your concern seems to be."

"I've always been concerned."

"OK." Jeannette switched off the radio. "I think I'll sleep in the cab tonight, Dad. No offense." Inside the house, her bedroom was decorated with fading pink curtains and wallpaper Maeve had chosen.

"No, no offense. You'll call about the drilling?"

"Said I would, didn't I?"

"Thank you." There was no reason for him to continue but he remembered the skinny girl, crying. "I thought you would want to know. I sold a Betty."

"Oh." Jeannette's single syllable fell out of her mouth, tumbling toward him, her breath supporting smooth undertones of accusation. "Which one?"

"Not sure, I've been tagging them so long. Somewhere in the twenties."

"Right."

"I'm too old to change, Jeannette. If I've said it once I've said it a thousand times—"

Jeannette interrupted, placing both hands against her father's head. Her fingers were soft despite hours of clinging to a plastic steering wheel. "I know Dad. *That's what they're for.*"

Turning away from her, Gerald saw the kitchen's light unblocked by movement or shadow. A few steps beyond his daughter's truck, he tripped, catching himself with his good hand against hard-packed gravel. He did not know if Jeannette watched him continue, worn boot soles flapping, as he covered ground separating her from the house.

The next morning, Gerald woke with the sun burning his bald scalp. His bedroom window faced east and he thought of the years he had worked without wearing sunscreen, slowly killing his skin. Sticking his head out, the sun hit his face and he knew, without hearing the forecast, how high the day's temperature was likely to climb.

He left the room, leaving the door open to circulate any breeze. A note lay on the kitchen counter, next to the coffee pot. Jeannette wrote that she would be on a round-trip haul to Omaha but she had contacted the drilling outfit. The drillers were due to arrive on the first day of August, early in the morning. She had negotiated a good rate, she wrote, due to 'my friendship with the owner.'

Gerald was at a time in his life when he was done thinking he would ever understand people, but his resignation did not preclude curiosity. Gerald was curious about where Jeannette spent nights she was not on the road and he was curious about the people she spent them with; curious why she had gotten tattoos around each wrist, green circles with jagged points like barbed wire; curious if his daughter would miss him when he joined his severed hand in the family plot.

Using his good hand, he poured a cup of coffee, unsure why he had not heard her engine. His mind was less willing to be roused by foreign noises, he decided, either a blessing of old age or a nagging infirmity.

The previous day's newspaper lay on the counter, open to the community events page. Red ink circled a block of text. His eyes focused, shutting out sloping fences and cattle gathered at the first gate, anxious for the truck.

The sun came through the east window. Smothering heat crept over his head and shoulders. Jeannette had written 'see you there' next to a picture of the heifer to be offered at the Spook light auction.

The first day of August, Gerald woke early, before the sun splayed color across the pasture sloping downward to his house. He drove upward toward the hickory stand, hauling two round bales he'd bought from the son of the neighbor who had wanted to hire a diviner.

"Didn't let the old man do it," the son had said. "He's got this crazy idea but I told him it was a snowball's chance, if you know what I mean." The son admitted that during firecracker week, he had hoped his barn would burn. "I'm insured, for now," the son had mumbled, looking at the ground. "And the insurance company's too smart for an accident. Anyways, you're welcome to the hay. I'm sending my old man's head straight to Martha. It's the best way."

"Yes, I guess so," Gerald had replied.

Driving in the south pasture, he noticed his three watering tanks were half-empty. The sun was level with the easternmost tree-tops. Light singed his forehead and Gerald pulled his cap lower as he worked from the back of his truck, feeding the expectant cattle.

The feeders were large steel rings standing three feet off the ground with edges punctuated by iron teeth every eighteen circular inches, requiring each heifer to make room for the others. If Gerald had help, he would have pushed the bales into the feeders. His weight was insufficient, so he raked hay into the feeders with a pitchfork, losing strands to the wind with every toss.

The wind also carried rumbling, like ghosts of cowboys moving up from Texas, slowly, to keep weight on their stock. The sounds changed, pulsing like the stamping noise of penned cattle waiting to enter the slaughterhouse. Gerald stuck his pitchfork through a bale and crouched, carefully bracing against the tailgate before allowing his feet to swing down. His good arm ached, shocked by each step across the acre of distance to the road where a steam shovel with a drilling rig sat on top of a tractor trailer.

"Mr. Richter, I'm Sheila Lundy. Jeannette tells me you need some water." The woman extended her right hand over the barbed wire. Behind her, another woman sat in the driver's seat of the red double-cab. Still kicking up dust, a black sedan idled by the ditch.

He wiped his hand against his overalls before offering it to the tiny woman. "Nice to meet you ma'am. You should call me Gerald."

"There's no need to worry about things like that with me." She gripped his hand tightly then pointed to her laced work boots. "I plan on getting dirty myself."

Sheila Lundy looked like a hundred-pound yellow bird. Her short blonde hair was cut into bangs covering her forehead and as she talked, her neck swiveled, affording her blinking eyes a complete view of the pasture. She seemed to be counting the head, assessing the scope of Gerald's operation.

"We need to cut your fence here, take out a couple of posts. Can't get the rig through that gate near the house." Sheila had a roll of paper tucked under her right arm. It bulged with muscles exposed by her white tank top.

"That a map?"

"Yep. We already did a title search. Gerald, you should be satisfied to know you possess rightful deed to this land. With your authorization, I can drill on it. We also verified there are no other wells out here," the woman pointed to the open pasture, "that anyone knows about."

"You mind me asking, Sheila, how much this will cost me?" Memories of his previous exertion floated past. They were going to take out the new posts, erasing his labor like swells covering muddy footprints.

"I'm waiving the deposit, so assuming we get to one hundred feet and hit nothing—and you want to stop—then I'm out a day's work and gas and you don't owe me anything. After a hundred feet, it's twenty bucks per foot, including the first hundred feet, plus parts.

Steel pipe, drill bits, tubing. And anything else we need. I've got my own survey system, but you're free to pay for someone to come here to give you the best idea where to drill. Of course, that's going to cost you, oh, probably six weeks of time. Those guys keep busy."

The black car's engine shut off and a woman who looked as though she could be Sheila's daughter emerged from the driver's door. The rig's driver also emerged, climbing onto the trailer to unhook steel cables holding the equipment in place. Next to steel tubes buckled to the trailer, the female driver looked like a feathery wisp that might be carried aloft and set down under mountains where no wind could pass. "Gerald, one more thing and it's a little delicate."

Sheila placed her hand on Gerald's good arm. Her skin was smooth and he wondered how women with rough jobs, women who might drive tanks or lug ammunition belts if needed, kept skin so smooth. He wished for Maeve, wished to clasp her hands because he could not remember how his dead wife's skin had felt against his own, whether she had been soft and yielding after baking pies and grilling steaks. "What's that?" he asked.

"Now if my crew was a bunch of guys, I'd never ask, but—"

Gerald interrupted, "I'll help carry the heavy stuff. I see you ladies don't have a man here."

"No, you misunderstand me." Sheila laughed, pointing to the sedan. A hunched woman relying on a cane emerged, lifting her feet carefully as she stepped across the ditch. A piece of metal clutched in the old woman's free left hand flickered. "What I need to ask you is, since things with us are a little different, if we might be allowed to use your house facilities."

"Of course," Gerald nodded, twisting his good hand over the stub. "Of course. Just don't mind the place. I'm a widower, you know."

"I know," Sheila said, placing her smooth hand over his left arm's ending. A blue vein popped from her wrist, hidden life revealed by her motion. "I know."

The morning after the drilling crew arrived, Gerald discovered a pain in his lower left back he could not massage with his stub. He could only press the stub into the sore spot, angry with limitations he usually forgot.

The sun came through the window directly, indicating he had slept late. His good hand throbbed, connecting with his back pain. Shuffling to the bathroom, he extracted three tablets of aspirin from a container the pharmacy clerk had opened for him. He splashed water on his face, shutting his eyes to avoid the mirror. He knew stubble sprouted from his nose and ears, the sort of hair he had laughed at on old men when he hadn't been one. Noise from the drilling hummed through the open window, the cadence dipping and rising with changing gears, reminding him of the foolishness he had allowed on his property.

He clumsily fastened both straps of his overalls and fumbled to locate a clean white shirt from the pile inside the wooden wardrobe his father had helped him carry inside nearly fifty years earlier. Even then, with his youth and strong muscles, he'd needed help with bulky pieces and was never comfortable asking anyone outside of family to assist him without offering payment. The wardrobe, along with everything else in the house would be sold, he assumed, when Jeannette was ready. Gerald guessed she would tidy the small rooms and then offer the keys to a realtor, glad to be rid of one more impairment.

Opening the bedroom door, smells of coffee and toasting bread reached him, repudiating Maeve's breakfasts, all steak and eggs, sausages, and fried potatoes. His wife would stand in the kitchen, switching her head from side to side, reluctantly inhabiting the farmhouse even when she had been alive. Perhaps, he thought, Maeve had become a ghost, a spirit warning Jeannette away in whispers. It would explain his daughter's absence, her stretches of solitude, and careful attention to privacy, as if she were responsible for hiding a treasure.

Reaching the kitchen, he squinted. Heat sucked moisture from his lips, forming canals in his cracked skin. "You never told me they was going to be witching for water." Gerald extended his stub. He had never gotten out of the habit of pointing with missing fingers.

"Good morning, Dad. I'm glad to be back home, safely. I missed you too, while I was gone."

Jeannette ripped the plastic seal on a bag of cat food and

poured contents into the pink dish. Cats skittered across the floor. "I'm feeling fine. Hope you can say the same."

"What about this witching? What about the damn crazy women I got running around outside?" Lowering his arm hurt. Movement hurt, stretching his tolerance.

"What about them?" Jeannette's wrist flicked, snapped a dish towel and then wiped crumbs from the countertop into her left palm encircled by long, cupped fingers.

"Don't play stupid with me. I'm too old for that." Gerald sat, heavily, in his seat at the kitchen table. He looked past the fence line, sighting the rig that appeared opposite cattle hunkered in the shadeless north pasture.

"You don't like them?"

"I like them fine. They would probably bake great pies. But I got a ninety year-old Granny out there shaking a stick around and I'm paying for it!" His daughter set a mug of coffee in front of him and he reached for it. Under the table, he felt one of the cats rub against his legs, shocking him with static sparks. The animal ran from him, disappearing down the hallway.

"You don't pay until they hit one hundred feet and chances are you strike water way before then."

"We hit a hundred and nineteen yesterday. Of course, Granny tells me she's feeling it." Gerald raised his cup but a spasm shook his hand and the liquid spilled over his wrist, bubbling into his skin. "Damn it! Granny says she's feeling as good as she's ever felt before about finding water."

His daughter swiped the white towel, blotting it wet and brown. "She's Sheila's grandmother. The other one's Sheila's sister." She paused, twisting the towel. "The young one's Sheila's daughter."

"You didn't have to tell me that. They're all birds out of the same loony bin."

"You didn't have to keep them. They would have left, you wouldn't have owed anything."

"That's true, except I need the water. Bad. The pump's about gone and when it goes, I've got thirty-three dead cattle. I can't risk sending them girls away."

"What did Sheila say?"

"She told me how far she got and that they'd be back this morning."

Gerald stood up, pointing to the newspaper, still open to the heifer's picture. "You going tonight?" he asked.

"Maybe." Jeannette's eyelids dropped, partially obscuring her pupils.

"I'm going. I want to see what kind of trick they plan on pulling."

"You took me there all the time when I was a kid. I know you said you saw it."

"I never saw it." The sounds from his throat felt like moments sliding out of him, escaping his failing grip on time. Opportunities, dried and blighted leaves, were sliding past, disappearing into cracked kitchen tiles.

"You said Mom saw it too."

"I courted your mother there. We never saw it. Except maybe once and it might have been someone's headlights or someone playing a joke with a flashlight." More memories slid past, white night lights, his daughter's dark hair in pigtails, her wide gray eyes, her pink elbows braced on the dashboard as she strained to see through the windshield. Colors seeped out, emptying him. Brown and gray work of pitching hay, stepping through cow manure and scraping dead fungus from the empty water tank appeared. Sweat seeped out too, the sun sucking his skin's moisture, like a greedy baby working a bottle's nipple. Pain sprouted from the knotted black seed in his back and spread up his spine.

"Dad, please, wait just a minute..." Jeannette's tall form sank to the kitchen table, her head bending. "I want to know what it was like. The divination. I've never seen one."

"I wouldn't expect you would care."

"What was it like? Sheila has never let me see one..."

Dead earth swirled in the kitchen, illuminated by a backdrop of red and gold light. Gerald saw patterns, squares, and triangles assemble and then, blown by the energy of movement, disengage. Topsoil had blown all summer, coating furniture and floors with a translucent coat that, although delicate, reproduced, reappearing within hours of being chased by a dust rag or mop. Topsoil that had once kept cattle in tall, green grass and sweet-smelling hay settled in his house, a nuisance to be swept away.

Gray soil had dusted the old woman after her flashing wire cutters clipped a wide swath in the fence. She walked through the opening, assisted only by her forked wooden cane. When the south wind gained force, dirt under the hickory stand rose up, bearing down on the figure with white tufts of hair sticking from beneath a white hat. Dressed in a yellow sleeveless shift, she had not stopped walking through the dirt storm. Gerald reached her, offered his good arm to the figure with crooked shoulders and fingers curled against her palms, common disfigurements of arthritis. Shrugging him away, the woman had tilted her head, smiled and revealed two perfect rows of teeth and green eyes the color of trout teeming in a year of plentiful rain.

"I'm here to find your water." The old woman pushed each sound as though the heat of words burned the fleshy meat of her mouth. "I'd be grateful if you moved those cattle so we can work undisturbed." She had turned, bending each leg above dead weeds, keeping time with the wind's trajectory. She pushed against her cane, driving the forked wooden stick into soil. Every three steps she created a new hole, punctuating the hill with a trail of tiny dots. From the north pasture, Gerald had raked hay from the truck. He paused when his arm tired and stared at the women setting up equipment on the hilltop. The old woman's dress flapped, like a flag caught in a gale.

"Dad, what was it like?"

Jeannette's breath fell inside his ear, her exhaled curiosity tumbled past his lungs to his belly, where it burned and twisted. He lost patterns in the light. The sun had shifted, pitching shadow across his daughter's eyes.

"I spent the rest of the day moving cattle. I didn't see what she did."

"Oh. I thought you might have been curious."

"No. Wasn't curious." Gerald had hauled an empty tank to the north pasture. He had only been able to fill the tank halfway. The pump whined and afraid of blowing it out, he had shut it down. "No more curious than I am about a stupid ghost."

The water would last only through the day.

"I'm going to town today, do some errands and then I'm going out there. Maybe I can give them a hand." Jeannette rose. "I'll see you."

Two steps from the door, she turned and though her body was competent and lean in her denim jeans and short-sleeved blouse, Gerald saw lines cut into her cheeks and around her eyes. Her lips tightened, twitching as though she might speak. The door to the kitchen opened and he saw her truck. Unhitched from its trailer, the rig could be easily turned to navigate the tight corner separating Gerald's driveway from the main road.

"Jeannette," he held his arms apart, reopening the throb of messages carried to cavities of his brain. "Jeannette, I'll see you tonight," he called after her, listening for the departing engine.

Spook light sightings traditionally occurred an hour after dusk, when lower light provided more favorable viewing conditions. Sometimes, the ghost walked over dark patches of velvet sky, picking her way through invisible molecules, climbing astral steps. Sometimes, she tumbled toward the ground like an adolescent gymnast. No one could predict how the ghost would reveal herself, but old-timers, grandsons of land rushers and fence-cutting ranchers, claimed she would always come back.

When Gerald arrived, the fiddle and banjo were rolling, greeting him as his truck bounced against the unpaved road. The notes swooped, settling in his ears, then giving over to the next chords of mountain music and three-part harmony. The Chamber of Commerce had raised a plastic, printed banner above the stage, welcoming the television show back to Vinita. A cherry-wood podium had been erected on the stage and the state senator was seated at a small table behind it. The senator's face appeared on a large screen supported by metal scaffolding. The senator smiled and nodded as one of his constituents was interviewed.

"She likes music," a bearded fiddler spoke to the man holding a microphone, "and my Granddad used to tell me how he'd ride his mule out here before there was a road or a fort and he'd sit and blow on his harmonica and watch her dance."

"Why do you think the ghost keeps returning here for so many years?" The man with the microphone pronounced words energetically, without skipping syllables.

"Because it's the only thing she knows. The ghost don't know this place is done with her. So she stays, keeps on haunting the only place she knows how to haunt."

"Thank you. Well, if she doesn't make an appearance tonight, it certainly isn't because of the quality of music," the newsman finished and twisted his lips into a crooked line. "Now, stay tuned for tomorrow's weather forecast."

Women crowded around tables filled with coleslaw, pickles, potato chips, and baked beans, scooping food onto donated plastic plates bearing a superstore's logo. Children stretched across tables to select hot dogs, hamburgers or ribs from hot platters. The Women's Auxiliary group members dipped large plastic cups into coolers of ice, offering soft drinks and juices. Twenty yards behind the group, next to the tree line, young and middle-aged men had gathered around a keg, tilting cups to cut through foam. Two sheriff's deputies assigned to the event overlooked the alcohol, acknowledging the county commissioner and judge in the group.

Around the smoking roasting pit, men wearing tall white chefs hats and greasy aprons took turns carving the roasting pig. Crisp skin harboring white flesh fell away from the skeleton. The pig's nose, ears and as eye sockets remained intact, although the pig's head had been severed from the body and rested on a side table, its exposed throat steaming in the air.

Gerald passed the barbecuing men, shaking his head at a plate of steaming meat. Heat and smoke drifted, settling in his ears and eyes and he coughed, moving as quickly as his body would allow. Pain navigated the concavity of his back, circling his torso to rest in his chest.

"Oh, I'll take two," he replied, extending his hand to the man pumping the keg.

"It's been that kind of day, right?" The man pouring beer was young, no older perhaps than twenty-five, both hands unscarred and with clean fingernails.

"Suppose so," Gerald said, bracing one plastic cup in the crook of his stub, holding the other in his good hand and drinking from it in long swallows. The spotted heifer was staked ten feet from the smoking pit. He drank two beers then extended his stub and good hand for two more.

Gerald recognized the girl scratching the Betty's ears. The biology girl, skinny as she had looked on television, held a blue cooler to the animal's mouth as it drank. The girl was like a walking stick disguised by the thin wood of a young tree. She matched the animal's curved lines and markings with her beige skin and brownish hair disappearing behind her head. The cow's red spot was bright, like the last spit of a roadside flare, a small spark lingering improbably, for too long and across too much distance. Gerald walked past the heifer but the skinny girl did not notice him. He remembered the difficulty of ripping her check in half with only one hand, dexterity had eluded him. He had crumpled the draft and tossed it into the trash.

Past the Betty's stake, plastic carts were filled with metal lighting poles and tripods. Young people wearing identification cards clipped to chains around their necks unloaded the items, positioning some lights against concrete blocks remaining from the foundation of the army fort. Other lights were placed closer to the tree line, to illuminate the crowd's reaction should the ghost appear above the heads of those finishing barbecue suppers on picnic blankets. Speakers stacked on the stage broadcast music but Gerald guessed the microphone hanging from the scaffolding was for the auctioneer.

Martha sat at a picnic table in front of the stage, hunched over a slice of apple pie. He sat next to her, swallowing the last of his beer.

"Here, you can have mine." Martha slid her plastic cup toward him. "I have a six pack under the table. I'm not on the wagon, like some people. I can have fun."

Gerald laughed, lifting the cup to his lips, thinking how Maeve had only met Martha twice. Maeve had disliked Martha's tight pink skirts and high-heeled shoes.

"Any particular reason you picked one of mine to donate?"

Martha's face was shadowed, the lines of age forgiven in the quiet pause between day and night. "She's the prettiest…it was a shame to send her to the packers."

"They weren't cullers, Martha."

She exhaled, a long wisp from accumulated disappointments. "We got no other bids. Guess you didn't look at the paperwork I sent you."

"Your check was for too much then."

She said nothing, jerking her head at the men gathered around the keg. Her husband stood, sipping from a bottle of water.

"I made him. I liked the looks of that heifer."

"It's not right." The insinuation of his need crept through him, digging rivulets in his forehead.

"I've seen too much of it, this summer, every summer. Haven't you seen too much?" Martha reached under the table. Her hands reappeared, each holding a can of beer.

"That's what they're for." Crowd members ambled, leaving each other laughing and insulted, tired and hopeful, young propositioning young, the old reaching to each other, scratching the tired, rough surface of habitual apprehension. Tightness twisted in his chest but the pain smoothed, flattening with each drink.

"I don't mean that. What I mean is that it's wrong to keep doing what we're doing when it's not good for any of us. The land's dried up and we keep on going, pushing it. What are we going to do?"

Martha finished her beer then produced a flask. They passed it between them, leaning into each other and the thud disappeared from Gerald's chest. People in the crowd reclined on blankets spread across dead grass. The minister on stage asked for prayer. Gerald did not close his eyes or move his lips. He stared at the heifer and girl, fifty feet from his table. Behind them the sun tucked under the arm of the horizon, emitting a final flash. Gerald knew the red spot on the animal shone in relief of the retreating sun. The blazing dot multiplied, bursting like sparks. His heart beat quickly and he tried to push back the swell threatening his balance.

He did not hear the prayer end but felt Martha's hand pushing his head toward the television monitor. The senator thanked the sale barn for donating the unusually marked heifer but the voice was muted, as if Gerald's ears had smuggled the words to ricochet inside his chest. He clutched his good arm across his torso. Martha leaned toward him, her eyes wrinkled and a small black cavity formed from concern separated her lips. Men held their fingers up, bidding in five-dollar increments. This was not, Gerald understood, an auction like those at the sale barn, measured in cents per pound and the notion people were bidding on the Betty too poor, even, for the packers, made him laugh. He knew men and women were staring, shaking their heads, blaming his plastic cup and Martha with her smeared pink lipstick. He laughed so drunkenly long and loud that bidding stopped. The senator's stern chin was replaced on the screen by his granddaughter holding a sign in front of her thin body. Large letters, formed by running splotches read *Animals are Your Neighbors. Love Them as You Love Yourselves.*

The girl's body incorporated the breadth of the camera but in a few sliding moments a camera operator opened the lens. She and her grandfather's image were cast opposite each other, unmoving except for their lips. Hers, quivering and glowing with a faint pink sheen, chewed and bruised. His, tight and unrelenting, tucked inside his mouth as if he was devouring them. They shared this pause with the crowd, the intimacy of common disappointments. There was no relenting between them. The auction continued with the girl's white face disappearing from the screen, confrontation pushed aside by breaths of resumed bidding.

And Gerald knew if he could summon water from the sky, an indulgence of gods or ghosts who walked the heavens, he would stand in the floodplain, to have dry dust coating his heart consumed by roaring water. He would throw his arms around the skinny girl and give her the keys to his house, tell her to occupy his bereft land and he would wave to her as the water bore him away, filling his lungs with promises of numbing relief in the mouth of an estuary. The river would carry him south, overpowering low-built bridges and he would find rest in the meeting of river mud and coral sand.

Laughter flowed again from the rumble of Gerald's stomach and his shoulders shook, heaving painfully. His torso doubled, he fell from the bench, feeling sharp pressure against his knees. Hands surrounded him, touched him, and he knew Martha's arms wrapped around his chest. Her hands clasped his shoulders to the warm small spot of her heart.

Gerald vomited under the table, releasing a sour flood on the packed earth. He stood, grasped his stub and walked away from the stage. The noises receded and faces were blank and fixed, tracking the walking incarnation of an old man. They saw a spirit of ritual suffering rising, repetition of fattening and bloodletting collapsing. Instability of the earth, fickle bounty of the land floated, beyond the reach of the price per pound of flesh and he knew their fears were honest, driving them across barren lands from misplaced trust, misplaced faith. His chest tightened. He walked away, lifting his eyes when he recognized Jeannette's red sneakers. Her hand was raised in bidding, signaling against men and women. She, like the others, stood aside for the exodus of the limping man, his face reflected in broken light.

Moments slid past Gerald. Pain crawled to his skull. Bidding continued. The girl's sign was raised high and the Betty shuffled, agitated by her caretaker's absence. The skinny girl's fingers pierced the air, signaling her bid and Gerald stumbled past the thin flesh, speculating what sum of money a twenty-year-old girl possessed to bid on a poor heifer, what treasures she held in her chest. A man raised his hand and nodded. The girl's head shook and she lowered her arm. Jeannette raised both hands, indicating her commitment but the man nodded again, keeping his hand high. There were no counter bids and the girl's arm and Jeannette's arm tumbled, relinquishing their claims to gravity.

Gerald crossed the dirt road, hearing applause and the senator's voice. Bracing his stub against the truck, he struggled for balance, struggled to anchor himself to familiar objects. He strained against the thrust emanating from the ground, a push on his slight flesh that might send him aloft.

Beside his truck, Jeannette stood with her arms crossed and her feet anchored apart, appearing impenetrable to erosion or wind. White light swirled over the treetops, enlarged, engorging on spectators' shrills. Gerald looked to his daughter's face, dark in front of the moon's silver outline. If she saw the ghost she did not acknowledge it and his head fell against her chest; pain driving holes through him, loosening his claim on infertile earth.

His head tilted to catch a lift of wind, his tears caught in the moving atmosphere's course. Blinded by crying, by a sting of silent professions, he climbed into his pickup, ignoring exaltations from people he had passed by.

Noise from the third day of drilling woke him; the clock on the nightstand read 11:30, later than he had slept since the day after Maeve's funeral, when he had been unwilling to rise from the cocoon of unconscious relief.

He moved his head, testing for a hangover. Angry nerves confirmed his punishment, his tongue felt like a dirty sock and pressure pulsed in his skull and chest. Remembering the girl's white face, her small round mouth, Gerald ran to the toilet, releasing the night's mistakes. Thinking of the groaning pump, he decided to forgo the shower, running instead a small towel under the faucet, wiping necessary places of his body.

Wheat toast rested on a white plate next to the pot of coffee. It was too hot, he thought, to drink bitter liquid and his stomach would not cooperate. He found a note from Sheila written with strange block letters, as if she were trying to disguise her handwriting. The crew had reached two hundred feet the night before. *If you want to stop let us know.* The note had been signed at six AM and he had no memory of being roused by sounds of women entering his house. The continuing failure of his faculties frightened him.

The rig hummed and cattle strained against the fence separating them from the shade. There would be no water left in the tank.

33

How long could they last in the heat, he wondered, until they fell on their sides, tongues distended and swollen, eyes bulging and infested with flies? How long would they all last, he wondered and retched over the kitchen sink, feeling his body shake.

His body seemed to resist the walk to the south pasture. Gerald watched the terrain, staring inches ahead for dangerous footing, like a pioneer exploring a new country without benefit of compass or chart. Moving his body across the earth slowly, he knew there could be no other pace toward the hill where they drilled. The land had its own pace, calibrated to rhythms unseen and buried, circulating air and water at secret tempos as unpredictable as when the bounty would cease to nourish dependent, palpitating recipients.

He climbed halfway up the hill, carefully, because the contractions of breathing hurt his chest. Oxygen, he thought, was becoming scarce. Only the impenetrable pile of stones and hickory trees, indomitable after years of drought, would continue unharmed. Those trees would grow toward the sky, he imagined, spreading branches and reproducing until the entire pasture was shaded, the sun blocked from its exertions against the land.

Nestled halfway up the swell, the drill churned and throttled past layers of earth compressed by millions of tons of glacial weight. The land had once been a frozen mass not beholden to winds or sun but sealed and protected by solid, pure water. The woman operating the drill raised one hand, confident in her ability to control the machine with the other. Fingers appeared, acknowledging him, and then resumed guiding and prompting gauges.

Jeannette stood next to Sheila. Jeannette was smiling, her lips slightly open and her fingers bracing the blonde woman as though Sheila were a bird on one of her branches. Jeannette wore white cotton slacks cropped close below her knees and a pale shirt with an oval cut below her throat. The sleeves of her blouse puffed with each gust of hot air. Her cheeks were white, she had protected her skin from the sun and the paleness of his daughter's flesh reminded him of white starlight, unaccompanied by the moon's illumination. She was tall enough, he thought, to sway like a tree in the wind, but her constitution was too stiff, unyielding.

"What do you expect for today?" Gerald's voice came to him slowly, dredged from places hidden from his tongue. Jeannette's hand slid to Sheila's elbow and he saw pale, blonde hairs, like tufts of baby grass sprouting from the smaller woman's pores. The old woman stood ten feet away at the top of the hill, leaning against her cane and clutching a sprig of hickory leaves. The lines trespassing the leaves' surfaces were slick and glistening.

Sheila answered, though Gerald had been looking to Jeannette. "Little past three hundred feet now. If we don't hit water, we'll get to four hundred before the day is over. Assuming we don't break down."

"And if you don't hit water?"

"Then we keep going or call it off. Your choice."

"We'll keep going." Jeannette's voice intervened, squeezing Sheila's hand. "I'm taking responsibility, Dad. Sheila can keep going."

"What if I don't want to keep going? I think it's time to stop, time to send all those stupid, skinny cows to slaughter. Make some dog food anyway."

"It's not just your decision." Jeannette swept her arm above her, creating an arch above her head, a perfect and airy gateway to the sagging fence row behind her. "You've been hanging on here too long and I've had to hang on here too."

"Sometimes," the words came from him, more harshly than he intended, raspy on air that he should have conserved. "You hang around sometimes."

"Yes, sometimes."

"That gives you no right."

"My rights have got nothing to do with living here, Dad."

Pressure, like anticipation, bulged, then escaped his mouth and nose, leaking blood and spit to dry, grasping wind. Like the single time he had worn a formal jacket and tiny black tie, he wished to be invisible, so the woman walking toward him could not see his weaknesses. Jeannette offered him a small towel but he waved it away with his stub. Drilling noise continued, the sun's heat continued. Cattle pressed against the fence, straining for relief. Gerald's heart skipped, jarring organs he had manipulated without thought for when he might be called to account for their care. "You have it your way. See how you like hauling off thirty thousand pounds of dead carcass."

"I'll take responsibility for that," Jeannette's hands clenched, unclasped and then opened, relaxing the muscles of her palms. "You don't have to worry."

Walking toward the old woman cost Gerald. His breathing attenuated, his legs responded reluctantly. He wanted to kneel, to brace his stub against the earth and hold his good hand to his heart to test for fidelity. But knowledge that flesh more frail than his own occupied the highest point of his property pushed him on. Less than a foot separated him from the old woman before he paused, retaking energy lost to the rising land.

"This how you run your business, taking orders from someone that don't own the place? That's what I want to know. I don't tell people how to run their business." His breath broke over the words, but he continued. "I may look like an old man to those women, maybe I look like a cripple, but it hasn't kept me from running this place for longer than they've been alive. Your crew down there is acting without my permission."

"Mr. Richter, don't you want water?" The leaves in the old woman's hands twirled, catching light like batons in the hands of adolescents. "Or maybe there's something else bothering you?"

"There's nothing I can't do with this." Gerald held his stub out to her, brushing leaves tangled in her fingers.

"Our infirmities are not always obvious," the old woman answered. The fresh leaves cast a green hue against her skin, green shadows flitted from the recently broken foliage, green shadows darted across her hands, her face, against the white scarf covering her head. The bright, fresh light hurt Gerald's eyes. He blinked like a small boy searching the current's surface for red-spotted bobbers indicating where the catch would be suspended, caught under cold fresh water carrying five-point leaves away from weeping green branches.

The sun would not relent and he turned his back to the woman and walked down the hill to Jeannette's pile of stones. The stone pile cast no shadow at the high hour, offered no respite but Gerald squatted and braced his back against it. He breathed dead soil and thought he should cross the few acres to the north pasture, where his stock was thirsting, some already capsized to the ground, others standing stoic and ignorant of the capriciousness of bounty but ignorant, also, of the long grip of despair. The old woman walked toward the stand of trees surrounding the crown of the swell. She did not totter with an old woman's pace but extended her legs from under her white dress purposefully, as though she were a bride inspecting her property.

Heat shimmered in waves, rising off the road and from the piled stones. Waves crossed his face and he tried to lift his hands, to signal that he was being carried away. Gerald's tongue swelled, his face burned and the cattle strained against the flimsy fence of his creation. His body lay under the sun, surrendering its moisture.

Gerald did not feel himself rise, as he had always believed he would when his time came. He had expected his old flesh to fall from his skeleton, cast-off detritus of human foibles. Instead, his lungs compressed and in the collapse, the earth unwrapped like a ball of dry brown yarn, rolling toward his flat and fixed body.

From his prone perspective, the ground heaved as though an army of low-sighted moles were tunneling, pushing the earth upward, rising to meet the sun with pointed, blind faces. His perspective widened and more ground turned upward. Thick layers of dirt separating him from the planet's belly were flung outward, roots and rocks, volcanic fires and glowing elements careened into the vacuum of space. Deep water too, a hidden beauty, streamed away from the flat earth in a fury of blue and white waves, dissipating energy gathered from the sea.

There was no air, no gravity left to the flat world. His lungs, involuntary bellows, squeezed and his dusty body slid through empty riverbeds. Heat choked him and ridges and clefts formed in the flesh of his mouth, hardening and drying, convincing him the end of all things was reunion with heat from creation, low fires from the belly of birth.

The sun subsided, a reprieve for the heat-cracked topography. Gerald recognized his daughter's shadow, her body blocking the sun. The shadow knelt and he felt his head raised from its nest against the rocks. A soft, wet cloth traveled across his forehead and the buttons of his shirt loosened, rushing air traveled across his throat and chest, ghostly white fingers tickled his flesh. The outline of Jeannette's right arm curled around his body and she held a hollow yellow gourd, like an oversized fruit plucked from a flowering vine. Drilling noise subsided, the earth stopped sliding and he occupied moments of quiet recognition, forgiveness spread across the mouths of stern-faced women, their eyes pouring rivers to irrigate seared, needy flesh.

"Drink from this," she whispered. "We've broken through."

The Bereavement of
Eugene Wheeler

N o trees shade the cemetery. There is no place to spread a blanket to sit and reflect. There is hardly space to move without walking on top of a body. Eugene Wheeler's long legs contort as he steps over a wooden cross or, for the more prosperous, an etched concrete block. There are no marble headstones in this graveyard but he shows proper respect, lifting one leg, extending it over a plot, placing his foot carefully. Though the graves are closely situated, he does not stumble, does not trespass on the mix of red clover and fescue growing from the allotments because he has memorized the layout, in fact has supervised its design. Anyone competent enough to walk through this crowded burial ground should join the high wire act. Yes, walking among the dead is a bit like being part of the circus.

Eugene is not thinking of performing under the big top or the irony of directing another indigent's burial when he can earn thousands of dollars for a fancy memorial service. He is not thinking of his son Scottie's refusal to enroll in college or of his wife's demand to take a vacation. Eugene is thinking what a shame it was to pick

Goldenrod Cemetery, the public poor folk graveyard, as the final resting place for the dead criminal Bertram Biggs.

The debate began before the incarcerated Biggs died from cancer. The convict was in his late fifties, serving the eighteenth year of his sentence for the poorly concealed killing of his wife's boyfriend when the prison doctor informed Bertram that neither he nor his liver were going to remain as guests of the state much longer. Biggs' court-appointed attorney tried to parlay the grim diagnosis into the sick man's early release but, true to form, his client was unwilling to express remorse for the crime. The newspaper quoted Bertram telling the parole board that, "The only thing I'd do different is throw my shotgun in a pond after I got him. Would have made it harder for them sons of bitches to pin it on me." Bertram added, "And I'm gonna tell them to bury me beside my dead wife, so I can torment that cheatin' whore for the rest of eternity."

Bertram Biggs' wife had suffered heart failure a year earlier, after being born again and publicly forgiving her imprisoned husband. Ruthie Biggs was buried in Goldenrod in one of three plots she had purchased when Bertram was sent to prison, recognizing that her family, due to the length of her husband's sentence, would only be reunited in death. She had designated one spot for herself, one for her husband and the third for their daughter.

Baby Regina had an olive complexion, blue-black hair, and green eyes. Bertram and his wife were pale, with freckles and brown eyes and the newborn's attractive but inexplicable coloring was a source of suspicion to her father. When Ruthie announced she was driving into town to purchase baby formula, Bertram hid under a tarpaulin in the bed of their pickup truck. Instead of turning into the grocery store parking lot, Ruthie pulled into a parking space at a roadside motel. Bertram loaded his gun and waited for the man meeting his wife.

Eighteen years later, Bertram's recalcitrant statement to the press, his last shot across the bow of Protestant penitence, set the Goldenrod County Council into action. The special meeting held at the courthouse was attended by families who had purchased cheap plots in the cemetery and by relatives of the murdered man. A cousin of the victim circulated hand-printed flyers that read: *'Don't Bury Murderer Bertram Biggs. He is NOT a CHRISTIAN and should not be buried with GOD-FEARING CHRISTIANS.'*

Because Wheeler Funeral Homes had directed all the burials in Goldenrod Cemetery, Council President Tom Bunt asked Eugene to speak against the idea of allowing a known criminal to occupy the public graveyard. An hour before the debate convened, Bunt explained his views outside the meeting hall. Residents filed past the two men, dripping from rain that had been falling unusually hard even for the month of April.

"Eugene, I expect you to support a resolution asking the state to send Biggs somewhere else. Why, you know, my own mother is buried there!" the council president exclaimed.

Tom Bunt was a foot shorter than Eugene and had worked as a part-time justice of the peace before his election to the president's full-time position that required him to perform no more than twenty hours of labor per week. Eugene knew Bunt had chosen to save money by burying his mother at Goldenrod instead of the more costly graveyard behind the church where the woman had worshipped for fifty years. There was no headstone at her grave, only a decaying wooden cross.

"I'll speak my opinion, but I don't know if you're going to like it much," Eugene said.

"Why's that?" The shorter man stepped back and looked up at the funeral director.

"Because if Bertram Biggs has got a piece of paper with his name on it—title for a plot the County granted to his wife in exchange for payment—then he's entitled to burial in that plot. But I agree the state shouldn't put him in Goldenrod." Eugene's height and slim build often evoked grim reaper jokes but he enjoyed his height advantage over Bunt, his feeling of a higher plane of perspective.

"Where do you think he should be buried?" The nose on Bunt's face twitched, as if Eugene's words stank.

"Bertram Biggs is a Vietman vet; he did two tours and was one of the bravest damn enlisted guys the infantry ever had. At the least, he's entitled to a military burial and probably qualifies for interment at a veteran's cemetery. But he's the one who has to want that sort of thing." Eugene had not known Biggs, personally, but had become acquainted with the convict's story eighteen years earlier while directing the victim's funeral. The murdered man had left behind a devoutly Baptist wife and a stack of hundred dollar bills that, as it turned out, were loans Ruthie Biggs had extended to her unemployed boyfriend by writing checks on Bertram's bank account.

"You shitting me?" The shorter man shouted. When three representatives of the Ladies Sunday School Society looked his way, Bunt lowered his voice. "You think he should get buried in a fancy service at my mother's graveyard? There should be a law against that!"

"The burials at Goldenrod are anything but fancy, Tom…" It was hard for Eugene to disguise his dislike of Bunt but he refrained from adding, *as you should know*. Eugene would not discuss the cost of burial after a funeral. He would not entertain *ifs* with the survivors because the ceremony of death should possess dignity and no one found him second-guessing the service when it was finished.

Eugene continued, quietly. "Federal law prohibits individuals convicted of a capital offense from receiving veteran benefits. Biggs was convicted of *second degree murder*. That's not a capital offense in this state and technically, he's entitled to a military burial, if he wants one." Eugene smiled because he knew Bunt had avoided service by enrolling in college for two semesters and dropping out when the lottery was instituted and student deferments had ended. "But I wouldn't want to advocate exploiting legal loopholes."

Council President Bunt turned his back to Eugene and walked to the podium. Bunt shouted, "Quiet down, everyone. Please be quiet. I now call this meeting to order."

Eugene strode to the back of the room where he was grateful to find an unoccupied bench in the last row. He wanted to remain unnoticed until it was time to give his opinion, to avoid questions about rumors that a so-and-so thirty-year-old single mother had been strangled or that a so-and-so eighty-year-old man had been found dead wearing women's lace panties. Wheeler Funeral Homes held itself to discreet standards and he had too much work to do, signing invoices and ordering office supplies, to waste time nodding politely and shrugging off inappropriate questions.

The meeting began with residents speaking out against the interment of Biggs' remains at Goldenrod Cemetery. Some offered impassioned pleas on behalf of their departed loved ones, insisting their dead deserved better than to rest beside such an unremorseful character. Several middle-aged men testified to knowing Bertram Biggs in high school; they agreed Biggs was a scallywag before he went to prison and that time could only have made him worse. A representative of the Ladies' Sunday School Society read a passage from Revelation, explaining that people who followed Jesus would be outfitted in white garments in heaven. Those who refused to fill their souls with the blood of the lamb would be cast into the pit to writhe with worms in their stomachs, condemned to burn for eternity. Eugene shuffled invoices and wondered if the writhing worms were fireproof.

After an hour of speeches, Eugene realized Bunt had skipped the printed agenda section calling for 'Expert Testimony.' It appeared he would not be asked to speak, so Eugene studied paper samples for Wheeler Funeral Homes' letterhead. He was evaluating the merits of '44 Beige' when he heard a voice, a familiar voice, emerging from the speaker hanging from the ceiling.

"…and it's also disgusting that anyone here would make threats about Biggs' body even before he's dead. Don't you people get it? When he dies, his debt to everyone will be paid in full. You can't punish the man after he's dead by not allowing him to be buried where he wants. Don't you people understand anything?"

The paper samples slid from Eugene's lap onto the floor, spilling under the bench. His son stood at the front of the room wearing torn blue jeans with holes in both knees and a red T-shirt with REVOLUTION printed on it. Eugene could not make eye contact with his son. Scottie was looking at the opposite corner of the room where a teenage girl dressed in a black mini-skirt and tank top occupied a bench by herself. Long dark hair hid the girl's face from Eugene.

A man in the front row booed. Tom Bunt rose from his seat, to signal that Scottie's speaking time was finished. Eugene felt cold and still, momentarily losing control of his motor functions. There was no reason why Scottie should be at the debate, no reason why he should even know the name Bertram Biggs. Eugene became aware of many faces looking at him and he was tempted to shrug, as if to say *I don't know anything about this* but he waited for Scottie to continue.

"Finally, I'd like to read a short statement from Regina Biggs, Bertram Biggs' daughter. As she will be the sole survivor when he passes on—"

"That's enough, son! Your time's up." Tom Bunt grabbed Scottie's hand and Eugene wondered if Scottie, lean as a bone but tall with broad shoulders, would wrestle the short man. His son slid away from Bunt and was gone quickly, passing through the hall to the exit. The girl with the dark hair trailed after him.

"Folks, we're moving on with the program. I'm sending around a petition calling on the state legislature to pass a law taking away the right of a convicted felon to rest beside honest, hard-working folk who have gone on to a good reward. Now, we're gonna need a lot of signatures and a lot of phone calls from everyone. If we can't get satisfaction from our representatives, then we need to discuss our legal options…"

Bunt's voice faded as Eugene stuffed paper samples in his briefcase and took long steps to follow his son into the rainy night.

Mourners are certain of the poignancy of their sorrows and anxious to pass them on to the living, like delicate pastries from a silver platter. *Here, take one, it's an original and so hard won.* From those who gather beside an open hole in the earth there are murmurings, the assertions *he was so vital* or *she was always kind.* For an infant, because there can be few descriptions and no caption to the life, there is instead optimism, that *it is resting in the hands of God.* Mourners toss handfuls of dirt on well-constructed coffins and let praise of the dead fall from their mouths, determined to persuade listeners that their degree of loss, like the departed, is *unique.*

Eugene is not convinced. He knows there is nothing special about anyone's grief, nothing to distinguish bereavement. Like death, the frequency of grief is *statistically predictable*, given a few demographic parameters he stores in a mental chart:

- Population: an average of 5,430 people live in or nearby each of the twelve towns where he operates a funeral home.

- Sample behavior: residents of the area (considerate Christians) have the courtesy to knock off in frequency and numbers that closely track statistical averages published by the Census Bureau.

- Abstract of the most recent Census Report:
  Location: Midwestern USA
  Sub-location: Rural-Remote
  Ethnic category: White
  Total mortalities per annum per 100,000   871 (.87%)

Eugene ignores the negligible 1.50 percent of the area's "Non-White" population (they die in higher percentages but pay less for funerals) and can predict within some ten mortalities, the amount of money his regional monopoly of funeral homes will earn during any given year.

Wheeler Funerals Homes, Inc. is not a public corporation required to disclose financial statements. The company is a privately held concern, and as such, its fiscal health (and the 300 percent markup it charges for a burial) is information Eugene shares grudgingly and exclusively with the Internal Revenue Service. Of course there are morticians' and other employees' salaries, fees for medical waste removal, overhead on buildings and black limousines, but after twenty-seven years the business of burying has made him rich; richer than even his wife Lois guesses. He feels grateful to his deceased father, a mortician, for encouraging him to save the down payment for his first funeral home when he was twenty years old and the forbearance of area entrepreneurs who are too squeamish about the business of death to enter the market.

Eugene's chosen line of work is not without challenges. There are diplomatic difficulties associated with collecting money from widows (which is why he requires half the estimated fee as an upfront deposit) and the inevitable squabbles between children of first and second wives as to which family plot the departed father will occupy. There are long debates about flowers, about the suit or dress the deceased will wear to be laid to rest and the infrequent, but most vexing problem of religion: what to do if the departed has broken faith with the core Presbyterian/Methodist/Baptist constituency and has elected a non-religious service, or potentially more problematic, a *Catholic* ceremony, requiring everyone to drive fifteen miles to the only area church reporting to Rome.

Eugene expects these difficulties, has dealt with them throughout his career, and addresses such matters as *issues to be discussed* and not *problems to be solved.* He personally directs one-third of the burial services; wears a black suit and crisp white shirt over his tall and lean frame; slicks back his hair (dyed brown but still plentiful); is always ready with information about insurance claims, estate attorneys, and Social Security benefits. He has not let his monopoly on death in three counties diminish the quality of his services.

The only problem Eugene has not been able to avoid with a dose of expressed concern is the matter of indigent burials. Not that there are so many of them; he receives on average ten per year. The counties pay for indigents, mostly old and transient men, at cost plus a modest charge for embalming and grave digging. This arrangement was forced on him at the start of his career, when a county coroner told Eugene he could either bury an elderly heart failure or risk having potential competition from the state capital called in to do the job. Eugene agreed to contribute his services and now oversees all indigent embalming, selection of caskets (the cheapest pine) and is the only one watching when these clients are laid to rest in an easement a cattle farmer granted to the County in exchange for a paved road to his property.

The land donated for poor folk burials is surrounded by a barbed wire fence and at the entrance, a swinging metal gate with barbed wire coiled on top. The gate is padlocked after hours to keep out vandals; the fence keeps out the farmer's cattle. Eugene is not overly fond of animals but always notes how underfed the creatures appear, bloodying their heads on the barbs to pick at grass on the cemetery side of the fence. The unusually wet spring has not helped the cattle; rather, the weather has created an enormous expanse of red clay mud that never dries out, causing inconvenience to humans and beasts alike. Because the parking lot has turned to mush, Eugene has parked his car on the shoulder of the paved road to avoid getting stuck.

He steps over headstones carefully, until he arrives at the Biggs' family plot. Eugene identifies the hole the groundskeeper has dug with a front-end loader but curses under his breath— *godamnit*—though there is no one to hear him. Dirty water is pooling in the grave. Probably enough water to float Bertram's coffin. The entire cemetery lies in a soft clay depression and is prone to flooding when the water table rises after heavy rain.

In the same month of April that Tom Bunt announced his opposition to allowing Bertram Biggs to occupy Goldenrod Cemetery, Eugene was scheduled to speak to the seniors of the high school during Career Day. Scottie sat in the back row of the classroom next to the dark-haired girl whom Eugene had learned was Regina Biggs. Scottie's long blond hair touched his shoulders and he wore pants that dropped from his hips and bunched around his ankles. The state of Scottie's appearance had been only one of the points of family discussion following the teen's aborted speech at the county council meeting. The other points of discussion had addressed his lack of motivation to attend college and the revelation he was involved in a "spiritual" relationship with Regina and the "special nature" of their love required him to become her public advocate.

"Regina," Scottie had informed his parents, "is afraid to speak in public. Plus, since her mother's dead, she has no one." Scottie had pointed at Eugene. "And *you* should be ashamed of yourself. You know better than anyone that when Bertram dies, he's paid back his debt to society. Like, it's about comforting the living and Regina wants to honor her mother's wish to be buried with Bertram."

Scottie smiled and said, "I don't have to go to college to stand up for what's right."

Eugene and Lois had always encouraged their son to be civically minded and because they could not see a philosophically consistent way to punish him for exercising his right to speak at an open forum, they relied on a technicality. They had grounded him for two weeks for the unauthorized "borrowing" of his mother's sedan to drive to the meeting and Scottie had not spoken to either of them since. Scottie had, however, informed them via email that he would maintain a vow of silence toward his parents until Eugene spoke publicly on the topic of allowing Biggs to be buried according to his wishes.

"What I'm doing isn't rocket science," Eugene said to the teenage audience in the room. Of the businessmen present, he was the longest-running participant at Career Day beating out the two bank presidents, the owner of a tire dealership and even Tom Bunt, who spoke about a career in civil service. "Everyone will die, eventually. I've never been afraid to say I'm in an annuity business. Does anyone know what an annuity is?"

"It's something no one's ever thought of before!" Eugene recognized the grandson of an expensive mahogany casket client. The elderly grandmother had set aside money from her estate to truck in fresh white roses for her ceremony. Money which, Eugene thought, might have been better bequeathed to pay for some tutoring for the boy.

"Not quite, young man. An annuity is an investment that pays off on a regular schedule." Eugene pointed to a girl in the front row, the only student who had been writing notes on the talks.

"Mr. Wheeler, how does it feel to bury someone you know?" The studious girl was the granddaughter of an exorbitantly priced steel casket client. She couldn't have known that her great-uncle, a church deacon, had set aside money for a private ceremony for his aging buddies from the VFW. Upon the deacon's death, Eugene made arrangements to bus in exotic dancers. The celebration with five blondes in swimsuits included party hats, balloons, and a portable defibrillator. In the event that one of the invitees inconveniently became a client, Eugene had not wanted inquiries with regard to his company's liability for negligence.

"Death is the only outcome of life. The inevitable end. I am always sad when someone I know passes on. We all have to hope that when our time comes, we're ready for it." Eugene continued. He had recited the words so many times. "In our bereavement of the dead, we understand how valuable each life is."

The blonde girl wrote quickly, committing each of Eugene's words to her lined notebook page.

"What about someone who dies in prison?" Scottie interrupted, speaking loudly from the back of the room. "Is that person's life valuable?"

The murmuring in the audience did not come from the students. The adults seated behind a long folding table leaned their heads together. Tom Bunt smiled.

"Well, Scottie, it depends a great deal." Given the local controversy on the subject of Bertram Biggs, Eugene had prepared for a variation on this question. But he had not thought Scottie would be the one to challenge him so publicly. He had believed his son possessed more loyalty.

"On what?" Scottie asked. Regina Biggs' head slumped forward, covering her face with her long hair. None of the students turned to look at her. The adults wrinkled their foreheads and twisted their mouths. The school principal whispered into Tom Bunt's ear.

"On whether or not that individual has undergone a personal transformation," Eugene heard more whispers and continued. "But I must also stress that everyone should avoid passing judgment on the dead. There isn't a person in this room, or a person in this world for that matter, who can claim to be without flaws. I am not in the position to assess the content of a character."

The adult whispers were unintelligible, but loud. The students were quiet, most staring at notebooks on their desktops. Regina Biggs hid her face with her hair.

The principal rose, cleared his throat and asked for a round of applause to "thank Mr. Wheeler for coming in today to speak to us." Eugene walked to his metal chair, never looking away from his son's face. Scottie settled his hands into Regina's dark hair, stroking its strands.

The other students thumped their palms together. The noise sounded like rain falling hard against the earth and the loud rush of water flooding a road, pushing past speed limit signs and concrete medians to pour into cars and trucks of motorists caught unaware by the storm.

One part of Eugene's job requires him to listen, to purse his lips and nod, to grasp a mourner's palm and press it between his two hands—a variation on the embrace. Another part requires him to stand, feet in line with shoulders, so that he balances when a client leans into him. He must be prepared to catch someone who may faint from shock or grief. Grieving people are fatigued when they arrive at the business of burying their dead. Eugene is patient and kind. Comforting the bereaved is only an ordinary task associated with the operation of a funeral home and he does not consider it a difficult part of his job.

The truly difficult part of his job has nothing to do with anyone's grief except his own, on the occasions when he must give instructions to the Goldenrod Cemetery groundskeeper, Vernon Skelton.

Skelton came from a long but not overly prosperous line of prairie dirt farmers, some who ran skinny cattle across the scrubby landscape and some who broke their backs mulching so they could grow wheat. Goldenrod Cemetery is full of Skeltons; their wives, cousins, and in-laws have owned or occupied nearly every farm in the region. The cattle farmer who donated the easement to the county was a Skelton and by some method of genealogical reckoning, which Eugene has never understood, claims Vernon as his second cousin once removed.

Vernon maintains his monopoly on the post. His extended family constitutes a significant percentage of the county voters. The elected county officials renew the groundskeeper's contract each year despite Eugene's complaints that Vernon is lazy and drinks on the job. Because Wheeler Funeral Homes must fulfill state requirements for the proper interment of human remains in accordance with the terms of an undertaker's license, Eugene considers Vernon a threat to his personal cash flow and is vigilant about the man's work. It is not a rewarding exercise.

The groundskeeper has not been digging graves deep enough. During the pounding rains of spring, the water table has risen, pushing freshly buried caskets upward, higher than some grave markers. Although Vernon has reburied the coffins, he has not been able to rectify the appearance of the gravesites. Next to the wet hole designated for Bertram Biggs' body is his dead wife's heaping mound of moist red clay and rocks. No marker identifies the spot. Even if she could afford it, Regina could not have placed a headstone on her mother's grave because the weather has been too wet. It will take at least one year for the soil to bear any weight.

Staring at the empty hole, Eugene feels tired. Tired of the hassle of burying this dead man for which he will receive little compensation and most certainly will not profit, and tired of his son's refusal to speak to him. But Eugene is a professional and because he is proud of the quality of his work, and mostly because he is anxious to finish this job, to return home to Lois, and consult travel brochures for a fall vacation, maybe a cruise along the New England coast to check out the famous leaves, he stretches his legs over the wet hole and follows a gravel path up the hill to where a shed stores Vernon's tools and equipment. The groundskeeper is leaning against the aluminum siding in a wooden three-legged chair, tilting a bottle against the back of his throat.

There was no need for niceties and Vernon must be aware of the problem, so Eugene starts in, "The casket will be here in three hours, that's *three o'clock*. What do you plan on doing about this?" Eugene subscribes to the management theory that shifts the onus of responsibility to the laborer. Part of running an efficient business is the delegation of labor; Eugene does not believe he can execute every duty related to a proper burial himself.

Vernon makes no effort to disguise the malt liquor he braces between his legs. "I can't do nothing," he replies, his face twisting. The groundskeeper has never been handsome. He has an asymmetrical chin that slopes downward on one side and juts upward on the other.

A jaw broken when he had been a toddler, probably a product of the scripture *'Spare the rod and spoil the child.'*

"Please elaborate. Why can't you do *nothing*?" Eugene has long since dispensed with the pretense of politeness with Vernon. But this too is useless because Vernon does not understand sarcasm.

"Two things. First, you ain't told me to pour no concrete, so that's why you're getting water in the hole. I ain't gonna pay for concrete myself. Are you? Second thing, Sheriff's gonna be here later to serve you with a restraining order some folks got. They're getting it from the capital, I hear, to give to you about burying time."

There is no wind in the graveyard to distort Vernon's voice but Eugene thinks he hears a high-pitched whistle, the shooting of air as it moves through a long drainage pipe. He looks overhead. The clouds are gathering.

"I want you to get your backhoe, dig out the hole *deeper* and backfill it with gravel. That will firm it up. I'll call into town to get the casket here earlier. Shouldn't take you more than an hour to do the job and then we'll have a decent burial."

As per Bertram's request, there will be no minister present. The state requires only one witness to a burial and Eugene will serve as that lawful designate. "I suppose Tom Bunt will make an appearance here with the Sheriff?" Eugene realizes he has not been vigilant, has not acted in the best interest of his deceased and indigent client. He should have insisted that Bertram apply for a veteran's burial, insisted the body be shipped away for a military farewell. He could have avoided this nonsense, this controversy distracting him from other funeral clients. *Paying* funeral clients.

Vernon tosses his empty bottle on the ground, nimbly springs onto the tractor and turns the engine over. "Tom Bunt's an asshole. He couldn't get laid if he ran in a whorehouse with a fistful of hundred dollar bills."

"You'll dig out the hole?" Eugene looks up at Vernon and feels in his pocket for his mobile telephone. He'll need the hearse driver to come immediately if what the groundskeeper says is true.

"Yep. But it's up to you to explain to Regina Biggs why her Daddy's coffin ain't gonna sit right in the hole when it goes down."

Vernon stares at Eugene, in much the same manner that Scottie has taken to staring at him.

Eugene is tired all over again, tired of unpleasantness and the implications of Vernon's statement. Goldenrod Cemetery is not obligated by state rules to pour concrete vaults into the graves because of the cost involved. Some clients, a very *few* of Eugene's clients, have been lowered into concrete vaults, *at their own expense.* Wheeler Funeral Homes has never absorbed, *gratis,* the cost for a vault and Eugene does not consider it good business to do so for anyone.

"She's not coming Vernon. She says it's too much for her. And by the way, that's not the issue. If you were digging out the holes deep enough, and by *deep enough* I mean six feet, not just about five feet, I mean, a *full* six feet lined with lime and gravel, then I don't need to pour concrete."

Eugene does not, as a matter of professional policy, swear when speaking to his employees but he is angry enough to abandon his practiced professional demeanor. "The *effing* coffin will lie fine if you dig out the hole!"

"Whatever you say, *Boss.*" Vernon smiles, revealing his yellow teeth, making it clear that Eugene *is probably fucked* and what is he going to do about it?

On the first Friday in June, Bertram Biggs passed to whatever reward was waiting for him, as his doctors predicted. The newspapers quoted the prison warden as saying that, "In his final hour, Biggs behaved more cooperatively than at any other time of his term in prison." The town newspaper also printed a front-page photograph of Regina Biggs hugging her father during a visiting session. Although the caption under the photograph did not identify the blond teenager in the small holding room with Regina and Bertram, the accompanying story reported, "Scottie Wheeler, son of the prominent businessman behind Wheeler Funeral Homes, lent Ms. Biggs moral support."

Again, Eugene and Lois found themselves sitting down with their son for a talk. This time, at issue was the lie Scottie had employed to gain use of his mother's car for the three-hour drive to the state penitentiary facility.

"I didn't do anything wrong," Scottie insisted. "I asked Mom in an email if I could borrow the car for the day to give a friend a ride and she replied yes. I have the email to prove it." Scottie had not broken his vow of silence with his parents except to respond to their questions regarding his trip to the prison. Bertram Biggs had died the day before and Scottie was dressed in black jeans and T-shirt to demonstrate sympathy for Regina. He was dripping, having been ordered by Eugene to come in from the porch where he had been sitting in the Saturday afternoon rain.

Lois sighed and Eugene knew what she was thinking. It would be easier to punish Scottie for his deceptions, for his sullen silences and for his public betrayal of his father at Career Day if, otherwise, he wasn't such *a good kid.* He was due to graduate the following Wednesday and would be at the top of his class. Every college to which he had applied had accepted him, but so far, Scottie had refused all offers to matriculate. Scottie wanted, he indicated in digital correspondence, either to join the Peace Corps for the next four years *or* to attend college with Regina Biggs. He further indicated to his mother with a series of bolded letters and exclamation points that the *only* college Regina could afford was the area's junior college *and* that Scottie would *only* attend if his father spoke out publicly on the injustice of the Bertram Biggs situation. Otherwise, Scottie informed his mother, he would *definitely* join the Peace Corps and would *renounce* his membership in the Wheeler family.

Lois leaned forward and grasped her son's chin. "If you were the parents, Scottie, what would you do about this? Would you want your son running off in a car for hours at a time when his parents don't know where he is?"

Lois was a small woman with brown hair and nervously shaking hands. She had given up smoking ten years earlier, when a surgeon found cysts in her lungs, removed them and warned her that she wouldn't be so lucky the second time around. At the onset of the cancer scare, Lois had instructed Eugene to send her body to a crematorium. "I never liked the idea of being stuck under the ground," she told Eugene in a revelation.

Lois had kicked her nicotine addiction but had never managed to control her need to keep her hands close to her mouth. Her nails and cuticles were chewed and often bled, but other than the appearance of her hands, she kept herself up well. She was a great cook and a better tennis player and Eugene believed that whatever problems he might have with Scottie, his marriage with Lois could be defined as *well-organized.*

"If I were my parents I wouldn't worry about my son driving their car to take his girlfriend to see her dying father." Scottie lowered his mother's hand to her lap. "I'd say to myself, hey, here's my kid who doesn't drink, has never even tried drugs or cigarettes, and makes better grades than I ever thought about. I'd back the hell off, that's what I'd do." Scottie folded his arms and slung his head backward, to shake off the water. "If I were in your position, I'd come out publicly on the topic of where Bertram Biggs should be buried. I'd do the right thing, not be a coward."

Eugene rubbed his eyes. It had been a long week. Twelve funerals and one of his limousines had broken down. He didn't have time or willpower to maintain his composure with each living human being who thought his or her dead person was the most important dead person in the world. He had no patience to explain to his son again, via email, that whatever he said was likely to be ignored by half the county's population and disliked by the other half and so, speaking up in the face of such strong public sentiment would do him and Wheeler Funeral Homes no good.

"*It's not my job* to figure out who deserves to be buried where, Scottie. I can only say that according to the title papers his late wife had filed with the probate office, Bertram Biggs appears to be the lawful owner of the plot. *It's not my job* to say this or that about his character. I had suggested to his court attorney that Biggs consider a military burial elsewhere because it appears he was entitled to one." Eugene stopped, out of breath. He wished the sound of the rain on his three-story house would subside, so that he could walk in the sunshine to breathe fresh air. "I'm going to do my best to follow the wishes of my client and act within the parameters the law allows."

"Siding with the law keeps you out of jail, Dad. It doesn't put you in the right." Scottie stood up, spraying water against Eugene's face. "I'm still not talking to you or Mom unless you can come up with some other charges against me. I want you to know that I'm not letting this go when I speak at graduation." Scottie opened the sliding glass door that led to the outdoor porch. "Hope you're not afraid to get wet."

Eugene looked at his wife and shook his own head, flipping secondhand water off his face. He knew Lois wanted him to follow Scottie outside, to talk to his son, to agree with him, to bring Scottie back to their home. But he was feeling tired. Though he had not napped in years, he thought he might wander into the guest bedroom on the third floor of his home, lie with his eyes closed and listen to the sound of water hitting the roof—the new tight roof he had paid for after the books had closed on his last fiscal year. Lois turned her mouth into a stiff line. Eugene left the room thinking he would never have permitted one of his clients to carry such an unattractive expression into the Afterlife.

The sky is drizzling when the casket arrives. The driver is on time. Eugene has trained his employees rigorously, ingraining the importance of customer service and *flexibility in the face of adversity* but he experiences less satisfaction than he should in the affirmation that meticulous instruction of his employees has paid off. Vernon has finished lining the grave with gravel and, overall, they are running exactly one hour ahead of schedule which puts them one hour ahead of anyone coming to serve injunctive papers against the interment. Eugene has never experienced this particular brand of funeral controversy but he does know that once the body goes in the ground and is even *partially* covered with earth, then any troublemakers would have to obtain a court order to disinter the body *legally* and should that happen, then Wheeler Funeral Homes would gracefully bow out of the thankless and money losing task of burying Bertram Biggs and ship the casket COD to another cemetery where people care a little bit less about who sleeps next to their dead and care a little bit more about minding their own business when it comes to a poor bastard who died from cancer in prison.

As Eugene helps the driver slide the casket from the belly of the hearse onto a rolling cart, he suddenly, desperately, wants to be on open water. Bounding over the swells of the ocean during a time when no one faulted a husband for shooting the asshole who had stolen his money and knocked up his wife, and when no one cared about proper burials other than tying the body in a gunny sack and dropping it with a prayer into the ocean, where the dead flesh would feed the scavenger sharks and the skeleton would settle against the bottom, lending structure to a coral formation, and then, hundreds of years later, a woman would snorkel in the blue water to spy on brightly striped fish feeding on the reef, safe from the long lines of fisherman who feared to power their boats into shallow water.

Rain falls harder and Eugene looks upward, expecting a roll of surf, but instead sees a darkening sky. He abandons all hope of keeping his clothes in order and peels off his jacket, throwing it across a concrete block sunk so far into the earth only SKEL is visible. Vernon hooks the cart to his tractor and turns the machine toward the part of the cemetery where Bertram is to be buried. The wheels spin before the groundskeeper shifts into four-wheel drive and powers out of the wet ground. Rain soaks Eugene's shirt and his pleated pants sink into ankle-deep mud.

Eugene does not pretend to be calm and shouts at Vernon to hurry. The weather is bearing in on them, only slightly ahead of those who want to disrupt the burial service for Wheeler Funeral Homes—potentially a nasty and newsworthy event. Vernon's attempt to navigate across firmer ground causes him to cut his tractor close to the barbed wire fence separating the burial ground from the cattle. Eugene curses, this time not under his breath, but loudly. "Fucking watch where you're going Vernon! You're going to hit the fence!"

The groundskeeper does not acknowledge Eugene and continues to navigate closely along the fence line. The yellow-toothed man is drinking from his bottle and laughing and Eugene swears to himself that he will *have this man fired*, if for nothing else, acting like a complete *white trash stereotype* and bringing disgrace to a final resting place for dozens of people.

Eugene reminds the driver of the hearse to wash the car thoroughly of the cemetery's mud. Then the funeral home director takes long but mindful steps across the cemetery toward Bertram's grave. Halfway, he stops to wipe his upper lip with a handkerchief he carries in his pocket. Several horseflies set upon him, circling his head and buzzing in what he interprets to be a threatening manner. He has been raised on the prairie and knows flies never stray far from livestock. In one horrible second, Eugene understands there must be a break in the fence and he runs toward the eastern side of the cemetery where three fence posts have been pushed over. Hungry cattle drift from their overgrazed field, tearing at the grass that is unusually lush and tall as a result of heavy rains and Vernon's lack of proper mowing technique. The trespassing beasts are not spooked by Eugene as he waves his arms and shouts, hoping to drive the animals across the wounded fencerow into the barren field where they belong. They are undisturbed as they feast on the grass of the dead, enjoying what looks like their first good feed in all the years people have been fertilizing the soil at Goldenrod. Eugene glances at his watch and sees he has forty-five minutes until the sheriff is due to arrive.

Eugene runs back toward Bertram's hole. Under the deluge, the cemetery is no longer a sacred resting place but a mud pit decorated with gravel and plastic flowers and chips of pottery. He realizes this is no place to bury anyone, but remembers that *this burial is what Bertram wanted*. Wishes of the dead should be honored by the living and he, the proprietor of the memorial ceremony, the man who can responsibly claim *to care about the dearly departed* will only be carrying out his client's wishes here in this muddy corner of poor man's death.

Vernon avoids a cow in his path by knocking down three wooden crosses and then resumes pulling Bertram Biggs' body to the only piece of property the deceased convict had ever owned.

The county's high school commencement ceremony was held outdoors on the football field because neither the gymnasium nor the performing arts auditorium contained enough seating for parents, relatives and acquaintances of the two hundred graduating seniors. The janitorial staff had erected a series of large white tents on the field to protect students and school officials from the afternoon downpour. As parents of a student speaker, the Wheelers were seated in the front row of the stadium, affording them a view unobstructed by raised umbrellas. Eugene held his own umbrella over his wife and lightly touched her arm. As they were being seated, Lois shrugged away his touch.

"What's the matter with you?" Eugene hissed at her, quietly. Tom Bunt was in the second row next to a church pastor. Bunt had not returned Eugene's nod of acknowledgement and Eugene knew the council president was still angry with Wheeler Funeral Homes. Bunt had failed to convince the state legislature to block Biggs' burial. The day before, Eugene himself had signed for the convict's body when it was delivered to his mortuary facility by state authorities. Normally, Eugene buried an indigent client the same day he received the corpse but out of respect for Regina Biggs, he had scheduled the service for the day after graduation.

"I told you I need a vacation, that's what is wrong with me." Lois did not attempt to mute her voice. "I'm exhausted." Lois wiped at her eyes. "I'm the only one who seems to realize the irony involved here: you're burying Biggs tomorrow, even though you won't publicly support it. My son is graduating first in his class and won't agree to go to any of the colleges that want him." Lois stopped speaking and chewed on her right thumbnail. Eugene did not try to comfort her. Instead he handed her the umbrella and turned up the collar on his raincoat.

The high school band played the traditional march and graduating students filed out of the football locker room, shielded by the tunnel of tents. When Scottie emerged out of the tunnel and ascended the steps to the wooden stage, he was wearing a white sign with large block lettering attached to the front of his commencement gown. The words read A DECENT BURIAL FOR THE DEAD. Eugene pulled his fedora low on his forehead. He was thankful, again, to be seated in the front row so that he would not have to watch the crowd turn to interpret his reaction.

The noise of the rain mixed with the sounds of the speeches. Eugene listened to the principal congratulating the class, acknowledging its accomplishments and asking Scottie Wheeler, the class valedictorian, to come to the podium to reflect, briefly, on the moment.

Scottie rose. Lois tensed and murmured, loudly enough, "Bless his heart," giving clear signal that she was *a proud mother* and that her husband was *a heartless bastard* for driving away their son. Lois raised the digital camera she had purchased for the event. Eugene calculated he had hawked one steel-casket ceremony to pay for the device.

Scottie took long steps across the stage to the end of the second row of students where, due to her early alphabetical listing, Regina Biggs was seated. Scottie grabbed her hand and pulled her toward the podium, pushing past the school principal who had risen from his seat, apparently surprised by the valedictorian's detour. Regina trotted behind him, her hair falling in front of her face and her arms crossed across her chest.

The class speaker grasped the podium microphone between both hands.

In Eugene's peripheral vision, Lois held the camera high and adjusted the tiny silver knob controlling the microphone's volume; Tom Bunt leaned forward, his lips pulled into a genuine snarl. The woman seated behind Eugene whispered, "Scottie Wheeler beat out my son because his father *bought* his grades. *Tutors!*"

The voice emanating from the microphone was the same one Eugene had known through the course of his son's post-pubescent life but this was of no significance to him because, at that moment, he was not listening. Though he resolved never to admit to it, even if someone would ask him on his death bed, when all the old mistakes would be forgiven and forgotten, Eugene decided *not to listen* to the phrases his defiant son appeared to be delivering extemporaneously. Instead, the funeral home director imagined that he and Scottie were locked inside the dark basement morgue. The scene he pictured had Scottie delivering this speech, presumably an intelligent ethical admonishment for the edification of the graduates, to the dead convict. By virtue of scientific tissue regeneration or the mystery of old-time laying-on-of-hands religion, Bertram's body would begin to breathe. The recently dead man would ask Scottie who had covered him with faggot makeup and then would ask for his shotgun. The recently dead man would touch the spot where his diseased liver had been healed and would throw his naked legs over the edge of the metal table, swinging them above the floor. Scottie would fall on his knees in the presence of such an accomplishment, the likes of which had not been seen since old Lazarus limped out of his cave, stinking and smelling of oils and decaying linen rags, and Bertram would point at the boy and yell *goddamn you for bringing me back* and would touch his blue-veined feet to the floor and flex his fingers, testing them for the task of strangling both witnesses to his latest crime of unnatural entrance into the living.

"…and I thank my father, Eugene Wheeler, for preserving the right of a member of this society to be laid to rest as he wants to be. My father is an honorable man. I know that he will…" Hearing his own name briefly brought Eugene back to the football stadium but the booing from the offended attendees caused the funeral director to hurtle away again, escaping the echoes.

Recalling that heavy rains often caused flash floods, Eugene decided he could be comfortable underwater, underneath the melée of cresting waves. He would hold his breath and deliberate on the morality of wishing a murderous flood onto the football field, carrying away the sound system and folding chairs and microphones, drowning the electronic accessories of the moment in the slap of a fast-moving river. He would swim toward his son and lift him above the waterline and insist, *Scottie, take a look and you decide if you want to come back underneath to tell me what you see.*

Eugene heard sparse clapping. The force of the rain had relented slightly and the notion of flash floods diminished to the real fear that rising water might prevent the proper interment of the father of the black-haired girl who appeared in front of him, extending her hand and whispering, *thank you.* The force of habit saved the prominent businessman from offending the teenager because without years of practicing bereavement etiquette, he would not have been prepared to extend his long arms around her when she threw her head against his chest and sobbed.

The rain is gathering force over Goldenrod Cemetery. Eugene instructs the groundskeeper to pull the casket-laden cart closer to the edge of the open grave. If what Vernon says is true, there are only thirty brief minutes left to bury the casket before Tom Bunt arrives.

"Asshole!" Eugene sends thoughts of painful death unaccompanied by a dignified memorial service through the air to Bunt and his posse of holy rollers. He stares at Vernon, defiant, hoping the drunken gravedigger will mistakenly take offense and get off the tractor. Despite the impending threat of an injunctive intercession, the three-ring circus of comedy that could ensue, Eugene feels like starting a fistfight.

Laughing, Vernon shifts the tractor into gear. "If I sit here a minute longer, my engine's gonna flood. Looks like we'll have to bury him by hand." The rain courses harder, flattening the gray whiskers against the groundskeeper's face. Vernon tosses a shovel that had been strapped to the tractor seat; it lands on the ground and sinks into the mud.

"You cracker! You hillbilly!" Eugene follows the retreating tractor three long steps but stops when mud from the tires sprays his face. "I don't care what I have to do, *you are fired*!" A wave of hilarity invades the corners of Eugene's head, causing him to anticipate his own time to drop dead. When someone else will have to lower his stinking corpse into a hole. He will leave no instructions, not a scrap of paper as to how he should be buried or burned or tossed aside because he *doesn't give a flying rat's ass*. Even if the worms of hell consume his intestinal tract in the fiery pit then *at least* he won't be standing in this puke-colored dirt trying to frighten an alcoholic half-wit with the information his grave digging services will no longer be required.

The tall man pries the long-handled shovel from the mud and strains against Bertram's casket, edging it forward. The box tips slowly at first, then gathers momentum and when Eugene pushes harder, the box turns one hundred eighty degrees and Biggs is lying inside his coffin face down in the hole that has not been cemented, his painted lips and nose filling with water. The dead criminal is drowning in his grave as Eugene shovels dirt on top of him until the rotten wooden handle cracks and the tool splinters into useless pieces.

Eugene does not hesitate to fall on his hands and knees, to employ the full reach of his long arms to embrace and then sweep heavy wet dirt over the box, hoping to cover this criminal, to rid himself of the misery of bearing this client's load, and to rid himself of this burden, this grief, this corpse of an unrepentant man who caused nothing but trouble when he was alive and is now causing significant heartache to Wheeler Funeral Homes now that he is not. The reason why *he*, Eugene, should be the one to suffer under pouring rain, is one he cannot fit into any moral order except that it is his *job* to do so and if this is the only reason, then why has he ever pretended to care about *honoring the living* because he has conducted the *business of death* and he understand it is about time he stops *pulling the wool* over everyone's eyes and screams the truth at them: that the business of burying the dead is *pointless*; that they are silly and self-absorbed, all of them, in their sorrows and sadness and if he had his way about things there would be no embalming, no caskets, or flowers but only a nicely limed and shallow dirt hole. A shallow grave to prevent any contamination of underground aquifers and plentiful lime to eliminate unpleasant odors and to raise the pH of the soil, to hasten decomposition so the poor dead bastard could get on with the business of rotting and pushing up daisies or maybe red clover so the cows could enjoy a nice meal.

He pushes and scrapes in the mud, forgetting that Vernon is supposed to rejoin him, to assist him. He forgets to read the quote he has typed on a small piece of paper and folded in his wallet. The passage is from Psalms and is one that for all his years of directing funerals he still has not been able to memorize, the one about walking in the valley of shadows and something about overflowing cups and sleeping in green pastures. There is only the rain and the earthworms and the pine box that is slowly disappearing under armfuls of wet earth. Eugene rests when he is convinced the coffin is completely covered with a layer of dirt. Bertram Biggs may not be fully six feet under, but *by God* the dead criminal is buried.

The man in charge of the ceremony rises from his hands and knees and believes he is the last and only man who can understand how loss and grief are great betrayers, the final evils of impulse that lead people through the rites of death like fish swimming around a living reef grown over detritus from shipwrecks. Ennobled by these thoughts, he is satisfied that he has performed the duties required of him.

Eugene turns away from the site, the hole a reminder of everything that *remains undone.* He is fatigued and breathing hard. A throbbing settles comfortably in his ears, like the relief of the ebb of deep and quiet water.

People are watching him. From across the cemetery, Vernon Skelton is watching him from atop the tractor parked in front of Goldenrod's gate. The gate is closed and Tom Bunt is pointing at the groundskeeper, issuing threats of arrest and detainment while the county sheriff is watching Eugene from the shelter of his patrol car parked further away on the road. The sheriff is laughing and holding a radio to his lips.

Eugene cannot guess how many minutes they have borne witness to his wallowing in the mud.

Outside the gate, Scottie is shielding Regina with a large red umbrella. The girl is crying into a handkerchief and wearing Scottie's raincoat. This time, Scottie must have obtained permission to use his mother's car because Lois is watching from the driver's seat of her sedan, idling roadside. They are apart from each other, the distance between them greater than the length of Goldenrod Cemetery. Their distance, their chosen consequence of doubt, is *the privilege of the living.*

He is not careful this time as he walks under the pouring clouds, moving among the cattle dispersed throughout the graveyard, eating the grass of the dead. Eugene steps on the bodies of everyone in his way, ignoring the rules of respect for people he has buried.

His steps are without purpose, knocking against etched blocks and rotting wooden crosses. He does not think about Scottie or his wife or how he may have to answer to Bunt's people and the state licensing board. Eugene Wheeler decides he will travel over the wet ground until he covers the several miles to his firmly roofed home, his protection from the open sky, and thinks as he leaves the graveyard behind: *it is absolutely indecent how close the dead people rest next to each other.* He strides across them, arms outstretched like a penitent, head tilted back so he can feel the full force of the rain.

Counting Coup

I will steal these words from my grandmother. "They are facts," she writes, "that are not copyrighted." I will steal these facts because she is old, because she will never hear about my theft. Even as I steal them, I will acknowledge her contribution. I will steal these facts from her because they compose a story I would like to have invented, would have enjoyed stringing together like her blue and white bead mural depicting the stormy pull of the ocean. That picture hangs on the sliver of wall space between the refrigerator and the scarred wooden door leading to the front yard. The home she lives in has only one door and everyone who leaves must look at the single decoration hanging on its walls.

I will steal these words from her though she might grant me permission anyway. If I were brave enough, I would ask to copyright her memories and inflate them like the pig bladders she put her lips against, blowing air to manufacture toys for me, her only grandchild. But I am not brave in this way, not brave in any of the ways required by an open telling of these facts, not copyrighted, how she killed a man and never repented for that act.

"It's a fact," my grandmother says, "that you have to do some things and hope people will understand later and if they don't, that's too bad. I'd do it again."

"Grandma, it's also a fact that hell is where you're condemned to repeat your sins for eternity." My eyes wander from her face, past her hunched shoulders to the image of a stormy sea. No jeopardized people or boats, only waves crashing against each other.

Her lips shake, she is afflicted in that way but nerve problems do not affect her thinking. "Then I'm prepared."

The land she occupies is not hers. Someone had stolen the land from her before she was born.

She lives in a subsidized tract house that does not belong to her. The tomato garden in the front yard does not belong to her. She has no title, no fee simple claim. The half-acre with its garden on the reservation is held in trust for her by the people of the United States. Indulgences from the great Congress to people from whom the land was stolen.

Stolen, stolen, stolen.

So you think if you are a descendant of natives. So you think if you remember when your own grandfather donned a black stovepipe hat, a feathered vest, and a black homemade suit of the best wool his wife could procure from the Indian Bureau's General Store, all to put his mark on paper promising black hills to his tribe. So you think if you are my grandmother and you are only one-quarter Indian—the rest of you is white—but the native portion of you refuses to be dissolved in the sea of solutions, *compromises* offered after that paper—and another and another and another—are voided.

One bad turn deserves another. So you think, if you are my grandmother and the Prohibition is on and your husband is distributing to the wealthy as far away as Boston and turning the proceeds back into a hog farm. The imprint of flying arrows has not quite abandoned the blood of your heart, you, the one-quarter native with bright blue eyes, and when the Indian Bureau's representative discovers your husband has been bootlegging, you have no hesitation in deciding what turn you will take. And no remorse once you have taken it.

She has lived a long life, if you define eighty-nine years as long, and she has lived it consistently, if you define a marriage of sixty-six years to the same man as consistent. There are other attributes to speak of: she was the first to pour herself a whiskey at a party and until a few years ago, when her bones began stiffening, was the last person to leave. Now she sits quietly at reservation parties and will accept a drink if it is offered, but will ask within an hour to be driven to her allotted home.

Outspoken tendencies thicken her native blood. As a young woman, she was victorious in a regional beauty contest but was disqualified when the officials discovered she was mixed. This humiliation in 1930, when the five-dollar prize money from the lady's magazine could have fed a family for a week

"You shouldn't have told the woman your real last name," I said to her when I heard the story for the first time. I was seventeen years old, her age during the contest. The distant lost dollars during those famously hard times hit me hard, like watching treasure swept out to sea.

"I was angry. She passed a comment about the reservation girls' hair. She said *they* all had lice and advised us to pay nineteen cents to buy the formula from the back of her magazine. Said it would kill their lice before they could infect *us*. She didn't give me the prize money but told me I didn't look like an Indian."

As a younger woman, my grandmother had the thick, blue-black hair of a native. Her hair has now turned a color befitting her age, but the rest of her remains dark. Her husband's people are strapping, thick men with thick accents. They marry light-haired women. They work in mines in Kentucky, trading their sunny days for above-average working men's wages underground. Their chests are broad, like curves of utility vehicle bumpers, and they wear tartan plaid shirts, heavy work boots, and canvas pants naturally, as if they were born wearing the uniforms their grandfathers wore a hundred years earlier.

When I think of these men, I imagine them striding across windy and elevated plateaus, bearing rifles and swords and singing and I do not understand how I can be related to them through my father and his father. There is nothing in my blood that feels like bagpipes and heaths and I have joked with my grandmother that in our women the Celtic blood is thin, diluted by viscous native fluid that simply refuses to bow down to one more white man.

My grandmother has never met her Kentucky relatives, the children and grandchildren of her in-laws, though they would, if I asked, send for her to live in their homes. It is part of the family legend, what she has accomplished. She and her husband produced monthly checks for his three brothers and two sisters—sums enough for private school tuitions piano lessons, summer camps, and linen suits. Both recipients and providers were gracious in the exchange, with the manners that extended families with well-to-do relatives adopt. A form of tribal sharing, differentiated by genetics, the facts of different blood overlooked or dismissed as topics too relevant or precarious to risk.

Marital finances were my grandmother's responsibility and accounts were solely in her name, Nelly Slimfeather. As did her mother, she took a white man for her husband and kept her maiden name. I, too, bear the native appellation but have shortened my given name to Nell. I do not know if my life will constitute the end of our bloodline. I have no brothers or sisters. Those siblings of mine, stolen from me by a woman who did not trust her fate.

"There are too many things that can happen to me. Suppose there were three of you kids and something happens? I know my mother could handle one of you but how could she raise three? She was already sixty when you were born and besides, I haven't found a new Daddy yet." My mother repeated these words to me when, like all children, I pestered her for the reasons why I couldn't have a baby brother or sister.

"Grandma wouldn't have to raise them. I would raise them. I could be their mother." Like dolls, I thought, babies were surely no more difficult than dolls to bring safely into the world.

"You wouldn't want that." My mother puffed on her cigarette

as she prepared for her date, brushing her hair upward, into a bouffant over her expensive red, knee-length skirt and her white, soft leather pumps.

I dabbed my mother's rouge on my cheeks but secretly I hated her for thieving potential brothers and sisters from me.

Most grandmothers have pictures hanging on their walls, portraits of grandchildren captured by the school's hired photographer. It is an annual event, students lining up outside the gymnasium where the photographer has set up a large camera on a tripod. Parents send checks to order the size and number of prints. Kids trade wallet size photos; larger shots are hung with pride in small living rooms of reservation families long after the children are grown. As reminders, I think, when children have left the reservation, are unemployed, or in jail. Reminders of what might have been, the buck-toothed smiles captured under glass, their hopeful trajectories static and unaltered, except by dust.

In a custom she observes from the old ways, there are no photographs on my grandmother's walls. No pictures of herself to be stored in a scrapbook; no pictures of her daughter, no pictures of the granddaughter who came into her care. Nelly Slimfeather is locally famous for not allowing it. Says the human soul is not meant to be caught and trapped under a glass frame by the same idiots who would snare butterflies to pin on boards. Says the spirit needs to course and pulse, needs to flutter in the veins. Once that spirit is captured, dammed like a river, then dust is all it will gather.

My mother did not observe this custom. Once married, she had hundreds of pictures made of herself and my father and when I came along, of me. She was not afraid to attach our images to paper. Though I cannot remember, I sat with my parents for portraits, black cloths behind us, smiling for the photographer who asked my mother to position one hand over the other so the family portrait would be perfectly posed.

Those pictures are gone, destroyed, except for the one with my mother's carefully folded hands. This print is still pressed into a book of American history I never returned to the school's library. The one place I knew Nelly Slimfeather would never look. She distrusts history as much as she distrusts photographs and laughed at homework assignments asking me to choose correct dates for the "establishment" of American settlements.

I know where my grandmother destroyed the photograph albums, the Polaroid shots, the negatives. She did it behind the abandoned hog barn. I found the ashy pile weeks later, charred metal frames jutting from a gray and black pile of soot next to a rusting trough where she and my grandfather had spread slop.

"I can't quite decide if I'm angry with you for burning the pictures." I tell this to her during my vacation from pushing papers around the top of my enormous wooden work desk, papers recording financial transactions of multinational corporations and different papers disguising the same transactions. Records of loss and records of profits, legally and illegally gained. No pictures though. Pictures of the people involved in negotiations, closings and deals don't exist in my files. Perhaps this would be considered too personal, too unbusinesslike. Or maybe too dangerous. Not many people I work with would want their images attached to their words.

"I was within my rights."

"They were my records of myself. And my parents."

"You don't need pictures for records. You have your brain. You have your memories."

"It's hard not to want the pictures, Grandma." I sip my red wine, liking how the drops slide down my throat and liking the knowledge that someone has grown these grapes in a vineyard with lush soil and attention to the living vine's perpetual care. I don't drink her liquor, mostly because it came from a still underneath my grandfather's barn, from a dark and airless room with an entrance disguised by piles of hog manure. I know that hidden still provided my rarified education, the private school with ivy on the walls, the large law firm—yet I dislike the whiskey and dislike how my grandmother drinks from cases stored in her root cellar, neatly crated reminders of all the money to be made by stealing the customs of other people.

"Well, it was hard for me to move from the farm to here. Sometimes things are hard."

She sips her drink with three ice cubes. Just three. She hasn't changed since she started drinking whiskey seventy-two years ago. I think her memories come easier if nothing changes.

"I didn't have a choice. No one could help you if you're living out on the farm."

"Your grandfather and I worked like dogs to get off the reservation. Then you bring me back. That's not helping me."

We are tipsy, no—we are drunk and fall into the easy silence of people whose brains have lapsed into neural cruise control. We drink through our evening, our tongues forming accusations. But I know she is guilty of more than burning photographs, her guilt runs deep as the furrows she dug in the ground. Pig blood spilled into those holes at slaughter and when my grandfather finished, my grandmother pushed fresh dirt over the ditches. Pig entrails, remains of corpses were covered, left to decay and vanish under the dry dust of this long-disputed land.

In my profession, we use written words to validate our agreements, not beads or feathers exchanged with our counterparties. Those beads and feathers, formerly possessions of some value, were used by my ancestors as what we now call consideration. No contract exists without consideration, the mutually agreeable exchange between parties. Contracts without consideration are indulgences from one party to another and indulgences can be rescinded, renewed, or amended on a whim. Like treaties. When there is nothing for one party to offer the other, when threats of war are empty and hollow as the cheeks of starving men, there can be no valid contract. Indulgences can be washed away from parchment by long, red lines of a people's blood, as ephemeral as the pulse of a calf crated for veal during the few weeks of its life. Each day of the calf's life, a deceptively protective indulgence.

It's because of the words. Words that have been lost, words that have become famous, words etched into monuments, words engraved into plates to print money and words that have been ignored. Better they should have photographed events, captured the souls of those making promises, to render their enemies impotent. Because words didn't help my ancestors. And my grandmother's words don't help me understand how she could have ignored threats, spoken publicly, by the native relatives of a Bureau man gone missing. According to the statement my grandmother gave to the county newspaper, despite what his schedule noted, the Bureau agent never arrived to discuss her application for a government subsidy.

Or it could be that by avoiding the camera's lens, she preserves herself. Someone glimpsing a picture of my grandmother when she was possessed with her youth, beautiful with long hair and long fingers would not recognize her shrunken hull. Would not recognize the once tall quarter-blood who decided she was tired of trading her favors for the favor of the Bureau man's silence. Would not recognize the quarter-blood who swung a hatchet across the throat of that drunken full-blood. It could be my grandmother refuses to pose for the camera to avoid becoming the culprit responsible for her own deterioration.

So there is only one picture of me as a child, though as an adult, I confess to having broken with my grandmother's beliefs. I possess photo albums chronicling my adventures in college, law school and now, pictures of myself vacationing with the blue-blooded friends I acquired on the way. They are thin women with straight blonde hair and cheekbones that seem sculpted by the same cosmetic surgeon's hand.

Their own tribes, their own breeding. Not so different from mine except their family criminals are generations past and can be discussed in romantic tones. Fur trappers who amassed fortunes annihilating whole species; cattle ranchers who shot small landowners and raped their wives; steel and railroad kings who founded banking empires by shooting Irish and Chinamen. And I don't forget the Christian ministers who received land grants in exchange for civilizing the Indians who cooperated and relocating the ones who wouldn't. For this reason, I am suspicious of Evangelicals. My beliefs are strong, but my pulse rises when money is solicited to preach the single path to God, through the blood of His son.

When I think of my own blood, I know it is a gift from Nelly

Slimfeather. As I lay in my crib, she slipped past my dozing mother and cut a line in my palm, pressing it against her bleeding one. Steeping my blood with hers, replacing watery white blood with the thicker, darker liquid that had coursed through her heart for six decades.

She stole my blood from me when I was a baby, let me bleed and bleed until finally, my mother woke to the burning smell of my grandmother cauterizing my split flesh with the flat edge of the heated knife. A dark, raised scar appears when I extend my hand at cocktail parties, when I greet clients, when I run my hand across a lover's chest.

I did not cry, she tells me, because she held her hand over my mouth and distracted me from pain with whispers of greater pains I would meet, of potent warriors for whom I should save my fear. Warned me about the shadow of the long spear of revenge haunting women with our blood. "The shadow appears," she said, "raised high in front of your eyes and you will see it the last moment you breathe in these hills."

But I feel safe, beyond the retribution my grandmother believes waits for us. I do not live under gloomy hills and do not feel called to answer for false words and native sins. Past arguments with my grandmother have exasperated me, kept me away from her reservation, her dry slop yard and dusky flesh.

"You should tell me everything," I said three years earlier, when I moved her from the farm to the reservation with its grocery store and doctor. "It gets harder to remember what you told people the longer you live after the telling of it."

"Remembering has nothing to do with the truth." Her words came at me like a sharp projectile. I believe Nelly Slimfeather enjoyed piercing me with her speech.

"More of a reason to tell me everything."

"You're putting me in this house to die."

"I'm putting you in this house so you can live better."

"That's what you tell yourself?"

She despises the reservation house because she misses the sweep of fields running upward to the tree line and she misses the cold air blowing out of foggy depressions. But the house is sturdy and safe and unless she is willing to move into an assisted home, it is the best I can do. Nelly Slimfeather is free to leave the reservation whenever she chooses, free to leave behind the cement block foundation and cheap paneled walls. Free to trust me with her cares and free to trust me with her fears, if she chooses.

I look at the wind and the waves crashing in the landscape she keeps—a picture of the ocean she has never seen—and I imagine small, white birds lifting themselves from the frothy waves, transformed by teary salt and raindrops into spirits imbued with long, free lives.

You should tell me everything. I think these words but I doubt if Nelly Slimfeather would speak the truth.

When my mother died, I had not seen my father for fifteen years, nearly the same amount of time I had been alive. He had reunited with his family, all miners and loggers. I received letters describing how hard he was working and how much he missed me. There were phone calls, usually on my birthday and Christmas and we spoke about schoolwork and which team might win whatever major sporting title was being decided. I last spoke to him on the birthday after my mother's funeral.

"Grandpa's teaching me to drive in his sedan." These words were only partially true; my grandfather had offered to let me drive on country roads but I had not worked up the courage to do so. But this self-enhancing lie comforted me. To my father, hundreds of miles away and far from the hills of the reservation, the fabricated words made me feel brave, deserving of the flesh I had inherited. Warrior flesh. Flesh that did not cry and weep because her family had either been killed off or relocated.

"That's great, Nell," my father said, his voice the most familiar part of him. I knew that if I saw my father passing me on the street, I would only recognize him if he called out. But he would have to use his phone voice because I would not recognize his voice shouting, singing or crying. He had not attended my mother's funeral; instead, he had sent flowers. It wasn't a good idea, my grandmother said, for him to visit. Too much bad blood.

"And he's going to give me his car when I pass my driver's test."

"He's a generous man." My father's voice paused and when he exhaled his breath, loudly, I understood. This part of his voice I had heard before. I would recognize his silence from any distance.

"How are you doing?" he resumed.

"Fine. I'm doing fine, Dad. It's OK. I'm really OK." I spoke the truth. My mother's death was only surprising to me because it hadn't happened sooner. She had always claimed something would be coming. She had inherited a sense of doom. Though she hated the poor and scratchy schools, the drinking, the peddling of cheap crafts to tourists, she stayed close to the reservation to face whatever fate was hers.

"I loved your mother."

"Yeah, I know. So did I."

"Your grandmother tells me you're going away to school."

"Yeah, I want to go. It's the best school, I guess."

"Your grandparents are generous. They will take good care of you."

My father did not call again, nor did I call him although I occasionally receive a Christmas card from my mother's cousins telling me he looks well and that his drinking is controlled. I infer that living far away from the reservation suits him.

"She would not have wanted you to live with us, on the farm," my grandmother said to me after the crowd left my mother's grave. The funeral happened three days after the autopsy had been finished, with its inconclusive ruling as to whether my mother had died by her own hand or somebody else's.

My mother and I had lived off the reservation, in town. She owned a two-story Colonial house with a garage large enough to hold three cars. She worked only occasionally, taking on part-time jobs as a secretary or ringing totals in the checkout line of the supermarket when she wanted to pass her time. We were lucky, my single mother and I, because of my grandparents. She never worried about money because it appeared in the account that bore her name, Lilly Slimfeather, just as a magician's white rabbit appears inside an empty box.

After she died, money appeared in my accounts, like pirate's booty I stumbled on every month. The treasure was plentiful and mine to be spent with the ink of my signature. I practiced signing my name when I left my grandmother, enjoying the taste of hidden labors, hidden crimes.

Counting coup. This is how the Sioux touched their enemies—sometimes their relatives—with sharpened spears. A humiliation, really, to be touched that way, though mercifully harmless to the flesh of the conquered. *Keep your enemies alive if you want to humiliate them.* These are words my grandmother spoke as I boarded a plane to a private high school that would prepare me for life. *Kill them if you want a good story to tell.*

My grandmother has many good stories and she writes them freely as she fills each page of her life, recording hours that belong exclusively to her now my grandfather is gone. She writes in an enormous, leather-bound volume that begins with a page devoted solely to her name. A luxury. Every other page contains rows of tiny writing that I can only describe as spidery, though that term is antiquated. Of course keeping a journal is antiquated, but I do not attempt to convince her that words will fail her as surely as human flesh. That words can appease, amuse, and sadden but are quickly forgotten.

She believes differently. Nelly Slimfeather uses words to trace deep paths in towering black peaks topped by sparse needle trees. She creates tales where men and women of similar blood summon benevolent spirits from boulders, cliffs, and water. Tales in which people meet death because they acted with greed or malice. She scorches paths into her hillsides with the energy of her burning blood, marking her way as clearly as if she had anchored bright, flowing flags.

When we speak together, she professes that stories have comforted her people for centuries. That death is only a marker on the path traveled under the shadow of a long spear. I do not trust in her paths and do not seek comfort in her habit of stories. My native blood is drying and leaving me, like a snakeskin shed in the sun, its former inhabitant slithered and disappeared into the woods, under the rocks or perhaps into the water with only a diamond-cut head and a hissing, stinging pink tongue visible. Waiting to grow a protective new skin and seek refuge under the shadow of a large and unmoving mountain.

There are lies people tell because they *know* someone will disapprove and lies people tell because they *hope* someone will disapprove. I tell lies to my friends, stories about men I've known, or if I'm really on a spree, women. I tell lies to my colleagues, exaggerating how much I drink or how much I gamble or how rudely I behave toward women pushing baby strollers on the wrong side of the sidewalk. There is the thrill of watching their eyes widen, listening for even tones and the practiced quenching of judgment. There is something in me, they must think, so much raw, native blood of the kind that could kill and be killed with stoicism, native blood that forbids women to cry out in childbirth.

Do they believe me? When have they seen me career out of bars, man on one arm and woman on the other and when have they seen me push pregnant women out of my way or miss my mortgage payment because I spent the day at the track? I wonder when my grandmother speaks of her own life, that in this our blood runs the same. I wonder if her tales are meant to push her listeners and bind their spirits with misgivings. Setting her free, I suppose, to laugh at all of them, even at me. *Say what you will*, I imagine her singing and flying above the ground, drifting in and out of the cover of cloud banks, *you will never know me*.

"I dated a man from the Indian Bureau," my grandmother tells me, sitting hunched and still in the red chair with the small brown pillow on the seat, to cushion the pressure on her old bones. I wonder about her bones, how sturdy their composition, how long they can hold out before they snap.

"Grandpa's problem?" I have attempted to pry this story from her, demanded it of her. I do not care whether it hurts her to speak of it. So I ask it of her again, testing for the softness that should reside in old women. I am many glasses into my wine and my cheeks flush. I can feel it. I need no mirror to indicate my blood is rising.

"Yes. He didn't know what else to do about the problem with the Bureau."

I understood. The agents from the Bureau of Indian Affairs distributed Congressional money. Making sure, however, to include fees for themselves. The representatives were usually natives with wives, children, and in-laws who became dependent on the bribes, an accepted method of redistributing the white man's money.

My grandmother motions and I comply. I lift the silver tongs, pluck three cubes from the sterling silver ice bucket and deposit them in her glass. The serving set is a relic of my mother's. She enjoyed expensive objects and could, thanks to my grandmother, afford them easily. My mother and I—also beneficiaries of redistributed white man's money.

"What happened to that man?" I ask, hoping she will slip, hoping the alcohol will overcome her age and prudence.

"You know I don't know." Nelly Slimfeather is not ashamed of her crime. But she does not want to be caught. Even now, when gossip about her capital offense would be dismissed as the type of romanticizing about ancestors that I endure at blue-blood parties, she is cautious. Cautious about what might happen to her money, *my money*, if someone knew or suspected. Blackmail is never out of the question—as she understands—and so she is circumspect about who gains access to the home she has been allotted and the words she guards in her journal.

"When did you date him? Before or after you were married?" I ask, though I already know the answer. She has told me this story before, whispered it to me the night my mother was killed with a bullet to her head. I do not know if my grandmother remembers sitting in the darkened kitchen with me, drinking whiskey while my grandfather sobbed loudly in his upstairs bedroom. Yes, she whispered facts to me that night, but because of her drunkenness, her grief, and at the end of that cold night in late spring her body's rejection of the day's ingestion of alcohol, I do not believe she remembers. I held her over the toilet, scared that she, too, might die but curious about the long-past affair, curious if my own mother had known. I am curious still.

"After." She reaches for the crackers, the only food she eats now. The crackers were my discovery, soft baked bread that does not hurt her teeth. She has not softened in her old age but perhaps this will not serve her well and she will break. I watch for signs that she is breaking.

"What do you mean by dated?" I am being crude, but hearing these related facts is like taking relief in a familiar lover. I feel sated during the caress of the words but want them to last longer. To last so long I grow tired of them and leave them behind.

"What do you think I mean?"

"Do you think Grandpa knew when you did it?"

"Probably not. I've always told myself he didn't. It wouldn't have helped him to know."

"What would he have done?"

"You know as much as I do."

"I really don't know what he would have done." This is true. I never knew much about my dead grandfather with the slight frame and the emphysema. He was kind to me, but he was not a life force, only the man who disappeared for days at a time to deliver pigs feet and *other* products. I was at the hospital when his lungs collapsed and he smiled at me while he suffocated, drowning in pulmonary fluid. He seemed content to leave the dusty cinderblock medical facility allocated to him as a naturalized tribal member, content to leave his life as the husband of a blood native.

"I don't know enough about him. Maybe he would have killed you both." I am guessing, pushing, and feel I'm swimming through a river that runs along a white man's buffalo hunt; the animal blood is pooling, thickening the surface, hampering my progress. The alcohol, one of the great plagues of my ancestors, is hampering my progress. I am a shadow; my healthy, gym-trained flesh is dissolving into a flowing stream of stories, only my spirit hovers over the dry flesh of an old lady. My shadow is watching my body being swept away.

"Then you know as much as I do."

My grandmother signals for three more ice cubes. We sit and

stare, searching each other's eyes for clues about secrets we reveal to one another in the hope that our greater, more dangerous secrets will stay with us.

Thief. The word drops through the air, as visible as a falling barometer, the measure slipping away quietly and foreshadowing an awful collision in the sky.

I have stolen my grandmother's journal from its place at the bottom of her underwear drawer. Her underwear is not the kind I imagine most elderly women wear, though I have no basis for this assumption as I have never examined another old lady's lingerie. Even in these moments, the ones for which I may suffer in this life or the next, I am amused. I might have guessed that my grandmother is the type of woman who would buy and wear red and black lacy underwear with padded, matching bras. The expensive stuff I only wear when I know there is a possibility of someone seeing it.

She is prepared to visit the undertaker in a shocking lingerie set, although we have never spoken of her wishes, probably because she believes that she will outlive me. But I have decided to scatter her ashes over the tallest black hill looming over the reservation, the hill her grandfather occupied. Of course, I will have to trespass to carry out this plan because that particular hill was stolen from her grandfather when he wore a wool suit and a stovepipe hat.

When the time comes to bid farewell to Nelly Slimfeather's ashes, to travel land posted clearly with NO TRESPASSING! signs, I will know the nature of my illegal act. Sundering the remains of a bloodthirsty warrior.

I have read her journal and I know the old woman has lied.

She has lied, not about the nature of her crime, no, on that point her written account matches the one she gave me in the kitchen years earlier.

Nelly Slimfeather has lied about her motivation.

Stealing from the white man. That's what my grandmother did when she took her body, the long brown figure she had promised to a poor white coal miner's son and gave it to a Bureau agent.

Stealing from the government. That's what my grandmother did when she slept with the full-blood more than twice her age. Slept with his ability to dole out subsidies to those whom the government decided deserved compensation for past treaty violations.

Stealing a safe life from her daughter. That's what my grandmother did when she ignored threats from children of the dead agent. They vowed to seek justice the old way. Like the patient wars waged by long entrenched people. People for whom two generations is a slim marker of time to wait to kill someone who would be not only a daughter, but a mother.

Counting coup. The vengeance Nelly Slimfeather's people imposed before the hills were stolen from them and the vengeance they still seek when one of their own has been wronged.

Keep your enemies alive if you want to humiliate them. Kill them if want a good story to tell.

I open another bottle of red wine and pour her another whiskey and we continue sitting at her kitchen table in the tiny room of the tiny house reserved for her. The summer has passed, the hot arid winds of late summer have retreated, making way for the first sliver of the harvest moon. Tomorrow, I will return to my job of creating documents for large corporations, examining precedents and conferring with regulatory and administrative authorities before I draft more documents. My specialty is navigating government bureaucracy, a talent which my grandmother never lacked. I have read her account of dealings with government agents.

"Grandma, I remember you had hogs when I was a little girl. Do you remember the hogs?"

"Yes, we had them for forty years before you were born. We owned hogs longer than you've been alive." My grandmother. Her way of saying, *Yes, of course I remember the damn hogs. I am not senile.*

"I remember the pigs' bladders. Balloons, right? You made them into balloons?"

"We used every part of the hogs. Bladders for balloons. Pigs' ears went to the dogs. Pigs' tails for barbecues."

"You didn't mind putting your mouth on the bladders?"

"No, I didn't."

"Even knowing what the pigs ate?

"The pigs ate our leftovers. The bones, the curdled gravy, old butter, old lard. Not so different than what we ate. There were people then that would steal from the pigs if your grandfather had let them. He never turned anyone away from a meal. And most of them weren't even his own kind."

"Not white?"

"No, he would feed my kind too."

"Because of you, do you think?"

"Because he was a fine man. Finer than most Indian and white men. Blood's got nothing to do with making a fine man." She smiles at me and tilts her head. "Surely you don't feel any better or worse for your blood."

"It's your blood that affects me."

We stare at each other and I drink from my glass while she rises from her seat. She does not need my assistance, but she must brace her arms tightly against the wooden arms of her chair. She steps to the window that looks over the narrow gravel road passing in front of her house. From my chair, I can see the stars because there are no night lamps in her sub-divided corner of the reservation. The lights were stolen, probably by teenage vandals who had nothing better to do than drink a Colt forty-five and squeal the tires of their beat-up cars after the theft.

"What are your concerns?"

"What you did. Why Mom died." I consider before speaking the next words, but decide that I have carried my suspicions too long. "You told me about it."

"I haven't told you anything." Her hunched back is toward me. I do not know if she looks at the silhouette of the hills or above them at the night sky. Or perhaps she has closed her eyes, blocking the images.

"Maybe. Maybe you lied that night she died. Maybe you didn't kill that agent. Maybe his son didn't plot to kill my mother. Maybe you didn't know his family learned about your affair because he kept a journal. Maybe you got the idea of keeping a journal from him.

Maybe you loved him or hated him. Maybe you didn't want to lose Grandpa. Maybe you forgot that you already told me. Maybe you forgot you've written all of this down. Maybe you forgot you're a murderer."

These are only words, I tell myself as I empty the contents of my second bottle of wine into my mother's crystal stemware. I am not wounding Nelly Slimfeather with the truth. She will have no standing as an aggrieved party.

"It's not for you to judge."

"Yes it is. My mother is dead because you murdered someone."

"Not murder." She swivels her body quickly, and I am surprised as she carries herself, erect and taller than I have seen her in years, back to her seat. Like a queen holding court, she motions to her glass and I oblige. There is nothing to deny her in this; she does not depend on me for this.

"I know things about you, Grandma." I extend the glass in my hand and after she grasps her whiskey, I spread my palm in front of her eyes. I feel the scar stretch along the length of my palm; it is a rubbery bit of flesh that has never moved easily with the motion of my hand.

"What do you think you know?" She sets the glass on the table, denying herself the indulgence.

"You chopped him up. Hacked the poor man to death while he was still alive. Fed his hands and feet to the hogs while he watched."

"Stories." Nelly Slimfeather leans toward me, stretches her palm and raises her long fingers. Her scar is even more prominent than mine; I assume she was bled longer by her grandmother, the one complicit in sewing a black suit for the treaty meeting. "You are only taking my stories, not the truth."

She raises her scarred palm and I imagine, or perhaps I am seeing, the glimmer of sharp metal and the chambers of my heart swell, pulsing full with dark, freshly oxygenated blood. The palm of her hand descends, I hear a high, wild whistle like the rush of arrows released from taut wooden bows. I feel the piercing sting of my flesh and smell the musty waft from the brown skin of her fingers.

We both reverberate from her slap and as she sinks in her chair my eyes close, dizzy with alcohol thickening my blood. In the cavities of my pounding chest, my grandmother is breaking. I feel the snap of her bones breaking and falling into the whirling red mass of a river bound on one shore by tall black hills and on the other shore by fields of blood, severed heads and sharp blades cast aside, useless, slowly being grown over by weeds and tall red clover.

My grandmother's head nods. I would use the word bows, but I know Nelly Slimfeather, and she does not bow her head to anyone, even in sleep. She is dozing in her hard-backed chair. Sleeping the sleep of innocents and children tucked under cool, white cotton sheets.

My grandmother's whiskey glass rests between her wrinkled hand and her bony, protruding knees. I lift it from her grasp, expecting her to wake and swat me away. Instead, her long fingers release the glass and I set it beside her, where she can find it when she wakes.

She will raise her head and stare at me and then we will smile and I will offer to cook breakfast before I leave. Leave her with comforts of stories and whiskey and surely, the tall and straight satisfaction she takes in stealing her past from me. But she is also leaving me. Leaving me with words that stream around my heart, erupting to the surface of the hand she scarred—but still, eluding me.

I watch the moon sliver trace a path in the sky. Even in its partial state, it holds my attention. I rise from my own hard-backed chair and walk to the window and wait. Minutes before sunrise, the smoky hills intercept light the color of newborn skin. The hills cast images in shapes that stretch long and low across the wet ground, like an army of warriors crouching, waiting for the signal to hoist their spears.

Host

Y ou were that early riser in 1962, an unmarried woman, assistant to the parish priest, and you were not unattractive. Not pretty like Bill Malley's wife, who had celebrated her thirtieth birthday the previous month (though you had not been invited to the party) but still, pretty *enough*. Enough to attract Bill Malley's attention when he dropped off his son, nine-year old William, for the morning's first Mass.

Your job was to open the church, at five on weekdays and six on weekends, to press the priest's robe, to lay out the altar boys' black cassocks, to bring forth unleavened bread, the flat, tasteless discs that would become host to the body of Christ. It was your job to place this bread next to the wine in a small mahogany cupboard. An altar boy, sometimes William Malley, sometimes another, would mix water with wine in the chalice for the priest who would consecrate these inanimate objects.

The 'old' Mass is gone and you regret its passing. There are no altar boys, there are 'attendants' and girls (girls!) are eligible for this reduced position. The 'attendants' do not ring bells, the parishioners, not the altar boys, are the respondents to a priest's intonations. The worshippers do not kneel and they receive the host in their hands, not on their tongues, for Communion. You attend this 'new' Mass, and are only grateful (in this old body) you do not have to kneel. You marvel that the attendant is no longer charged with holding the paten, a thin metallic plate, underneath the host to catch any crumbs of Christ's body that might fall toward the floor.

You are an old woman, the kind of old you can no longer ignore. Men of fifty (how ancient that age was once!) think you are frail; they offer you assistance crossing a narrow road. Your retirement, if it can be called that, is comfortable, no better or worse than your working days, if they could be called that. You, unlike Bill Malley's wife, did not marry for money because your father was a successful New England dairy farmer; you, unlike Bill Malley's wife, had lived alone in a sprawling ranch house built with glass windows to gaze across the pasture. She, a thin daughter of a dock worker, had occupied a hundred-year-old Colonial with a view of the town green. Her house, though elegant with a white colonnaded porch and shady oak trees, must have been *cramped*, its five bedrooms *full* of children and toys and schoolbooks.

You speculate, now as you did then, that had your own father *not* been so successful, had he *not* been so prominent a figure, that Bill Malley might have dated you, that *you* might have been the one waiting tables to support him while he worked his way through law school. You might have been mother to his four children, mother to William, the altar boy whom you supervised.

William was blond, like his mother, with a slight frame that kept him out of playing sports. His father spoke at length of William's desire to become a priest. You were obliged to say his son had learned the Latin Mass quickly and that you would watch over the boy. You knew Bill Malley loved his wife, you were convinced of it, but you admired the clean line of his jaw, the white that salted his thick brown hair. Like any decent woman, you acted appropriately when you greeted him at the door of the church, but you suspected, from the way Bill Malley's wife twisted the corners of her mouth when you crossed her path, something was *there*, (definitely!) and she knew it.

You believed Bill Malley had to keep his desire secret, out of respect for the sanctity of the body of marriage.

One morning, a bright November morning, William's aunt brought him early, an hour before Sunday Mass. She stood in the door of the church shaking, though she was wearing an overcoat, and said William's mother had died, had choked to death (in public!) on a piece of veal at a fancy restaurant, that the family would be along later, but William was to act as altar boy as usual. You suspected Bill Malley's sister had never liked you, never trusted your intentions and you saw her face, the look of accusation: you have *coveted* my brother.

William's suit was clean and neat and you knew it was not his father (competent esquire yes, housekeeper no) who had pressed it. No, William's mother would have cleaned her children's clothes before she kissed them and left them to the care of the teenage babysitter Bill Malley hired when he took his wife on a date. William's mother would have ironed three dresses, pressed the white ribbons the girls wore to tie their blonde braids and would have taken extra care to starch her only son's Sunday shirt. She would have hung the dresses and William's suit in each of the children's closets, told them not to wrinkle their clothes before Mass. Bill Malley's wife had not been the sort of woman to hire a housekeeper, though her husband could have afforded it, and you thought it was shame, how you would have hired a girl to help, to spend more time keeping Bill Malley happy.

You whispered the news to the priest so he could approach the boy, to speak a few comforting words. You told the two other altar boys who had arrived to mind themselves because William's mother had died. You watched William slip on the cassock you had draped over a chair with the other garments, watched him sit on that chair outside the priest's vestibule and rest his chin on his two small hands. He was not any more or less quiet than usual, his brown eyes following the priest, mentally rehearsing the part he had always performed without error. His hair was tousled, not neatly slicked away from his pale forehead and you wondered if that morning was the first the boy had tried to comb his hair without help.

You watched, later, as Bill Malley walked into the church,

holding his youngest daughter's hand while the two older girls followed. You wanted Bill Malley to notice you, so you could nod your sympathy, show your appreciation for his loss. But he stared ahead, as if there was no one to acknowledge. You took the chair William had occupied outside the priest's quarters and waited for the service to begin. The church was not very full, it was the early Mass and when the oldest daughter began to cry the noise from her chest filled the tall, empty hall. Bill Malley did not move, either to hush or comfort the girl as she sobbed (into a pressed linen handkerchief, no less.)

You knew then, as clearly as you know now in your infirmity and unsullied spinsterhood that Bill Malley would *not* re-marry. He would occupy the Colonial, graying and balding until he would die in the bed he had shared with his wife, grieving the loss of her body until his own end. He would attend Sunday Mass in a wrinkled suit and William, who would become the parish priest, would bless the wine and offer the body of Christ to his father. You would speculate until Bill Malley's passing how your lives could have changed had he had admired your breasts when they had been firm and your dark eyes that were not, then, shrouded in wrinkled hoods.

Your eyes were open, free of sagging skin that morning and although you kneeled, you were not worshipping, properly, the entrance of the heavenly host into the building, (a sin for which you would repent later.) Yes, you were somber and heard the altar boys chant *mea culpa, mea culpa, mea maxima culpa* while the priest recited the prayer, saw William beat his right fist across his heart. You saw the priest raise the bread and utter the blessing to bring the Eucharist into the holy house. But you imagined how it would feel to sit beside Bill Malley in a formal dining room, wearing red silk and your mother's antique diamond brooch, offering him fine wine and food from a thin china plate.

That morning, when you did not concentrate during the Mass, you drifted through European city cafés on the arm of Bill Malley. You shared champagne with him when the priest finished his blessing and the parishioners filed to the altar to kneel. You were listening to Bill Malley tell you how much he had always loved you when William, the slight son, lifted the paten and followed the priest down the row of communicants, past his three sisters to his father.

Then you were sitting on an uncomfortable wooden chair, hearing the priest intone *body of Christ* and Bill Malley's voice whispering the single word, *Amen*. You sat in the shadows and wished the church were better heated when the priest placed the host on the kneeling widower's outstretched tongue. You prayed for the service to be finished while William lifted the metal disc, hand trembling, keeping it close to his father's throat, to make safe the body of Christ, should parts of it fall from his father's mouth.

Dirty Laundry

I would like to tell you there is absolution somewhere. Maybe steaming up from the gutters where poor people sleep or maybe it's on the sidewalks where those women, the ones with the painted toes and strappy shoes, stand to admire more shoes and clothes. The forgiveness, that smell of bleach mixed with lemon to remove a stain, might come at you like that. From the gutters, where it's rinsed after the washing, or maybe from behind those square panes of glass where they advertise clothes that haven't been washed yet. Yeah, maybe that's the most logical place for it to come from, the clothes that don't have any stains. They have all the good stiff feeling in them and haven't had to take a bleaching yet. I'd like to say that's where you can find it, but like the dirty T-shirt says, "'This is New York Fucking City' and if you're looking for absolution you might want to consider relocating."

That is the manner she uses to speak. She speaks to everyone that can hear her and everyone that can't. Jane rehearses these monologues of hers, of this point I am certain. I see her mumbling and waving her hands as she traverses the sidewalk of Jane Street. Yes, it is too good to omit, this point of her name, it is too much real-life bad literary irony. Her parents, Min and Soon, named their first daughter Jane after the great American children's book and the great American street that plays host to their laundry facility. She has, in that Western feminist manner, insisted upon 'co-opting the language of fucking oppression' and makes it her mission to educate the citizenry one at a time. Of what topic or strain of religious belief, I do not know. I know little regarding her evangelism except that she favors synonyms of the infinitive 'to clean.' Her verbiage includes, but is not limited to, 'purify,' 'sanitize', and 'pontificate.'

"Pontificate?" I ask in my ignorance, thinking the word implies babble from the mouths of fools.

"Yes, ponti-fucking-cate. It's from the French *pont*, which means bridge, which of course, medieval oppressors commandeered to brainwash the masses that the pope was a bridge to heaven." Jane holds high regard for her duty as a public educator and drops the pile of boxer shorts she carries to devote her entire energies to her gesturing hands. "Pontificate is a cleansing word. It reeks so strongly of bullshit, that no one can do anything except call in the toxic waste experts and purge, purge the scene of the pontificating crime. Burn all the fucking bridges."

I do not care to argue with Jane. Who am I but her customer? She washes my laundry, has seen all of my clothes and the brutalities I inflict upon them with my coffee stains and the chemical burns from my workplace. She is the person to know when my period arrives because the laundry is bloody with leaks from my underutilized birth canal. Jane may also know that for three months my underwear was not bloody. I believe that Jane does not miss many details, but I do not know for certain.

"It tastes like cunt, Andy. Fucking cunt. You don't make pizza, which is yummy with tomatoes and cheese, and throw fish on it. Who wants to eat that? Bleach it. Fucking assholes that order this shit!" Jane bites into the pizza. No, to be accurate she *severs* the slice in the distinctly middle portion of the large serving. It looks as if she has burned her throat with her gigantic effort, but I do not know for sure. Her face often clenches in pain, "Existential pain for the world," she says.

"I wouldn't know," I reply and blow on my slice because I do not care to burn my tongue.

I also despise anchovies. But this pizza we are eating is stolen. It is not as if we had placed an order that was not fulfilled to our liking. Jane relieved a delivery boy of this meal when he chained his bicycle, but not his pizzas, so that he might knock on the door of my neighbor's house.

"As the old saying goes…do not look a gift horse in the mouth." I scrape the anchovies from the pizza and bite into the fishless-slice. Her beer and my beer sweat beside each other on my kitchen table, a comforting distance from the laundry basket with my clothes. The basket seems more full than if one of her sisters had folded the load, because Jane does not take time to press the air from between the items. Jane inspects clothes for the minutiae of dirt and will attack them with the full power of laundry lore available to her. But she does not fold well. Her folding takes up more space.

"It's not right to remove the anchovies. I admit this pizza sucks ass. It tastes like smelly cunt. But it's all about form. If you take the anchovies off, you destroy the form of the object, the form that was imagined by the pizza maker when he got the order from some shit-head to start a pizza that would have fish on it. It's the pizza maker's fault, more than whoever ordered this. He should have known better, known that this form sucks!" Jane bites into the slice again and it is gone. I have always been impressed with her appetite. Perhaps she eats heartily to spite her heritage, the one that dictates she should be shy about her consumption. Or perhaps she is not so political about her eating and really enjoys the taste of food.

"You eat a lot Jane, more than I can. I would be enormous." I wash the fishy taste away with her Budweiser. We are comfortable, Jane and myself. We drink each other's beer but not with sisterly camaraderie. A more precise description would make me the little sister that sips beer because her older sister gulps it. I enjoy drinking after Jane because she is sloppy and leaves lipstick and spit on the neck. Her spit smells and tastes faintly of soap.

"I know what I know and I'm the first to admit it when I don't." She points to me with her tiny fingers, the ones that do not look sturdy enough to manipulate the quantities of clothing that come through the Jane Street laundry. "You never say anything is true and so you will never be wrong."

She attacks another slice of the purloined pizza and garbles with her mouth full of half-chewed food. "I didn't go to six years of college for nothing, you know. I've learned intuition."

I trust that she has learned intuition. I would say that I trust her judgment more than my own in most cases but there are exceptions about which I am not sure.

"Andy, you need to let me in!" Jane often relieves my door of its lonely, closed position in the night. She favors nocturnal wanderings of the sort that I do not enjoy. My body retreats into sleep when the sun leaves, but Jane's body gains energy in the dark. I encourage her to make herself welcome, at any time, but my admonitions are unnecessary because Jane does not patronize the notion of private property.

"Easier to get forgiveness than permission!" She runs up the steps into my townhouse and I experience jealousy. She is only five years my junior, but she is thin where I am round and she possesses energy as though she is not subject to the laws of entropy. My own energies scatter before I am aware of possessing them.

Jane is high and smells of sweet pot and soap.

"You reek, Jane."

Jane has turned the two paintings hanging in my living room upside down. "Any particular reason?"

"No, just generally felt like fucking in the laundry room again." Jane lies on my sofa and lifts both of her legs to the ceiling. Jane is flexible and would make a master contortionist should she decide to run away with the carnival. I maintain my silence on this thought because I do not want to put such ideas into her mind.

"You have come to gossip? It is only two AM and I have to be at the lab in six hours. No problem at all." I watch her blow imaginary smoke, to puff-puff away my stodgy, working woman concerns. It does not trouble me, Jane's lack of respect for my responsibilities, but I am more accommodating than most.

"Oh that lady friend of mine was beautiful tonight, Andy."

She keeps her legs pointed toward my ceiling and I wonder if the blood is pooling in her head. "We drank tequila shots at the Hole and hit on the bartender's girlfriend, which pissed off both of those bitches and oh, we did it thirty times, at least! On the floor, in the suds and the soap and I told her that I would kiss her but only if she let me pour some vanilla lotion on her first and she did!"

Jane pauses to issue a dramatic sigh, which she does with much attention to theatric detail. "And then we lit up and my sister walked in on us! She heard a noise and thought it was her stupid, lost cat! No cat, only pussy, it kills me!"

"Well, I am happy you enjoyed yourself, but why don't you sleep at home tonight?"

Jane lives around the corner from my house in the apartment above her parents' laundry. "I have an important test in the lab tomorrow. I think that is worth a good rest, correct?" I climb my second set of stairs to the landing with the door to my bedroom. "Please lock up tomorrow when you leave."

"Locks are the means the landed elite use to oppress the poor masses!" Jane shouts after me and I look at her from above. She lowers her legs to my flowered sofa and smiles, I believe, at me. "Make sure when you clone fucking Hitler that you get it right! Evil, brilliant and definitely a closet homosexual!"

She laughs and lays her perfectly proportioned shoulders against my sofa. She is falling into a sleep of which I am jealous, for I believe it holds sweet dreams for her. "Oh, yeah and Andy…make sure to ask him what color badge you would wear…"

I pause before I enter my bedroom because I am tempted to return to the sofa and lay my cheek against her smooth brown one. The thought embarrasses me as much as the story about her sexual encounter. Jane enjoys shocking me. She does it well.

My laboratory is not unlike Jane's laundry facility. There are mixtures of strong acidic and basic solutions. There are long, empty tables that are cleaned rigorously by assistants who earn far less than the scientists who mix the solutions. There are pleasant people to work with and unpleasant people with whom I must deal. I derive great satisfaction from the fact most of the scientists in my lab are devoted to their tasks and do not fear to act because of politics. I instruct them to let everyone else bicker. In the meantime, we will work. I stole that phrase from Jane five years earlier when I heard her speak to a boy who was afraid to deliver a customer's laundry across the striking doorman's picket line. She answered him in English, though he spoke in a jumble of Cantonese and his second language. She told him, "Do your fucking job and let ass-kissing politicians sort it all out." I subscribed to her sentiment and adopted it for my own needs, although I have modified the delivery to suit my incoming residents' sensibilities.

My facility is a prestigious one for aspiring medical researchers and I am proud to be the woman in charge. I have found that medical research, unlike practical medicine, does not favor a sex or ethnicity and that my accent has only served to help me advance. It is a queer twist of ethnic stereotyping in which individuals that bear accents from their parents' native tongues are encouraged to pursue research. As if each child of an immigrant is engendered with special motivation! Perhaps it is an American notion with regard to their hard-working ancestors, those immigrants who are storied to have built cabins and cleared forests with their bare hands. Perhaps they look to immigrants' children to be inspired to achieve great goals. Perhaps this is the reason, but I spend little time considering accents or motivations in my laboratory. I prefer to utilize my time to decipher the mysteries underneath each body that bears an innate genetic composition and only secondarily acquires an accent.

The doctor who oversees genetic development is named Dr. Ivan Zhirovsky. He seems to believe that because our parents were born in the same country, we should share special confidences. He always attempts to speak to me in Russian, and at first I accommodated him. Now, I only respond to his advances in English. He is typically Russian, and by this I mean that he is appropriately morose when necessary and joyous when the occasion calls. Ivan knows the postures of both ease and discontent but does not seem to favor one more than the other.

Jane encountered Ivan at one of my cocktail parties and pronounced him 'a complicated motherfucker,' and on this point I queried her for specifics. Jane, who had studied chemistry in a stint at a very good college, told me that he was the sort of man whom she would want in the kitchen supervising the cooks, but would not want inventing the ingredients for the menu. Ivan's discipline is neither culinary nor chemical, but I understand her analogy. Better for Ivan to continue in his role as developer of current projects, rather than as creator of new ones. Ivan is an uncertainty in an environment where people and formulas need to be precise.

Jane conversed with each scientist the evening of my party and made herself pleasant. She is also possessed of Ivan's ability to don a persona. That night, she discussed the laboratory's new project with the partygoers and I believe she might have extracted information that should have been kept confidential. I speculate that Jane, in addition to having missed her calling with the circus, would have made a terrific spy. She puts forth the appearance of entitlement all at times and with all people.

Jane has been dismissed from three good research positions, one of which I arranged. She remains amiable toward the experimentation community and appears to enjoy discussing science. Yet it is unlikely that she will obtain a future role within a lab, given her reputation for disregarding the basic premise of scientific research that a scientist can never take credit for proving a fact, only for disproving a theory. Jane had great confidence in her work, even in her mistakes, and would commit to procedures outside of laboratory standards. I heard a story recited that she labeled one supervisor a 'gutless wonder of a woman and a lousy excuse for someone who should be trying to help people.' I understand Jane's frustrations but do not accept her view that scientists are meant to be good. Our role as researchers is to discover what is false. Jane could not abide by that rule and returned to her parent's laundry, where the form of her labor is always comforting to its recipients.

At my party, above the sound of the immigrant-tinged murmurs,

her practiced American voice whispered, "Dr. Ivan looks like a tre-
mendous fuck." She was correct in perception and pronunciation.

"Andy, why the new dress?"

Nothing is private, according to Jane. I learned six years earlier,
when I had turned thirty and undertaken the task of buying clothes
for the new decade, that Jane memorizes my wardrobe. She sits at
my kitchen table, sips her beer and pushes the buttons of my kitchen
television's remote control with a compulsive ardor. She finds only
evening news broadcasts that she pronounces "worthless" and lets her
chopsticks lie idle. Tonight, we eat noodles stolen from her mother's
kitchen. They are delicious and it is that rare occasion when I eat
more heartily than Jane.

"I have a dinner engagement this Friday."

"Can I do your makeup?"

"No, thank you, I prefer not to be mistaken for a vaudeville act."
Jane often offers her beauty advisory services but I always decline. I
have seen her appearance prior to her treks into wild New York bars
and do not care to have her sense of contemporary fashion replicated
on my face.

"Oh, come on …I'll give you five dollars off your next load."

Jane leans across the table. "I never get to do white faces, I
only get to do brown ones and my sisters won't even let me do that
anymore. Bet your date will want to suck your face off, I can make
you look so good." She pouts, but I am unmoved, primarily out of
caution for the safety of my skin.

"You should give me my next load for free. This load is poorly
done." I feel perturbed at her, this time for prying. She is my friend,
but she asks inappropriate questions. Despite her view on the subject,
I believe some aspects of life are private.

"No it's not." Jane drops the remote control and grasps her
beer, tightly.

"Yes, it is. The towels are not bleached and the clothes are not
folded. It appears you wadded my belongings and threw them into
my basket."

My words escape my mouth as I watch her body tighten. I

feel guilt that she may be angry with me, but I am eager to prove my point: she should not perform her laundry duties shoddily because we are friends.

"I guess I got a little distracted today, Ms. Vladko, seeing that my sister is getting married, and I'm not invited to be at the wedding because I'm a fucking dyke. I'm so, so sorry that your hideously ugly dress, which I am sure you were planning on fucking that asshole in, doesn't meet expectations. So sorry that I even bothered to come here." Jane stands and throws the beer bottle across the kitchen where it breaks against my wall. I watch the foamy liquid slide down the white plaster and listen to her low-pitched, perfectly American voice and wonder how she developed her speech faculties without acquiring her parents' native accent.

"You're the epitome of the unexamined fucking life. You don't think about anything except your lab. Most of all, you don't think anything about me! I deserve better from you, Andy but the part that really sucks is that you don't have any better to give." Jane raises her arms with her palms stretched toward me. "You're like this, with your arms in front of you, pouring out chemicals. Look at my hands, Andy."

I see her palms, they are chapped and rough and I remember that she has been working in the laundry alone. Her parents have been arranging her younger sister's wedding and have left Jane to direct the operations. I feel ashamed that I spoke poorly of the laundry because I know the volumes she handles each day. She should not be there. She was born with a higher intelligence, for better things.

"Jane, let's talk about your career. I can secure a place in my lab, with certain restrictions, but you can become part of our team." I watch her hands lower to her side. They brush against the orange canvas pants she wears and hang, limply. She does not respond and turns her back to me. "Jane, we can talk about this later if you like. I am sorry."

Jane does not speak and I notice the two paintings that she had turned upside down nearly two weeks earlier. I had forgotten and had not rectified their situation. From my perspective, the paintings are partially blocked by the two braids from Jane's head of black hair and seem to be enlarging as she moves away from me. I believe the paintings look better and more natural as they hang upside down. I think that I may leave them as they are.

Jane gives my front door a terrific slam. I walk to my street window and see Jane gesturing and mumbling. Her thin arms wave as if she was swiping gnats circling her head and I believe that she is proselytizing to nobody in particular but everyone in general, as she walks toward her laundry.

Ivan is charming me at dinner. He knows the manner in which to make a plain woman feel beautiful. He compliments my black dress with its white piping on the cuffs and the collar. It fits me as well as it might, with my firmly set hips and the legs that are too long to comport well with my torso. My hair is pulled into a bun behind my neck, that gives angles to my face. My features are round without the illusion of spatial contrast. I order one martini and then another, although I know that I should not drink too much in his presence. As in science, I feel there is little room for error with him.

I feel he acts in opposition to me. He abstains from drinking when I raise my glass and he taps the table when I rest my hands in my lap. We are discussing his role in the laboratory. He is explaining why he should be given a larger budget. While I can make suggestions, I do not have authority with regard to budgeting and Ivan knows this limitation of mine. He is only talking in the general sense to me, about his problems with science and his disgust with the politics necessary to conduct research in the lab. I remain silent during his soliloquy and wish he would stop talking about the lab. It happens when his entrée arrives at the table.

"Androika, why do you avoid me? It's been weeks since we talked. Have you found someone else?"

Ivan clinks his glass of wine to mine and laughs in a conspiratorial fashion. As with his attempts to speak to me in Russian, he is under the impression that I enjoy his familiarity. Four months ago, I did. Tonight, his thoughtless remarks assault my pride and cause me to become angry.

"You must ask? Ivan, that is an expression of ignorance that I do not believe you entertain. After what has happened to me?" I am certain that Jane would describe my emotional state as 'blown away.' It is the only appropriate label that I can attach to my feelings.

"You must know how much I care for you. I supported your decision and will always support you. I want you to be happy."

Ivan rests his utensils beside his plate, obligingly, though I know from the nervous twitch in his knee that he would rather attend to his meal. Ivan is clever at adopting an attitude, but certainly not expert at concealing all of his sentiments. I wonder which emotion he will assume next for me; which tactic he will deem appropriate.

"It wasn't only my decision Ivan. You had a part in it too. I do not believe you would have wanted me to continue."

Ivan decides which emotion he will don. I think that Jane would say he 'decides to run with hurt.'

"Not fair Androika, not fair at all, my love. We, together, are of mutual admiration and sympathetic companionship. We, together, are dedicated to discovery and advancement!"

He decides to relinquish the stage and slices his steak. "Time heals all wounds and we, too, shall heal."

I eat the food in front of me, but without any enjoyment in the nutrients that support my complex biology. I am unable to direct my anger toward Ivan for his foolish and inaccurate description of me as part of his "we" that would "heal." I am angry at Jane for causing me to care about this meal and this date with Ivan, for causing me to try and look better than I normally do, for taking more care with my appearance than I normally should. I realize that Jane, being more intelligent than even I give her credit for, has convinced me to place importance on this meeting with him when it should not be important to me. I have allowed her to inject herself into me when she has no business being here. I drink one more martini and find it easy to ignore Ivan for the remainder of the evening. Instead, I concentrate on how I will confront Jane.

Ivan kisses me goodnight as he hails a taxicab and says, "I still believe you made the best decision."

Why do I hesitate to confront Ivan about this so-called decision? What decision was there to be made, when only two days before the decision, I saw him put his hand under a laboratory assistant's jacket in the same fashion he had done with me? Unlike pure research, there are uncertain moral consequences associated with human behavior, but I believe that I decided appropriately with the evidence that I had.

I see Jane seated on my front steps, staring into a laundry basket nestled between her knees. I pay my taxi fare and open the door, carefully. I do not believe I am fully drunk but my synapses have not ceased their misfiring from the gin. I hold closely to the railing of the steps to my house before I attempt to climb them. Jane is crying. I cannot speak, because I do not know why she is here.

"I didn't know you would take so long, Andy. I waited for two hours. I'm cold."

"Have you brought some laundry for me?" Jane slumps and her braids droop across her breast. I wonder, in my alcoholic uncertainty, if they droop with sorrow.

"Not your laundry…maybe a dead cat. I think my parents shut my sister's cat in the cellar…it may be dead." Her voice cracks into a wail.

My perspective changes as my body climbs to Jane's level. I see the contents of the basket underneath the light of my porch. The form of the cat is there, yes, with a fuzzy gray and black coat. The white towel underneath the small animal appears bloody. I put my hand to the animal's stomach and feel an irregular rise and fall.

"Jane, it's not dead. Look here, underneath her belly." As I turn the panting female's belly aside, three small blind faces shift their slight mass to follow the heat of their mother's moving form. "She gave birth and she may be dehydrated and malnourished. She's not dead, not yet anyway."

I am surprised how gently my hand runs across three tiny noses. I pull back, and put my hand on Jane's shoulder. Her body, despite her assertion, feels warm to my touch and I wish I could lean into the heat that she denies herself.

Jane shudders and continues to lose her energies into the cold night and I become sad. Sad with the realization that I live where the kindness to rescue a birthing cat will go unnoticed. It is a loneliness that comes between us, like the shoppers so famous in our city, the ones with a great deal of time and money but for whom the object of desire is behind the window or hidden away. I feel cold, in this moment, as I relate the story that springs from the destruction I can cause with my slight indifference. Or perhaps there is no slight indifference and this moment, like all cold ones, will fade under the warmth from my hand but will not pass without leaving its mark

She whispers to me, "I don't know what to do." My heart tightens with a feeling I am not ready to describe. My hand moves to her breast. She frightens me with her warmth.

I do not let go of Jane as I unlock my front door and lift the basket of breathing life. I will bathe and nourish them to health. I will make a place in my kitchen and I will prepare warm milk and feed them, drop by silky drop, as I pet their soft fur and developing eyes.

But all of these things I will do with my other hand. For I plan to continue to touch and then hold Jane, tightly, and to put myself between her and the cold air spilling from the gutters to steal her warmth.

A View From Eagle Rock Mountain

T he lake was still and the old man who sat in the slim fishing boat, a fire red bass boat, hung his line into the water. Burow was not an avid bass fisherman; he preferred to fish for trout. But the Army Corp of Engineers had dammed Roaring River to create Eagle Rock Lake, named after the pointed mountain that rose high above the water. Schools of river trout had died next to the dam when its closed gates prevented the fish from swimming to shallow water to spawn. Burow had been young then, so much younger he had only a bait business and no wife or children.

Burow had fished for trout with his homemade rod when his mother needed something for dinner. His bare feet picked a path from their three-room house through the mountain fog, an hour's walk downhill to the water. When they had been very hungry, or when the weather was too cold, he ran trotlines from the riverbank. It had not been illegal then, to catch as many fish as they could eat with baited lures tied to tree branches. Even as an old man, he would not cut any bobbers he found strung from bushes beside the lake. Poor people, mostly women and children without men, lived a mile or more from the water and were afraid to risk trespassing on vacation properties to cast their lines.

The creation of the lake had reversed the geographical fortunes of the poor. As a boy, he lived above the river, the rockiest and steepest ground, and the cheapest land to buy and pay taxes on. After it became lakefront and zoned to accommodate vacation homes, the upland property had increased in value and most original owners had profited by selling forty acres at a time to residential developers.

In the time before the lake, the more fortunate children lived on flat stretches of land close to the river. The farming and grazing was easier in that well-loamed soil, but harder to acquire for those without fathers or money. The farmers did not object if Burow walked across their land on his way to the river, so long as he took care not to disturb the cattle and the crops. Burow admired the evenly spaced rows where men planted their seeds; he pulled weeds out of the ground when he saw wild grass choking the corn. Sometimes, a farmer raised his hand in greeting or offered a sip of ginger water from a wooden bucket and Burow brought the man part of his catch, if the fishing had been good.

As part of the great public works effort during the Depression, the Army Corps of Engineers had pronounced the valley *eminent domain*. The federal government paid the weeping and angry families to abandon their houses and rows of corn. Farmland that had been cleared of stones and trees became the lakebed, resting underneath millions of gallons of water and the reflections of fisherman who came in their fiberglass boats.

Kickapoo Indians inhabited the river valley a century before Burow was born. The tribe called their hunting grounds Eagle Rock, after the giant birds that flew above their heads. Kickapoo viewed the birds as omens, good or bad, depending on their circling paths and the sounds they made in the air. Burow knew how strange and large the birds' shadows must have looked to the Indians, like the shadows from low-flying planes shuttling tourists to the lakeshore resorts.

Kickapoo men fashioned wooden spears tipped with flint

arrowheads to impale freshwater trout, after the manner of eagles that speared fish with their beaks. When the river slowed because of a freeze and the great birds were hungry, Kickapoo left fish heads by the banks. The eagles' talons curled around the silver fish heads, their beaks pierced the skin and then the birds flew, shrieking, toward their elevated nests.

Indians left remainders from their kills because they believed the eagles to be their departed kinsmen's spirits. If a young Kickapoo found a white feather by the water or underneath a tree where a bird had nested, the parents re-named the child, a secret appellation to provide strength in the hunt or in childbirth. Parents carved these secret names into flat stones their children would keep hidden, as treasures, because to reveal the name was to lose the eagle's advantage of enhanced vision and long life. The practice of bestowing secret names stopped when the eagle population dwindled and the settlers' population increased. The last generation of Kickapoo to arrive at adulthood had no secret names to reveal; they had only learned to read and write English in their missionary schools.

The old man had learned Indian ways from his mother's memories of what her own father had told her. Burow was eighty-nine, but not old enough to have known anyone who was alive when the Kickapoo had been relocated, before the War Between the States. On the land reserved for natives in Oklahoma Territory, there were no rivers to fish. The ground was dry and rocky and completely unsuited for anyone except people who had no need to hunt or farm because the federal government promised to provide.

The old man knew the vacation people called him *Burl* because no one understood his pronunciation when he introduced himself as Burow, the bait salesman; neither could they imagine he bore the same name as a pack animal. Nor could they know his mother had named him for Officer Burrough, the man who had led her father in the Confederate Army, but lacking familiarity with the alphabet, had done her best with the letters she knew. Burow's mother struggled with more than her son's name; the baby arrived in the world only two months after his grandfather and father had been killed, shot as poachers. She would not lose her son to the woods and decided they would survive by eating fish.

Burow's mother taught him to make lures from metal scraps his father left in a box beside the tree stump they used for chopping wood. She heated the blacksmith's leavings on stones in a fire, then wrapped her hands in wet rags and quickly shaped the glowing metal into a curve. After the new hooks cooled in the ashes, she gripped a round rock in her right hand and the new lure in her left. By slamming the rounded rock against the edges of the lure, she formed the sharp points that would sink into fish gills.

Burow made his own lures when his hands were strong enough to bend the metal, taking care to mind his long blond hair when he leaned close to the fire. His mother would not cut his hair, telling him that in the Bible story it brought bad luck, that a man's power was in his hair, that to lose it was to relinquish the strength he would need to fish for food.

The pounding rocks they used to shape lures were old Indian grindstones Burow found beside the river. Kickapoo women had chipped the rocks into spherical masses they rolled, back and forth, over their harvested corn. He knew it was rare that Indians were allowed to occupy a patch of land long enough to harvest a crop and assumed it had been less work for the women to shape new stones than to haul their tools further south and west. Finding an Indian threshing stone had been easy when he was a boy and could trace the retreating tribe's path along the riverbank.

The hooks he made from his father's scrap metal sometimes lasted for years, but most were lost to large-mouth bass that snapped the lines he cast. In his old age, he used stainless steel store-bought hooks with masses calibrated by a machine. He fumbled with the store lures, finding it hard to thread the small openings, but knew he lost fewer of them. Not only was the metal of a greater thickness, the hooks were sharper, more precise and more likely to sink into the gills of a fish disposed to fight. What Burow had lost in strength since his youth he had compensated for with equipment and when he used the factory-made hooks, he rarely left the lake with fewer than he had set out with.

Despite his store-bought lures and durable fishing line, Burow had little luck finding bass the day the lake was so still. He had killed his high horsepower engine, so as not to spook any fish feeding near the cove. Nothing was biting. It was May, tornado season, and the sky's coloring had gone green, a familiar color to the locals who knew to watch for funnel clouds in the hot and rainless horizon. Burow suspected the bass knew something he didn't about the advancing weather and had found deeper water. The wind and the waves began to pick up and he was discouraged. At four o'clock that afternoon, he decided to run his boat back to dock. He cranked his reel and then felt the line pull slightly, and then go loose.

Nothing tugged again, but he heard a slapping sound against the boat's fiberglass hull. A fish, be it crappie or bass would take the lure and swim. When Burow looked, he was not surprised to see his lure hooked through the jaw of a cottonmouth water moccasin snake—a common disadvantage of the store-bought equipment. The lure's additional tensile strength pierced tires, sunken canoes and often, the thick skin of poisonous snakes.

The maddened reptile struck the boat with its exposed fangs. It was in a water moccasin's nature to attack the source of the hook and Burow kept a small knife ready for these occasions. A wave rolled under the boat; the cottonmouth, buoyed by the higher waterline, threw its body upward. Burow needed to cut the line, before another high wave dropped the snake into his lap.

Burow let more line out of his reel and walked to the bow of the boat to retrieve his stainless steel tackle box from the dry storage compartment. His daughter and his wife, both Helens, had presented him with the box for his fiftieth birthday. It had a smart design, with a hinged upper tray divided into differently sized sections for spinnerbaits, flybaits and the remaining stock of his own lures. The upper tray lifted up and out of the box on hinges to reveal the knife and a pistol. He had trouble with the leather sheafe, but when he was able to draw the blade, he sliced the line at the front end of his rod. The snake hit the boat a final time and then swam into the shadows of the trees hanging over the cove, the strong hook embedded in its jaw.

A year or two earlier, Burow would have shot the reptile for its hide, but it had become difficult to hold his hand steady. Worse than that, he had developed a dislike for the loud noise of the gun's discharge and the smell of blood. The harvesting of animals and their hides had become less enjoyable, too. It cost too much energy to pry open a trap clamped on a fox's leg or to skin a squirrel. He replaced the knife inside the box and flipped the latch, sealing the lid. If it rained later in the afternoon, he wouldn't lose his lures to rust.

Switching on his trolling motor, he guided his boat into the cove. Vacation kids swam in the lake, skinny-dipping and splashing each other off the sides of their parents' expensive pontoon boats. Where there was one snake, there was probably a nest of them. If he saw more snakes, he would tell the Lake Warden to mark off the area with buoys, to warn of the danger. There had been no such threat to bathers or fishermen when he had been a boy. The river water had been too cold, too shallow. The snakes flourished only after Roaring River was dammed, when trees shaded the still water and hid the reptiles from the eyes of the few eagles left on the mountain.

The auxiliary motor groaned, pushing the boat toward the bank. He would take a quick look before he covered the three miles back to dock. There were plenty of exposed tree roots growing in tangles at the shoreline, a comfortable home for cottonmouth breeding and nesting. Burow's eyesight was still good and, despite the dimming light and dark water, he saw several spots sliding across the water, ten feet from the boat. He would call the Lake Warden, tell him to get the buoys out before the summer season started. There was no need to risk sending vacation people into nests of baby poison snakes.

Burow turned his boat slowly, to avoid scraping the hull across the jagged wood jutting from the water, remains of trees loggers had felled decades before, in advance of the flood from the dam. The water rose against the boat, hard, and the wind blew hot. Still, he saw no signs of narrow clouds forming in the sky. He trolled away from the tree stumps and looked at his electronic gauge, flickering between twenty and thirty feet deep. A powerful undertow was working below his boat, a current strong enough to drag a swimmer along the lake bottom. There were always people who miscalculated how quickly the undertow developed, even in shallow water, when the winds started. Lake patrol found remains of bodies at the end of each summer, flattened against the dam's sluices.

Then he saw a naked man, balanced on two hands like apes, moved at the edge of the water. Burow watched him grab willow branches and weeds to pull himself to the top of the embankment, where he stood straight, shading his eyes and pointing. The man was tall, with long black hair and screamed in a language Burow could not understand.

Burow looked at the expanse of deep water and the clouds blocking the sun, above his head. The wind slapped his face and he laid his rod in the bottom of the boat. He thought he should troll back toward the bank, before the snakes and the wind could get to the stranger.

There had always been stories about crazy people around the lake. Burow had been learning to catch lake bass when he heard about a woman from the state capital who had scalped herself. A conservation ranger found the rich lady, dead inside her parked roadster, with a fistful of dried blood and blonde hair in one hand and several fishhooks in the other. Word around the dock was her son had been killed a month earlier in the first wave at Normandy, and that her husband, a state senator, had forced the teenager to enlist. A kid who sold bait to the tourists insisted he had done business with the dead woman. No one knew whether to believe the kid's claim the woman had bought twelve of his sharpest fish hooks, for fifty cents each. Burow heard the story and was shocked at how badly the woman had been cheated. It was then that he started his business, selling hooks for ten cents each and turning a profit.

Burow heard more stories the summer the lake opened to fisherman and boaters. He sold night crawlers and June bugs to the vacationers and the locals. All of them had tales. There was rumor of five-year-old twins who disappeared from their father's boat, despite his claim he never heard a splash. The father told the county sheriff's office, "When I looked back, to clear the space behind me for a cast, my boys were gone." The man was never arrested but people said he hanged himself from an oak tree behind his house in the city. Another story said a fifteen-year-old girl and her mother had gone missing from their cabin beside the lake. The two were assumed to have been overpowered by the current, until the next summer, when a local trapper found two female bodies in a tangle of weeds on the shore. The medical examiner announced the state of decay prevented anyone from knowing whether the women had drowned, or had been killed and then thrown in the water.

Burow listened to men with strange accents and shiny shoes tell these stories from under the brims of their hats as he searched his coffee cans for the proper amount of bait. He nodded his thanks when they paid him with silver dollar pieces and let him keep the change. The men went out with Burow's baited hooks in the mornings and returned in the afternoons with their stories: an Indian had been seen striding, in breechcloth and moccasins, carrying an eagle feather and a dead black woman over his shoulder; a man with a beard was diving in the caves, looking for the gold his grandfather had buried on the old farmland; a teenage boy who was afraid to go to war had fallen from the dam but because his body was not found, the draft board pronounced him a dodger 'until such time as a death certificate could be produced.' Burow kept his head low and wondered what his mother and wife would do if he were drafted, if they would take in laundry or find work at hotels.

The stories of the lake continued during the following summers. Burow heard them all, because through some point of chance, he was not called to the war effort. His customer base grew larger, due to the superior reputation of his metal hooks and long worms. Copies of the local newspaper rarely mentioned the strange circumstances of deaths on the lake. America was at war and people concerned themselves more with reports of troop casualties and monstrous activities in Germany than rumors of unlucky tourists who never found a way out of Eagle Rock.

The lake was no longer still and the wind blew so hard that Burow watched his rod, an expensive gift from his lawyer granddaughter, fly out of the hull to become entangled in a willow branch over the head of the man standing on the bank. The stranger was dark-skinned, and his body had the kind of large and defined muscles Burow had only seen in pictures of male movie stars. The thick hair that swirled around the man's face reminded the old man of his youth. His own long blonde hair had never gone gray; it had fallen from his scalp years earlier and disappeared, leaving his head bare.

"You OK there?"

Burow did not know what else to shout. The wind strengthened and branches of large sycamore trees were parallel with the ground. This was no place to be caught in a storm and Burow did not have a radio or mobile telephone to call on the man's behalf.

"My boat's sunk." The man understood English, but his accent was strong and of a sort Burow had not heard before. The man's fingers wrapped around pieces of his long hair, twisting the strands. Burow looked to the waves splashing over his stern. If he stayed in the cove, he risked having snakes in the boat, or flooding his engine.

"Can't help you, mister. I can only offer you a ride to the dock." Although the man crouched only a few yards away, Burow strained his voice to be heard above the rising weather.

"A tree made a hole in my boat. Who cut the trees?" The man pointed to the stumps that disappeared when a high wave smashed the bank. "My boat is down there."

It was unlikely the man had sunk a boat and swum to shore without being attacked by a cottonmouth; more likely, the guy had wandered from his campsite, drunk or stoned out of his gourd. Burow hollered, "So, do you want a ride?"

"Yes, yes," the stranger yelled, "I will swim to you."

The man lowered himself, backward, down the bank, until he hung from a branch above the water.

"You just aim over here, to my boat. I'll help you in." There was no need to spook the man by mentioning the snakes.

Burow leaned toward the tackle box, this time, to remove the loaded Buck Mark field pistol from the lower tray. The gun was for a snake, or in curious situations, for a person. He did not take time to fasten the tricky lock on the tackle box and hoped the lid would hold well enough to keep out the rain. Wrapping the pistol in the red handkerchief he used to shine up his lures, he hid the bundle under the steering console.

The man released his grip on the branch. The depth gauge flickered between thirty and forty-two feet; the water was getting rougher. Despite the high waves, the man swam toward Burow smoothly, covering the distance in a minute. Burow worried he would not have the strength to help, but the man lifted himself easily into the boat. His dark hair dripped with water and he crouched, his arms folded across his torso. The sky turned a darker green and a single cylindrical cloud dropped from the horizon. Burow tossed a yellow rain slicker that smelled of fish to the passenger.

"What's your name mister?" Burow asked as he turned the ignition key. The engine could do seventy miles per hour on flat water but the lake was so choppy he would need to go slowly, or risk flipping on a wave.

"Lightning hit me and the tree made a hole in my boat. That was three days ago." The stranger held his face in his hands and made no move to cover himself with the slicker. There were deep scratches down the sides of his arms and his shoulders, as though his flesh had been raked by claws. His toes were green and looked infected; he was missing all ten toenails. The man hunched over and held his stomach, as if he were protecting himself.

"You better cover up, mister. I got to get us back to dock, it's about to blow."

Burow pointed toward the cloud dropping in front of them and opened the throttle on the boat. He figured at a safe speed of thirty miles per hour, he could be at the dock in eight minutes. There was not much chance the twister would hold off that long. He had been fortunate, before, to never be caught in a full-blown tornado.

When the sky turned green, he had always retreated to his bait shop by the dock. When Helen had been alive, he had taken to their house where she was sure to have fresh water and canned vegetables waiting in the cellar.

"I was there for three days, I walked. I couldn't find anyone." The man clasped his hands together. "No one except the birds and the deer and the snakes!" The stranger stood and the motion of the waves caused him to lurch forward, toward the driver's seat. Burow concentrated on keeping the wheel steady, even as his right hand reached underneath the console, to touch the red handkerchief.

The man waved his arms and Burow saw a water moccasin, a small one, with its fangs clamped on the man's lower left arm. The passenger in his boat did not scream, but swung his arm back and forth, like he was rocking a baby in a cradle and sang in a strange language, something sounding like a gospel song.

Burow's heart beat more quickly and the sounds of the wind and the water cut into his ears. He unfolded the handkerchief to grasp the gun. The pistol was wet from the spray and he was trembling more than usual; it fell from his hand and slid across the bottom of the boat. The man swayed with the snake, waving his left arm and singing.

The boat bounced upward each time it hit a wave and the wind was so strong Burow doubted he could maintain control of the wheel. The large cloud mass parted over his head to reveal a setting sun and a gray funnel cloud dropping onto the water. Bright light breaking through the storm hurt his eyes; he blinked and saw the stranger's right hand, the one free of the snake, reach for the pistol.

The man pointed the gun at the storm; he waved his left arm around his head, the snake still attached. Burow heard the stranger scream when the tackle box was lifted from the hull, into the air. The lid flew open and lures flew from the compartments. One hook lodged in the stranger's ear and another, in his neck. The man tried to wipe the blood dripping from his head with his snake arm. The tail of the reptile curled around the stranger's throat.

Burow hoped to drive the boat under the cloud before it hit the water. It was impossible to turn the boat around, to try and outrun a tornado. Better to go under it, past the center of the storm to reach the shore. If necessary, he would take his chances in the water, until the twister tired of the lake.

The snake looked like a slender flag, flying stiff in the wind, with the man's arm acting as flagpole. The stranger moaned.

"Shoot the goddamn snake, you idiot!" Burow did not know if his passenger understood the words. "We've got a tornado coming our way!"

The old man realized how small and ridiculous the problem of the storm had to be to a man with lures and a snake cutting into his flesh. The stranger's dark body bounced each time the boat hit a wave and Burow ducked lower behind the wheel, hoping the gun wouldn't fire.

"You need to get down! Get down in the bottom of the boat!" The gray mass of wind in front of Burow sounded like a train. He opened the throttle even more and tightened his grip on the wheel. Inside his chest, his lungs squeezed as if someone had punched him and a sharp pressure traveled through his ears and his head. The passenger's legs lifted high in the air, as if the man were a gymnast performing a trick, and rolled toward the spinning cloud. The rain slicker passed over Burow's head and disappeared.

When the pain left his ears, the sun shone in front of him and the sound of the train had stopped. Burow thought he might have gone deaf. Then he heard his engine, churning against the water. He slowed the boat and glanced behind, at the retreating gray cloud and the tangle of tree branches and debris floating in the air. The stranger and the slicker were gone, the tackle box was too; but his pistol lay below a few inches of water in the bow. The dock came into sight and there were two lake patrol officers, waiting in a souped-up bass boat that could travel faster than his own.

The eagles that lived on the mountain when Burow was a boy were a bastard breed. The birds had become dependent on Kickapoo fish kills during the winter. Relocation of the tribe forced the pure-blooded birds to find other food: berries and bugs and, in the worst times, after the fashion of vultures, the dead flesh of deer and settlers. In time, the eagles mated with the vultures and hawks and when the lake was created, the species had been changed. The state's conservation officials insisted that kind of inter-breeding was scientifically impossible, but Burow had seen the mixed birds circle the docks in the mornings, searching for discarded bait from bass fisherman.

One of these birds waited for Burow, beside the old chopping block for wood, after the young lake patrol officer escorted him home. The white-headed creature flapped its wings and rose in the air, with one of the old man's spools of fishing line clutched in its talons. Perhaps, Burow thought, the mixed-breed bird was flying to the mountain to build a nest. So he emptied his coffee can of the worms and bugs he had not been able to use as bait that day, with the hope the bird would return to find the food for its young.

The pale, blond officer gave the old man a dry blanket and a ride to the house Burow had once shared with his mother and then his wife. Burow explained to the college graduate how he had encountered a dark, naked man before the storm, and that the man claimed to have been lost for three days.

"Well, Burow, we appreciate you telling us this," the officer smiled as he drank coffee at the kitchen table. "But we've had no reports of missing boats or men in the vicinity. You sure this guy wasn't a tourist, pulling your leg?"

Burow remembered how he had not believed the stranger's story; he thought over the scratches covering the muscular body and the way the snake had hung from the man's arm.

"Well, he may have been pulling my leg, but I'll tell you this: he had a cottonmouth clamped on his left arm and it didn't bother him none. He stood there and sung to it. He'd have been through a whole lot to get to that point."

Burow felt drowsy. The officer nodded in response and smiled— a little smile the old man had seen on the faces of tourists when they bought bait.

"You get some rest, Burow. I'll put in a report." The blond young officer rose from his seat and tipped his hat. "Not many men your age who could outrun a storm like that." The officer walked through Burow's front door and closed it, gently, as if he were leaving a child's room for the night. Burow sipped his coffee and thought of the naked man's strange accent and words and long brown hair. Burow hoped he would be on the lake, during the summer, to tell the story to tourists who came for the spooks and the legends that had covered the valley, after the trout were gone.

Clan of Marsupials

A glass of wine will put words onto your pages faster than a glass of water."

She gulped the last mouthful of her red wine and leaned across the table. There were white half-moons in her unpainted fingernails and dirt in her cuticles. Local laws prevented her from smoking so she inhaled habitually on an imaginary cigarette.

"That's only true for the first glass. After one, I'm too sleepy to write." Rob settled back into the booth, away from her yellow teeth. There was a beauty to her, with thick brown hair that hung in waves over her lean cheekbones and green eyes that seemed too bright for any woman's face. But many details of her personal hygiene had gone unattended and nature's contribution could only carry her so far.

"A professional would have an obvious response: if one drink puts you down, you need to build up your tolerance."

She pushed Rob's plate toward him, to make room for her elbows on the table.

"Baby, I shaved this morning for you. All over." She arched her back and lapped her tongue in the air.

"That's real fucking charming, Colleen." Then Rob was embarrassed, afraid he had been overhead by the people occupying the next booth. They were regulars at the diner. Twin girls, about ten years old, and a man with large shoulders to match his thick neck and barrel torso. A knit fisherman's cap sat on his head of red hair and he wore a white shirt that spelled out *Seamus* in red cursive letters. The girls concentrated on their hot fudge sundaes and the man stared into the coffee mug he held between his hands. Neither the girls nor their father appeared to have heard the conversation.

"If you don't like it, leave it. Let's go, I'm starving." She refused to eat inside restaurants, insisting on carryout because she couldn't taste the food unless she smoked when she ate. When Colleen motioned for the check, Rob noticed the thinness of her arm.

Rob Merrill had lived with Colleen for three months, since she had convinced him to leave his Manhattan apartment to split her lower rent in Brooklyn. "Come on, Robbie, you're banging me at my place all the time. Why not grab your ass for half the price?" she had said, tickling his side.

Colleen had persisted with multiple versions of her argument until Rob decided to break his lease. The move required unpleasant acts of writing checks to the moving company for its physical labor, to Colleen for his first month's rent and to his landlord to pay for damages to his apartment. Colleen had fallen asleep more than once on his couch, burning holes in the carpet with half-smoked cigarettes.

Promises were made to compensate him for these inconveniences, starting with a farewell ceremony for his bed. Before the movers took the mattress to the sidewalk to be claimed by the sanitation department, she had arrived bearing two cartons of cigarettes and a bottle of expensive tequila.

"Apologies for my appearance. Didn't have time to shower. I overslept." Colleen swayed over her polished red toes and waved two burning cigarettes under his chin. "Wanna shower with me, Robbie? Last romp through your mildew-free playground."

"I'll pass. I packed all my towels."

Rob remembered his first date with Colleen. After spending the night, she had emerged from his shower and announced that because she did not want to dirty his towels she was going to drip dry in front of him unless he wanted to do something about the wet spots on her breasts and hair.

"Up late last night?" Rob asked. He had met her for dinner before returning to his place to finish packing.

"Yep. Painting. You know. And cleaning."

"Right." Rob knew what he was getting into. There had never been "cleaning" on her part and there would be no "cleaning" when he lived with her. However, Colleen *had* agreed to his suggestion that they pay for a cleaning lady to visit twice a week. He believed their residence should conform to the minimum standards required by the city's health department. Colleen's method of housekeeping would not make the cut.

"You doubt me? I'll make it up to you. Here's a poem. Oh, hey, my hobby, my well-hung Robbie. Goodbye city, goodbye bed…. oh my, what a great big penis you have…"

"That the best you can do?"

With this too, Rob knew what he was getting. Colleen liked to drink. A lot. He encouraged her to go to group meetings and to get a job that would occupy her days. "You shouldn't let this become a problem," he had told her.

"I'm only high on life. Whistle me a tune, Robbie…if you can't, I happen to know a certain Russian-speaking mover outside who can whistle it for me." She dropped both cigarettes, still burning, on the floor and yanked her skirt and panties down with both hands. "I gave him twenty bucks, told him not to let anyone come near us until ten minutes *after* he heard me scream." Rob's back hit the mattress that he had already stripped of sheets.

"Robbie, I told you to whistle…Now, now!" Colleen was on top of him and her teeth bit at his earlobes, first the right one, then the left. It felt like she was chewing through his head and he liked it.

"What do you want to hear?" Rob smelled tequila when he breathed.

"How about Danny Boy? Love that tune." She stopped moving her hips. "No more until I hear something!" Colleen made demands like this in bed. "To test your concentration," she claimed.

Rob closed his eyes and whistled. Colleen rubbed her body against his legs and he forgot about the group meeting he had made her promise to attend later that evening.

Brooklyn wasn't so bad. The borough was home to hipsters with trust funds, artists who needed space, and a few former Internet millionaires living on their 401(k) withdrawals. There were also people Rob had never noticed in his Manhattan neighborhood. Real people. People with jobs that required them to punch timecards, people who had not attended college, and people who raised children.

Passing these people was part of his morning routine: traveling to a building occupied for the cause of printing news for the people of New York City. His job was a good one that his suburban parents were proud to explain to their friends. "Our son, Rob, is a writer. For the *Times. Entertainment.*" They enunciated the words they thought important, as if the subjects of his prose (statuesque women and sculpted men) launched him into the elite orbit of planets circling the stars, feeding off their lights.

He left Colleen each workday at seven AM. The sound of his alarm roused her from sleep, although she did not have anywhere to go. Her theory was, "If I give you a blow-job first thing in the morning, you'll be less likely to try to get it later from someone else." Rob couldn't argue with her logic. Colleen knew what she was doing. He had never cheated, hadn't even flirted with another woman. There was no telling whether or not they were in love but after three months of living together, Rob was not inclined to look elsewhere.

After Colleen put her theory into practice, he kissed her forehead and descended the four flights to street level. The last thing he saw was Colleen leaning out of the window, her right hand waving and clutching a cigarette. Rob didn't think she slept all day because there were at least two packs worth of cigarette butts in the ashtrays when he got home and not even Colleen could smoke in her sleep.

He wasn't sure how Colleen occupied her time because she refused to elaborate, had told him when he had pressed her, "Painting's a fine art darling. I'm going to be a famous painter. That's all you need to know." Rob had never been allowed to see her paintings and Colleen claimed to keep most of them in private storage. But he had cheated once, waiting until it was *their* bed to go under it, to pull out the plastic box of oils and canvases she had told him he was not to look at.

He found a stack of five seemingly unfinished portraits. All looked as if they had been smeared with tar instead of oil-based paint. The faces were wildly out of shape with no recognizable features except for bright red hair sprouting from the tops of elongated heads. Rob restacked the paintings in the original order and ignored his urge to question her. He knew that Colleen *did* leave the apartment; he often came home to find her cross-legged on the floor, surrounded by brightly-colored shopping bags from stores on Madison Avenue. Sometimes, she would be lying on the couch, ashing cigarettes into a cardboard box delivered from her favorite liquor store. On Tuesdays and Fridays he walked into an immaculate apartment, with a scrubbed kitchen, clean towels, and freshly pressed linens. Rob was especially grateful for this invisible cleaning woman when Colleen greeted him at the door, naked. He could throw his clothes on the floor and not worry that his white shirts would land in a puddle of red wine, or on top of an ashtray full of smoking cigarettes.

Before he met Colleen, Rob had never dated a girl who had attended a Catholic high school and college. His previous girlfriends had been wholly Protestant and half-heartedly sexual. He was surprised to discover Colleen's amorous enthusiasm and she demonstrated, even after they lived together, that it was not an act she had assumed to impress him at the outset of their relationship.

"So, it's not, stereotype about the Catholic school-girl thing?" Rob lay with the sheet covering his lower body and was grateful for the evening's diversion. He had endured an uninspiring day of work, carefully wording his review of a teen slasher film so that he would not offend the studio distributing it. Management was always reminding writers that their salaries came from the industry's advertising money. "Even if it's a bad cliché, I'm happy to live it," Rob teased.

"Sure, there's some life-imitating-stereotype stuff. When you're wearing the blazer and the skirt, you think you're perceived as a hot piece of ass. Then you start wanting to act like that hot piece of ass." Colleen ashed the cigarette that had dangled from her right hand during sex. The hardwood floor in their shared apartment withstood the onslaught of her nicotine addiction. "Maybe I got the idea to like sex from the whole repression thing, but I also believe that I'm a horny bitch. I mean, when I was like five years old they caught me taking off my clothes for boys who stood in front of my bedroom window. I didn't even know what a strip show was, but I wanted to put one on."

"Any deep secrets about your father you need to insert in the conversation?" His fingers stroked her left wrist.

"No, Robbie, as the other cliché says, sometimes a cigar is just a cigar." Colleen swatted his hand away to grasp a tumbler of bourbon on the nightstand. "I can't help it, I was born that way. And I have to say that most men I've known thank whatever god they pray to for it." She swirled the amber liquid in her mouth. "You don't complain." Colleen's teeth ground the ice from her glass. It was a familiar sound. Rob often woke in the middle of the night to find her on the couch, asleep and grinding her teeth, as if she was trying to chew through her own jaw.

"No, I don't. I love it. We're good together. Baby…you need… well, you need to not.…"

She interrupted him. "You know Robbie, this whole conversation *feels* like one we should have had a long time ago, like no one reading it in your stories would even fucking believe the two of us would live together for, like, over three months and not have this conversation before."

Colleen coughed and dragged on her cigarette. "What's that shit with the unfinished sentences? Do you go to the mall and memorize lines from paperbacks? Or is it plot research to write a story about an asshole who won't lounge in bed naked with his girlfriend? Do tell, because I am *soooo* fascinated by this exchange." She pulled the sheet from Rob's body and tossed it on the floor.

"I thought you might think it was rude if I was hanging out, literally." He covered his crotch with his hands, a mocking modesty.

Colleen dropped the cigarette on the floor where it burned close to the cotton sheet but did not catch fire. She rolled on top of Rob. "I've got no problems with literal, Robbie. Only the fake stuff. It's time."

The smell of the bourbon mixed with the smoke. Rob closed his eyes and resolved to practice whistling.

Somehow Rob had expected that by moving to the borough with families and blue collars and flowerbeds on the street, he would befriend his neighbors; be welcomed into their living rooms; be invited to share dinners of juicy roast beef and dry red wine. Colleen said she didn't want to meet anyone, that she didn't want a knock on the door from somebody asking to borrow sugar. Lacking introductions and encouragement, Rob walked the streets each day, a stranger to the residents of his neighborhood.

The only man he could put a name to was the one who had *Seamus* stitched on his shirt. Seamus was a familiar figure on Rob's block, occasionally emerging from a brownstone carrying a steel garbage can or a bucket of soapy water he used to wash the concrete sidewalk. Initially, Rob passed the big man and nodded, hoping to be recognized as a fellow block dweller and diner patron. Each time, Seamus only stared at Rob, hard. After a dozen attempts, Rob stopped nodding, abandoning hopes of making an acquaintance.

He had no better luck with the old woman who swept the steps of the brownstone while Seamus cleaned the walkway. Rob could set his watch by her, the stooped old lady with the paunch. It was as if she waited for him, so she could push leaves and dirt into his path. Some days she yelled, "Watch yourself now. Mind the dirt!" On other mornings she shrilled, "Get out of the way now, I'm trying to clean up here!"

Seamus, dressed in his green work pants and heavy-soled black shoes, would turn and scowl at Rob, causing him to become conscious of his blue suits and yellow ties. Rob hurried past them, toward the train that would carry him to his desk full of announcements for the week's television and film releases. Behind him, Rob heard water splashing on the curb and the pitch of Seamus whistling.

On the date that marked six months of cohabitation, Rob asked Colleen if she wanted "to do anything special."

"Do you mean sex or something else?" Colleen shrugged her shoulders and pointed the remote control at the television. She liked to watch three shows at once, flipping between channels about every forty seconds. If the three major networks simultaneously broadcast advertising, she quickly mixed a pitcher of margaritas. She maintained that following multiple storylines required her full concentration between commercial breaks.

Rob laughed. "I was sort of offering to take you on a more formal date, to celebrate, well, whatever this is with us."

"I want to eat at the diner. And this is our six-months-of-cohabitation anniversary." She flicked the mute button and rolled off the couch. "Let's go, I'm starving." The screen silently flashed an eighties sitcom in which the principal teen actor had matured into a real life of drug abuse. Rob turned the television off before he followed Colleen out of the apartment.

They both appreciated the little restaurant on their corner where the waitresses kept violets in the pockets of their white starched shirts. The courteous service suited Rob and as the evenings turned colder the waitresses did not care that he lingered over his cups of coffee. Colleen admired how the kitchen staff packed extra ketchup for her carryout french fries without having to be reminded and so she waited impatiently but without smoking as Rob consumed his meal.

Seamus and his twin daughters were seated in a booth, finishing their desserts about the time Rob and Colleen arrived. The big man ushered his daughters out the door with one hand on each of their shoulders while Colleen blew imaginary smoke at the departing figures. Seamus stopped, briefly, on the sidewalk to stare at Colleen through the glass window of the diner. Rob was curious; the big man had never expressed interest in her before.

"Have you ever met that guy?" Rob asked as he sipped his beer. One beer was the limit for him on work nights and he drank it slowly, so that he wouldn't be tempted to order another.

"Nope. Not really. I see him around." Colleen examined her red-tipped fingers. "I got a manicure today, to celebrate our living together thing."

"You look great." Rob fibbed. She was only partly beautiful. Her body was long and thin, but her shoulder blades caved inward and her teeth looked too large for her mouth. "Where do you see him around?"

"Like today, when I fired his mother from cleaning the apartment. Caught her looking at my paintings under the bed. I told her it was off-limits." Colleen looked directly at Rob. "He came over to pick up her last check."

Rob remembered the depictions of red hair. "The old lady is the cleaning lady? I walk by her every morning!"

"I know." Colleen drummed her fingers against an imaginary pack of cigarettes. "I watch you walk to the subway station all the time, hello?"

"Why didn't you tell me? They must think I'm an asshole. I don't say anything."

"You never asked about the maid, did you now? It's not a big deal. She's Irish. It's perfect." Colleen drained one of the wine glasses in front of her and started on the next one. She ordered her drinks in pairs, to save the waitresses a trip.

"What's perfect?" Rob was confused.

"Me firing the Irish maid."

"I'm not following you, Colleen. This is too much drama for me to figure out."

"Because I'm the slob firing the lady who is such a neat freak that she makes her grown son wash the sidewalk every single fucking day." Colleen exhaled in a loud rasp. "Plus, I paid her more to clean up our shit than he probably makes all week."

"Your shit," Rob threw back.

"Yep, right. It's all my shit." Colleen pulled her lips into a wide and long-toothed smile.

Colleen paid for the 'six-months-of-cohabitation' meal and placed the takeout order inside her red-crocheted bag. Rob had offered to pick up the check, but as usual, Colleen had declined.

"It's against the rules for you to pay. It's OK, Robbie, as long as I'm crazy and Daddy doesn't mind," she told him as they walked toward the apartment.

"I feel like a kept man." Rob grabbed her right palm and kissed it.

"Good, let me keep you!" She took her hand away, to dig in her bag. The wind blew at their backs. Smashed pumpkins left from the holiday lay beside the bed of purple flowers in front of the old lady's brownstone. Rob stared at the stoop where dirt balls were launched at him each morning. Perhaps he could convince Colleen to rehire the Irish woman. He would personally introduce himself to Seamus, to apologize for the misunderstanding. Dirt projectiles or no, the woman had done an excellent job cleaning their apartment.

"I grew up in a house like this. Of course," Colleen paused to light a cigarette, "my house was in a better neighborhood."

"I bet your mother didn't have this lady's flowers." Despite his reservations about the woman, Rob held her flowering plants in high regard and wondered how she protected them from the falling temperature. "How much do you know about the red-headed guy?"

Colleen continued to walk and said, "Nope, my mommy dearest only had a few hundred dead animals as outerwear. She left flowers to the florists." Then Colleen started to run, as if she had seen the devil appear from the smashed jack-o-lanterns. "Come on, Robbie, you're so slow!" Ten yards later, she stopped in front of their apartment building and examined the contents of her handbag.

"What's with the sprint?" Rob panted. He had not run since junior high and did not know how Colleen's lungs could have managed the exertion.

"You didn't see?" Colleen heaved, but inserted her hand in the bag, nervously searching. She had dropped her cigarette.

"No, I didn't. What was I supposed to see?"

"That damn dog. A fat, slobbering dog that shits in public." Colleen pointed. Under a fluorescent street light, next to the old lady's brownstone, Rob saw a short, thin man standing with a leash looped around his wrist.

"That's a bulldog!" Rob saw the square body, the massive front legs and the tiny tail that looked as if it had been cut off. "They're very friendly. No need to run," he heaved.

"How do you know anything about dogs?" Colleen lit another cigarette. She squatted, staring at the bulldog that was also squatting, quietly finishing its business. "I fucking hate those dogs."

Rob had never owned a dog but they seemed likable enough. "My high school mascot was a bulldog. They're harmless."

"They shit all over the place." Colleen ashed, then dropped the burning cigarette on the sidewalk. She stood up straight and kicked some fallen leaves on top of it. The small pile melted into a flame.

Rob ground out the fire with the soles of his black loafers, the most comfortable shoes he could get away with wearing to work, but still, an uncomfortable pair that pinched his feet so much that he often removed them when he sat at his desk. Rob's boss, a woman in her fifties, had walked into his cubicle that morning when he had been shoeless. Her nose had twitched underneath the pile of gray hair on her head. She reminded Rob of a dog trained to locate employees acting out against corporate culture. She had stared at him, then at his feet and turned away without speaking. Rob wondered if she had only been disgusted by his mismatched socks or had seen the envelope clearly labeled "Application for Employment" stamped by the office's postage meter. After work, he had ridden the elevator downstairs, hiding the address tight against his chest. He had dropped the packet containing his resume, academic background and some writing samples into a blue metal postal box. The packet struck bottom and he thought of a response, should his boss inquire about the envelope addressed to the Department of Journalism at a midwestern college. He would remove his shoes before informing her that he was considering teaching.

"Colleen, I need to talk to you…" Rob cut off. She had turned her back to him and was walking toward the building's door.

"About what? About how much I hate that fucking dog? You don't want to get into that, do you?" Colleen reached into her bag and took out the plastic carryout dish with her salad and threw it over Rob's head. It landed on the sidewalk only a few yards from the bulldog's snuffling mug. The thin man looked toward Colleen and pulled his dog in the opposite direction.

"Do you always throw produce at animals or is this something I missed?" He had seen Colleen pass dogs on the street. She had never reacted before.

"What I have against everything. It's a nasty beast. It pissed on the flowers." Colleen sniffed and breathed heavily. "I need a drink to clear my head." She yelled, "I dropped rat poison in the salad! Hope your mutt likes it!" The man did not look back at her but jerked the leash, pulling his bulldog across the sidewalk until it turned the corner and waddled out of sight.

"What the fuck is your problem?" Rob kept his voice low, to avoid including the neighbors in the conversation. An image of an irritated Seamus emerging from the brownstone flashed through Rob's head.

Colleen took no such precautions. "My father hates dogs!" she screamed in the direction the offending animal had taken. "I also happen to believe that idiot dog shouldn't be allowed to piss on the flowers." She lit another cigarette, puffed twice and dropped it on the sidewalk. "Robbie, would you get rid of it if I asked? If it was pissing on the flowers?"

"No," Rob considered before continuing, "I don't think the dog is guilty of anything." He watched Colleen's hands shake as she searched in her bag for a book of matches.

"The red-headed guy would kill it if he sees it." Colleen lit another cigarette, again puffed twice and dropped it. "He'd kill it because it causes us all a problem and I would love to see that happen."

"That dog's not a problem. The only problem is you. It's dangerous to fall asleep smoking and to drop cigarettes all over the goddamned sidewalk." Rob stepped on the butts. He was also tempted to step on her toes in their high-heeled red sandals. The shoes probably cost as much as his share of the rent and she had dozens of them piled in her closets, he assumed, courtesy of Daddy, the dog-hater.

"You never fucking know what's dangerous and what's not, right baby?" Colleen stroked his earlobes, sending a tingle down his spine. "Come on, let's go to bed. You've got a long day tomorrow and I've got…well, I've got all kinds of painting to do. I think I may go outside to paint tomorrow."

He followed her up the stairs, watching her thin hips strain against gravity and decided to wait to mention his job search. Rob was tired and anticipated the anniversary sex he knew would be forthcoming. When it came to sex, Colleen was a champ. Cigarettes and wine were the medals she awarded herself when it was finished.

A month later, the interior of the apartment stank and no amount of aerosol disinfectant Rob sprayed made a difference. He had stopped complaining about the odor to Colleen. She had promised to hire another woman to clean but claimed she had been too busy. Rob had not seen the old lady since the day Colleen had fired her. Every morning he walked in the *opposite* direction, circling the entire block to avoid passing the brownstone with the purple flowers sprouting in front of it.

"You should write about these battery people." Colleen was experimenting with the batteries for the remote controls. "I swear to you Rob, the generic batteries work better in the television remote. The fucking bunny rabbit batteries work better in the VCR remote. This has got to be against some law, some Better Business Bureau bullshit." Colleen was cross-legged on the floor in front of the television. Each time she handled a battery, ashes fell from the cigarette in her mouth. Too close, Rob thought, to his feet. He was sitting in his leather chair trying to read a book, despite the various cop shows blaring from the television.

"When the arts and leisure editor needs me to slap together a consumer report, I'll be sure to consult you for material." Rob's boss, the arts and leisure editor, had written a book which had been made into a mini-series and Rob was scheduled to write the review for the televised version. The story was a sentimental memoir of a stateside girl during Vietnam. The adapted mini-series was terrible. But the show's director was dating his boss and this meant he would write a warm and deliberately fuzzy review.

"Colleen, how does this sound? 'The director has achieved, admirably, the small goal he sets for himself in depicting the journey of one woman through the figurative landmines of her past.' No one could fire me for that, could they?" Rob closed the book and crouched low where Colleen sat. She had abandoned her experiment with the batteries and was picking at scabs around her toenails. Her feet were always scabby and bleeding because of the shoes she wore: high heels with tiny straps that cut into her flesh.

The leftovers from her dinner, feta cheese and grape leaves, lay on the floor alongside the ashes and a nearly empty bottle of bourbon. "Didn't make it to group today, did you?" Rob lowered his voice and inhaled. The smells of booze and old food wafted, reminding him of how his boss had sniffed the air in his cubicle. "You should know that I've applied for a job at a college. It's in the middle of nowhere. I expect to hear back from them soon and well, either way, we need to be prepared." Rob stopped, hoping Colleen wouldn't press him on the last point. Prepared. There was nothing for either of them to *prepare*.

Colleen didn't hesitate. "You know the Irish guy, the one with two girls? If I was going to write something, I'd write about him." She narrowed her focus to the scabs on her big toe. "I'd say he's like a koala bear or a kangaroo. Pouches all over him. Folds where his kids can hide. Folds and folds of muscles where anyone could hide. He's off the boat, you know, just like me old dad was before he got himself rich." She pulled off a large scab and her toe oozed gray fluid.

"What in the hell are you talking about?" Rob walked in front of her and picked a burning cigarette from the floor. "It's a goddamn miracle you haven't started a fire yet."

"I can talk about and do anything I want. It's my apartment.

"It's not your apartment. I pay half the rent and it's time for this shit to stop! Enough! You're welcome to drink yourself silly but you are *not* welcome to burn me to death in my sleep. Enough, Colleen!" Rob knew his anger would be lost on her. He had given Colleen the speech. Her response was always, "Enough with the intervention crap."

"Fine, I'll pay your half of the rent." She tried to stand up, but lost her balance and toppled into the television. It fell from the stand, crashing on the floor. But the picture was unchanged and if anything, the audio sound had improved. Sounds of gunfire pelted the room. "If you leave, I'll get someone else to live here. Like the red-headed koala. He could come and live here with me and I'll pay him enough so he doesn't have to go to the docks or to the meatpacking plant or whatever he does. He can sit here and I'll paint and we'll be a fucking clan of marsupials, that's how close we'll be."

Rob stood and listened. Colleen eased back into her cross-legged position.

"I'd tell him my last name and how it happens to be the name my father, the man with the same last name, gave to me." She struck a match and held it above the toes on her right foot. "Then he'd have to tell you everything about himself and *that* would be a great story. Not like that crap you're doing with movie reviews." She dropped the match on the floor and picked up the bottle.

"I don't have to do this crap here Colleen. I could do it somewhere else."

"Fine, why don't you think about that?" Colleen's arm shook, splashing bourbon on her jeans. "I need to work more on my painting, anyway." Her faded denim jeans swallowed her frame as did her white blouse with ribbons on the sleeves, like hippies used to wear. Her feet were a bluish color and her toes were bleeding. Rob felt afraid, suddenly, that she was more than drunk, that she needed a hospital or a doctor. He moved closer, to rub his hands against her dry hair. Colleen leaned her head against his thighs, briefly, before she poured more bourbon into a glass.

"Colleen, let me put you to bed." Rob pulled on her arm, but she shook her head and stayed on the floor.

"Don't bother with the…" Colleen examined her bleeding toe.

Rob interrupted. "I know, I know. I won't bother anymore." Rob walked into the bedroom and checked under her pillow for the matches he knew she kept there. He flushed them down the toilet before he fell asleep.

The letter from the university arrived a week later in a thick manila envelope, the kind he knew to expect if he were being offered a teaching position. Rob slit the seal with one of Colleen's sterling silver corkscrews and admired the heavy paper stock. Inside, he found several forms, including a health benefits plan and a housing application. He was required to notify the college if he would be sharing an apartment or if he would be living alone.

There was less ceremony to the occasion than he expected: providing his social security number, signing his name and dating the paper accepting his offer of employment. He needed a few stamps and knew Colleen would have them in her purse. She banked exclusively by mail and always kept plenty of postage to deposit checks from her father.

At the bottom of the red cloth bag with its wad of twenties and fifties was an assortment of matchbooks from expensive restaurants where she probably had only ordered drinks. He found three stamps and left a twenty-dollar bill and a note that advised her to buy a carton of cigarettes. Rob stuck the envelope under his pillow and fell asleep, leaving Colleen on the couch smoking and watching reruns as she mixed premium tequila with lime juice and salt.

The next morning, Rob descended the stairs with the stamped envelope in his hand and decided to take the short route to the train. Any uncomfortable encounters with the old lady or Seamus would be brief and then he would be gone. As Rob approached the brownstone, the thin man and his brown bulldog ambled toward him.

The owner scanned the sheets of a newspaper while the bulldog sniffed the flowers. Rob was surprised to see that the old lady's plants were still thriving and had managed to avoid the killing frost.

Rob increased his pace. He wanted to pet the bulldog before

he moved away to a state in the middle of the country where they probably had all kinds of animals such as chickens, cats, cows and dogs that Colleen would also hate.

The bulldog stuck its head into the bright blooms. Folds around the dog's neck swayed with the lateral motion of its breathing. The body and stubby tail shook, as if the animal had been tickled. The owner pulled at the leash and turned a page. The dog's lower fangs protruded, like two divining rods searching for water. Quivering, the dog wrinkled his muzzle and issued a terrific sneeze. The snot and the slobber spurted into the bed of dirt chips and wood.

Rob heard the shout first.

"Get your fucking dog out of there! I'll fucking kill that dirty dog." Rob turned to see Seamus, with his white shirt and cursive lettered name, standing on the townhouse steps. The veins in Seamus' arms bulged from his grip on the handle of a baseball bat and in two steps, the big man leaped to the sidewalk. The dog kept its face in the purple flowers and its square chest heaved as if it would sneeze again. Seamus raised the bat as the owner dropped the leash and his newspaper and walked slowly backward. The paper was open to Rob's section. *Entertainment.*

Rob hesitated for a moment. Then he ran toward the man with the bulging arms.

Seamus hurled the bat at the dog's wrinkled head. It caught the creature across the back of its skull and bounced, coming to rest in the cobblestone street. Flecks of liquid spattered against Rob's face and he saw that the dog's skull had burst open. Seamus fell to his knees and pounded his fists again and again on the head and muzzle of the animal. The dog's body buckled, until its head rested between two iron spikes that guarded the flowering plants. Its nose was shoved deeply into the dirt. Seamus stood in a quick movement of a much younger man and kicked with his booted foot at the bulldog's stomach. The dog's owner screamed, "Stop it! Stop it! Man, oh my god, oh my god! *Rocko!*"

The dog's body was stretched on the sidewalk with its head weirdly twisted, an eyeball hanging from its wrinkled forehead. Rob's stomach moved, but he had eaten nothing for breakfast and dry heaves twisted his abdomen. The dog's body convulsed and Rob wished it would die soon so its paws would stop twitching.

Seamus walked into the street to retrieve the bat. He raised it, as if he might throw it and Rob could only think to yell loudly, "Don't man, the dog's already dead!" He was ashamed to hear his voice crack, as it had when he was fighting his way through puberty. The big man advanced slowly toward the convulsing animal and Rob stepped in front of it. There was no large rock or stick nearby, nothing to defend himself or the dying dog.

Rob heard a door open behind him and the old woman's voice. "Seamus, enough already. It's time for you to be going on." The big man needed only five long steps to cross to the other side of the street. "I'm on my way," he yelled as he strode away with the wooden bat under his arm. The door closed with a quiet click that Rob heard along with the fading sound of whistling.

Rob knelt, running his hand against the dog's bloody fur. A few passers-by had formed a circle around the twisted body. He heard a woman using her mobile phone to report her location to the police. The bulldog's owner sat on the bottom step of the old woman's brownstone, weeping, even as a twenty-something woman ran to the body, carrying a bright blue blanket that looked like it might belong to a baby. The Entertainment section was spotted with flecks of blood. Pages were blowing into the street.

Rob turned from the scene of the woman covering the dog to look at the window of his apartment. Colleen was leaning out of it and clapping her hands together, a cigarette hanging from her lips. A rolling line of smoke issued from the open window. Too much smoke to be coming from an overly full ashtray. He did not look again as he walked toward the subway station, clutching the stamped envelope to his chest. There was no need to watch when the men with flashing lights and water hoses ran to save her.

Fee Simple

L oyce Cantrell listened to Principal Swims tell him he could not march in the Granby High School graduation ceremony. Loyce stood in the rehearsal lineup, sweating from his scalp and armpits, wearing a black tasseled cap and cloth robe too short to cover his knees. He got his long legs from his father and the black robe from the commencement rental booth for twelve dollars. To get the money, Loyce sold his old rooster to the cock fighter in his history class. The kid told Loyce later he wanted his money back, because the cock had lasted less than a minute before its throat was ripped out.

"You can't wear sneakers under your gown tomorrow night. The rules state you must wear appropriately dark dress shoes and dark dress slacks." Principal Swims looked upward at Loyce. "I'll pass your jeans, they're dark enough, but I can't let you in the ceremony with white shoes." Loyce was quiet, as he always was with Principal Swims. "Can you get a pair of black shoes?" The principal spoke slowly, as if Loyce were hard of hearing. Then the principal slipped his right hand inside the rear pocket of his suit pants.

"Loyce, you go to the Wal-Mart and find a pair of nice black shoes. Make sure to get black socks. You have to wear socks with dress shoes." The principal's hand held a twenty-dollar bill. Loyce stood still and stared ahead. The principal lowered his hand and folded the bill and said, "Ok, Loyce, if you don't want it that's fine. But I'll call the manager at the Wal-Mart and tell him to expect you. You won't have to pay son, you just need to walk over there this evening."

Loyce did not move after Principal Swims stepped to the next boy in the graduation rehearsal line-up. His face was hot and his chest was tight and he got hotter when he heard two girls in front of him whisper words that were not quiet enough. He examined his fingernails but was really looking at the tops of his canvas sneakers and how he could see through the hole in the right one, straight to the hair on his sockless big toe.

Loyce was Duane Cantrell's son. Duane Cantrell was a known pot-smoker and had been to the state prison at least twice that people knew of. No one had much against Duane except that he ran his horses down and no one liked to see animal cruelty. Loyce was in his junior year of high school when the heavyset wife of the County Judge came to represent the Humane Society and announced she would take Duane's six horses and make sure they got good homes. Loyce saw his father take a white paper from the lady. The lady asked Duane to see her out, but Duane stared at her and did not move. She walked quickly through the space where a door had been hinged until the night when Duane couldn't find his key and had kicked it in.

Duane put the white paper in a magazine about bullets and animal traps. Then Duane left the house and Loyce figured his father would check on the horses in the yard and so he peeked inside the magazine. He was a good reader and knew the words ORDER TO SEIZE LIVESTOCK. He did not have time to read the entire paper because Duane came back, smoking one of his sweet cigarettes. Duane said he had spilled a bag of corn on the ground for the horses and poured peroxide on them to clean out the sores.

When Loyce got off the school bus the next afternoon the horses were not in the yard. He was not sorry they were gone. Sometimes he liked combing their manes and patting their faces but they were angry and smelly and tried to bite when his father wasn't there to twist their noses. A few months later he attended the downtown Christmas parade and was sure he saw two of the horses clopping along with girls in red dresses sitting on top of them. The horses were covered with large green blankets and had tinsel tied to their manes. Loyce saw metal flash from their hooves and wondered how anyone had gotten close enough to the animals to nail shoes to their feet. When he went home later that night he told his father about watching their horses in the parade. Duane snorted and said, "Nah, not our horses. I sold 'em to the glue factory. Sorry kid, those weren't ours."

Loyce knew his father was wrong; the horses *had* lived in their yard. Both parade animals were missing their left eyes from when his father blinded them with hot pokers because they tried to kick when he mounted them. Duane said, "A blind horse can't see to kick me," then doused their oozing eye sockets with alcohol. Loyce thought the horses might die but their eyelids grew together, as if someone with thread had stitched them shut. The horses in the parade were so close he could have touched them. They had passed him at eye level, faster than they had moved before and he believed they had not stopped because they couldn't see from the left.

Principal Swims knew Duane because the two men had attended Granby High School together. There were pictures of their football team hanging in the school hallway. Duane had played quarterback; Principal Swims had been second-string receiver. Principal Swims started working the same year Loyce was supposed to graduate. The principal before Swims had a heart attack and died while he passed the collection plate at church; it was rumored they found bills stuffed into his pockets.

"You run into Swims yet?" Duane asked Loyce after his son started his senior year.

"Seen him in the hall." That was all Loyce told his father. The truth was that Principal Swims had called him into his office on the first Wednesday of the school year, the day when everyone got their pictures taken. The principal said he was happy to have him in school, that it was an honor to supervise the education of the son of a former Bobcat team member.

"Your father and I were friends. I would be letting him down not to look after you." Principal Swims tapped his fingers together as he sat beside Loyce in an aluminum folding-chair, instead of the leather chair behind his square wooden desk.

"Thanks, Mister." Loyce did not have much else to say, so he looked at the parking lot behind Principal Swims' two windows. The lot was full of cars belonging to the teachers and the students who drove to school. During class breaks, kids stood beside their cars, some of them smoking. It was against the rules to smoke on school property but teachers who were there also smoked and they didn't report anyone.

"It's my privilege. You come to me anytime you have a problem." The principal stood and held out his hand. It took Loyce a few seconds of watching the man before he realized he should also stand. The principal's head craned backward until his forehead was nearly parallel with the ceiling.

"I'm not sure the photographer will be able to get all of you in the picture, Loyce!" Principal Swims laughed and swung his arm toward the open office door. Loyce ducked his head as walked under the doorjamb but he was used to that. He fit best through barn doors, built higher for horses with riders.

"Thanks, Mister." Loyce said it again and walked outside the office toward the auditorium where students lined up for pictures. There were many students in the hall; most of the girls looked at mirrors and used brushes on their hair. Loyce saw a blonde girl rub her lips with her finger after she applied red gloss. She used her right pointer finger to go around the edges of her mouth and Loyce felt himself move and harden, in his private area. He decided to walk out the exit doors to the parking lot. He did not smoke but he thought he might admire the paint jobs on the cars until he was in a better way.

The fresh light outside caused his pupils to shrink and he tried to focus on the faces of the kids gathered around a car. He recognized two boys from history class who always wore black rock and roll

T-shirts. Loyce would have liked one of those shirts, but he mostly wore his father's Western-style shirts with long sleeves because none of his own shirts buttoned across his chest anymore. He made out a girl with spiky orange hair who wore a shirt that read OUTLAW IN TRAINING and Loyce thought she looked good even though she had a long scar across her nose. He moved past the crowd until he reached the end of the parking lot, where there was a three-foot tall concrete curb between the cars and the drainage ditch. He put his weight against the curb and wiped the sweat off his neck and wished Granby High had air-conditioning instead of a famous football team.

He saw the kids walk closer to the car. There was a boy with curly brown hair who wore the letter 'B' on his sweater and another, shorter boy who was lighting a cigarette. The spiky haired girl leaned into the driver's side open car door and her skirt was so short she showed the black stripe between her legs. She stood that way for a few minutes but the other boys did not look at her the way Loyce did; they looked inside the car windows. When she backed away from the open door, Loyce guessed what the other boys had seen. There was a skinny, gray-haired man in the front seat with his pants unzipped and his privates sticking upward. Loyce fell beside the concrete curb and crawled behind the other parked cars, where he was hidden. Although he did not recognize the automobile, Loyce knew Duane was the man reclining in the driver's seat.

The football, baseball, and the basketball teams had sent coaches to talk to Loyce at the start of that school year, though he had not played sports before. Principal Swims pulled him out in the early weeks, sticking his head inside the classroom door and telling the teacher Loyce "needed to be excused for a few minutes." Loyce left his books on his desk and followed Principal Swims to the gym, where the coaches sat on the bleachers and talked with him about being on a sports team. The basketball coach was most excited about Loyce trying out for the varsity team. "You've got the height son. What are you, six foot six? That's plenty enough to make up for lack of talent, or training." The Coach paused, to draw a breath around the toothpick sticking from his jaw. "Come around this evening, for informal practice. You can meet the whole team." The Coach's jaws worked the toothpick as if he had a wad of grain or carrots.

"Nope, Coach Fizzle, I can't come to practice." Loyce was not sure of the coach's name and the man never told it to him so he used the name the other kids called him.

The Coach stood and said quietly, "You can forget about playing for me young man." The Coach spit his toothpick beside the spot where Loyce sat in the bleachers. Loyce stayed there until an old lady in a blue flowered-dress yelled, "You get back to class or I'll write you up for skipping."

The next time Loyce saw Principal Swims in the doorway he stood before he was told. The history teacher said, "Better take your notebook with you Loyce." The kids whispered and shuffled papers as he ducked his head under the doorframe. He kept his head low and thought the dull brown and green tiles were easy colors to clean and that was why someone had picked them.

The plastic window covering was closed in the office and Loyce could not see if anyone was in the parking lot. Principal Swims sat in the chair behind his desk and instead of tapping his fingers he opened a yellow folder with words written in cursive that were too small for Loyce to read.

"You don't bring your history book to class?" Principal Swims licked his finger to turn a page. Loyce's lap was empty except for a spiral notebook and he shifted his hands to cover the scribbles on the torn red cover.

"Mr. Hively won't give me a book until I bring the money."

"What money, Loyce? Books are free."

"Not for me."

"For everyone. Books are free at the school." The chair creaked when the principal shifted. The bearings in the swivel chair needed a good oiling.

"Not if you lost one the year before. He says someone's got a hold on me." Loyce lowered his eyelids and waited.

Loyce heard Principal Swims stop flipping pages and then speak, loudly. "Mrs. Gideon, are you there?" Loyce raised his eyes to see the principal's face lean toward a long metal board with gray steel switches. The voice that came out of the long board belonged to the old lady who had chased him out of the gymnasium.

"I'm here Mr. Swims."

"I need you to take Loyce Cantrell off book return holdover. He didn't lose the books, it was a teacher's mistake."

The voice attached to the person got louder. "Mr. Swims, Loyce lost a lot of books and it was no mistake. Mr. Hively told me—"

Principal Swims voice was low and even. "Just do what I said Mrs. Gideon. Thank you."

Loyce looked at the white half-circles that grew out from his cuticles. He understood he was supposed to return the books, but last spring the septic tank backed up. The books had been soaked in stink and water and he told teachers he lost them during a hunting trip.

"Principal Swims, no teacher's mistake." Loyce knew he should not put guilt on somebody else. "I lost the books."

"It's fine. Why, if I had a dollar for every schoolbook I lost when I was your age…"

Loyce waited but Principal Swims did not finish those words and started with other ones.

"Did you see your father today?"

Loyce raised his head. The principal had a round face inside a round head and eyes that bulged under his pale eyebrows. Principal Swims had a lot of yellow, wavy hair but it was short compared to Duane's. The yellow matched the color of the tie around his neck and was shiny and clean. "I saw him this morning before I got on the bus." Loyce lied; he did not want any trouble for not knowing where his father was.

"Duane was arrested last night, Loyce. He spent the night in jail."

Principal Swims closed the folder with the pages inside and opened his hands as he talked. Loyce did not follow the exact words but he understood Duane was having sex with a high school girl and using her car to sell drugs to other high school kids and the police knew about it. The principal wanted Loyce to stay with an adult until Duane made his bail. "My wife and I would be happy to let you stay with us for a few days, until you get settled. She's busy

with the baby but I know you're a man who can take care of himself."
Principal Swims coughed and waited about half a minute before he
spoke again. "I knew your father in high school."

These words bothered Loyce, though he could not have said
why and he stood, rising above the seated man's head. "I'll stay with
Aunt Betty. She owns a house." Loyce did not want to meet this man's
wife or his baby or hear anything about this man and Duane.

"That sounds fine, Loyce." The principal put his hand forward
and this time Loyce shook it right away.

Loyce left the office and said, "Goodbye" to the woman sitting
outside. Her fingers clicked hard against the computer and did not
stop when she turned her head.

The wrinkles in her face pressed together. "Where are you
going Loyce?"

Her desk had a plastic covering over the wood to protect it
from being scratched. On top of the plastic, she had books, pens and
a coffee mug with the words JESUS SAVES on the side. Loyce thought
she could probably type and drink coffee at the same time.

"Lady, I'm going to stay at Aunt Betty's house, lady, so I can't
come back here. There's no school bus on her road." He opened his
hands in front of him, moving them in the air like Principal Swims
had done. He felt better, like he was pushing the words to her ears.

The old lady grunted, as if something bothered her from the
inside. She said, "Wait here a minute." She walked into the office
and Loyce waited until she came out and told him that Principal
Swims would send the school bus to his aunt's house. Then she held
out an envelope.

"Take good care of this. And call me Mrs. Gideon, not *lady*."
Her eyes widened and she leaned toward him, so close that Loyce
saw yellow teeth in her bottom jaw. "This card works anywhere in
the school. Mr. Swims gives it to special students."

Loyce took the envelope to his locker and opened it. There was
a card inside that said FOR USE PER RONALD SWIMS. The paper card
had his name typed over the drawing of a bobcat and was covered in
hard plastic to protect the words.

Loyce was glad he never slept on Aunt Betty's orange couch; it smelled like pee and did not have pillows. He saw Aunt Betty the first afternoon he was at her house. He opened the door to the bathroom and she was sitting on the toilet with her red underwear stretched around her knees. She screamed, "Get the hell out of my house!" He decided to get on and off the bus at Aunt Betty's place but spend the nights at his own house. Loyce knew where his father kept money in a cigarette carton under the sink so he could pay the electric man who checked the meter. His breakfasts and lunches were free in the cafeteria because he used the card Principal Swims gave him and he could buy pretzels and ice cream at the gas station beside the school.

He stayed there for two weeks and nobody visited his house and the plan worked fine. But one night someone entered the house and yelled. "Duane, you in here? You in here?" Loyce crawled under his bed and watched feet walk into the bedroom and tried not to breathe. He saw girl shoes and heard a girl's voice sound against the walls. "Duane I brought you the goddamn money. I know you're around here. Here's all of it, every goddamn cent." Something dropped with a loud bang and Loyce thought it was a gun. But he didn't smell gunpowder and when he heard a car spin gravel he crawled from under the bed. There was a square tin box on the floor. He turned it upside down and two red cowboy boots fell out. The boots had high leather sides with black stitching and were stuffed full of money. He spread the money on the floor and counted as high as he could. He rolled the money inside the boots and hid the box under a pile of old bridles in the barn. Loyce kept the boots under his bed, the place where things were most safe.

The next day, Loyce asked the shop teacher if he could take some scraps. He got permission and jointed two pressboards and screwed two mismatched hinges into the wood. Then he carried the project six miles to his house because the bus driver wouldn't let him on. He bolted the door to the frame but it was not a good job and the door dragged. He had to duck and push the door with his shoulder, especially if was holding something and could not use his hands. When he left the house, he locked the door with a lock he bought with boot money. He kept the boots hidden and never wore them. He did not want the original owner to see him somewhere and know that Duane had not gotten the money.

Loyce did not bother the money or the boots for the next few months, until the day after Christmas, when he took two bills and bought himself a pellet gun from the pawnshop. Loyce shot coffee cans and plastic bowls off fence posts on the weekends, even though the weather was so cold it hurt his fingers. When the days got longer and warmer, he practiced after school. He ran out of coffee cans and plastic bowls and started using rocks he found beside the road. He got better aiming the gun and could hit small rocks. The evening of his last day of high school, after the girls had whispered about his feet, he hit a school notebook and watched as pieces of paper floated to the ground.

Loyce would never go to the Wal-Mart because the manager knew him from when his father tried to return fishing lures and car tires. The last time, the manager said if he saw Duane again he would shoot first and ask questions later.

There were no shoes in his father's closet and Loyce did not know where else he could get them. Then he thought of something and for a second time, went to the teacher of the shop class and asked if he could have some materials. It was the end of the school year so there wasn't much left but he found what he needed. He was afraid the bus driver might not let him on so he walked to his house, carrying a burlap bag with his rented robe and cap and the things from the stockroom. He stopped a few times to empty the gravel from the sneaker with the hole.

There was no school bus scheduled for the trip to the graduation, so Loyce took the boots with him the morning before it was supposed to happen. He was the oldest kid on the bus because the seniors did not have classes that day. He sat in his usual seat in the front but instead of looking out the window at the spring corn, he stared at the hole in his shoe and clutched the burlap bag.

He sat in the parking lot that day, except for his visit to the bathroom and the cafeteria for lunch. The lady at the end of the line said his card was expired and took it from him, but let him keep the food on the tray.

After he ate, he returned to the spot in the parking lot where he had seen Duane in the car. He opened the burlap bag and took out both boots. The money was rolled tightly inside them and he did not want to remove the bills; instead, he tried to squeeze the money forward into the toes. When he put his feet into the boots, he had trouble walking.

The graduation line formed outside the gymnasium later that day. Loyce wore the robe and the cap, sweating and bending his knees, to try to conceal his bare feet. He carried the boots, one at each side, and had hidden the burlap bag with his sneakers beside the concrete wall. No one said anything to Loyce except a boy who told him his feet smelled. Principal Swims came down the line but Loyce saw him first and put his feet into the boots, working hard to slide his feet inside.

Loyce's heart beat faster but he felt better when the principal walked past his row, nodding but not looking closely at anyone's shoes. Loyce was afraid the man might bend and discover the black paint on the boots was not very thick and had already started to flake off; there was no time to brush on a second coat. He waited in the line, sweating and bending his knees until the band played and the people moved forward. Loyce did the best he could when Mrs. Gideon called his name to keep his balance. He felt clumsy, like one of his old horses, clopping along, but his boots stayed on his feet and he remembered to shake Principal Swims' hand. He stumbled on the steps of the bleachers but he did not think anyone saw him. After the ceremony, Loyce rolled his diploma into one boot and put the money in the other and gripped both boots tightly against his chest as he walked to his house in the cool night.

It was two nights after the graduation when Principal Swims and another man drove a car in front of the house. His heart beat faster and he thought of the boots. Someone must have recognized the boots, even through the black paint. There was no time to hide the money if the principal wanted to examine them.

Principal Swims spoke to Loyce after the car with a light on the dashboard stopped its engine. The other man, with a black hat folded upward on both sides, sat inside the car. Principal Swims gave Loyce a set of pink papers that were attached at the top. "Have you heard from your father?"

Loyce remembered the last time in the principal's office when he had lied. "Mister, I don't know. Maybe, I guess in jail."

"Loyce, it's been in the newspaper. Your father didn't pay his property taxes." Principal Swims coughed a few times and placed his fingers together lightly, in front of his chest. "Unless someone pays the money, fee simple title goes to the county. The marshal, that man in the car, will sell it. Anything left over, unless your dad shows up in a month, can go to you." The principal kept his head aimed upward at Loyce. "We need to find you another place to stay." He tugged at the knot of his tie. "Duane was out of jail five months ago, before Christmas. He owed taxes on this place for three years. It's a few thousand dollars and the marshal knows Duane's not coming back."

"I got money, Mister." The paper was smudging ink on Loyce's hands and he didn't like the way it smelled.

"How much Loyce?" The principal looked upward and smiled in the way the lady had smiled when she came to take the horses. "You'd need a whole lot of money."

Loyce thought of the boots. "Can I go inside, Mister? I need to get something." The principal looked at the man in the car with the light and then turned back to Loyce and smiled. "Sure, you go get some things inside." The golden hair on the man's head waved. "We'll wait for you here son."

Loyce folded this new paper four times, until it fit in his back pocket and walked inside his house, making sure to close the door. He thought about how he had not moved anything because he didn't know if his father would care and how bad the bathroom and the kitchen smelled because the septic tank mess had never been cleaned up. The high school certificate was rolled inside the right boot and the money was still in the left one. He put both boots in the burlap sack along with the key to his door and a bag of pretzels. He looped the bag around his hand and slung it over his shoulder. Before he left the house, he picked up his pellet gun and then he had everything he wanted. He ducked his head and threw his shoulder against the door that stuck and caused it to move a bit.

He swung his gun through the half-open door and pushed hard. It opened wider and he stepped on the porch. The man in the folded hat stood beside the car door and raised his arm in the air, as if he meant to wave. Loyce returned the wave, lifting his own arm. The pellet gun felt light and he thought he might get a heavier, more grown-up gun.

Principal Swims waved his hands and yelled something but the words did not come through because a loud noise rushed into Loyce's head, like an explosion, and he fell sideways. The burlap sack spilled and the gun fell out of his hand. A tight and burning feeling rushed through his stomach.

Loyce lay against the wall. The money from the boot was next to him and had blood on it. He saw the other boot and he hoped his diploma was rolled inside and would not get bloody. Some sound came back into his head and he heard Principal Swims yell curse words at the other man. The man yelled back, "He's so goddamn tall, I meant to hit his rifle hand."

The principal ran toward him and Loyce felt the piece of paper folded in his back pocket. The thudding in his head was like listening to horses go by and he wondered if he could keep the painted boots or if the principal and the other man would take them away.

Like Dancing On Both Feet

Above the static of his phone, my brother told me how they dragged the lake for the body. Every man who owned a boat and was family or friend brought yards of rope with grappling hooks tied to the ends. Women stayed on the shore with dogs to search the banks, both humans and animals sniffing the February air for a scent of the lost man. The black mutt that belonged to Collin whined loudly at a small circle of rocks on the bank where someone had built, and then abandoned, a campfire. Searchers from the sheriff's office walked a mile in each direction from the spot but found no indication anyone had struggled into the trees.

"Midnight's a smart dog. Maybe he smells where Collin made it to shore," I said to my brother after he spoke of the weather conditions. The sun had set on the first day of searching; the wind was blowing harder and the temperature had dropped to less than forty degrees in the water and twenty degrees on land. They had decided to resume looking at daylight the next morning.

"Rory, he's smelling where Collin built a fire a week or even a month ago." My brother, Jimmy, had taken off from his job managing a brokerage office and driven four hours to aid the effort. "He had five minutes, ten minutes max in the water until hypothermia got him. If we're lucky, we'll find the boat first. Then we'll know where to look for him."

"How's Aunt Helen?" Collin's mother was the only woman searching on the water. She had gone out in a small johnboat, the same type aluminum craft in which her son had launched. She wanted to look over the narrow coves for evidence of human activity. Aunt Helen thought her son might have swum to shore and constructed a shelter. My cousin was a skilled outdoorsman: he had built his own cabin and had been building a boat. It was not impossible that he could be waiting for someone to find him on the thin rock bluffs where the high-water mark met the tree line.

"She's not good," Jimmy replied. "We made her put on Collin's coat and a life-preserver." He hesitated, then said, "They made someone ride with her in the boat all the time…"

I knew the coat, an old buffalo hide that would have been resting across the seat of Collin's pickup truck. From what the family could put together, Collin had backed his truck and trailer to the water's edge around four in the morning on Saturday, waking a man with the sounds of country music radio. The same man, a sixty-five year old retired farmer who owned the boat launch ramp, reported Collin missing to the lake patrol early the next morning. It was not unusual, the retiree said, for someone to go out early and spend all day on the water fishing, so he hadn't been concerned until the second day. When the lake patrol arrived, Midnight was waiting in the bed of the pickup, having endured over thirty hours of the freezing temperature.

"They afraid she might collapse?" I asked. Our aunt was a widow, losing her husband only four months earlier. I imagined her long legs extending from the coat that would stop at her knees. Aunt Helen was a striking woman, as tall as her son and as tall as my uncle had been before cancer pushed through his lungs. I pictured her wrapped in Collin's coat, her brown hair blowing, tears on her cheeks. But she would not be crying alone; all searchers would have tears on their cheeks, brought up by the cold wind.

"No. Everyone is here with her." Jimmy sighed into his mobile phone. I knew he would be tired, like everyone in our family would be tired.

"Everyone except me." I lifted a glass and tossed its contents down my throat, thankful that Jimmy could not see me taking comfort from a bottle. "It's going to kill her anyway. It's too much for anyone." Feeling the pin pricks of inactivity, I bent my right knee, brought it to my waist and extended my right foot. I could still unfold my leg parallel to the floor without displacing my hip, a dead giveaway of poor technique.

"Probably." Then Jimmy told me he needed to retrieve a depth finder a fisherman had offered for the search. The electronic equipment was designed to send a sonar signal bouncing off schooling bass under the water. My brother was going to use it to look for something much larger.

Table Rock Lake is a flooded forest and the rotting remains of oak, sycamore, and cedar are misleading. A clump of these decapitated trees can be mistaken for fish instead of shallow water and it is not uncommon for a bass fisherman to scrape his fiberglass boat, costing him several hundred dollars in repairs. For other boaters, the jagged wood poses more than an expensive inconvenience. A leak in a canoe or pontoon boat is serious, especially in cold water and this is only one reason why boating at night with low visibility is dangerous. Especially in the middle of winter; especially if the boater is alone; especially if the boat is a work-in-progress and the captain is full of Jim or maybe if he had been feeling highbrow, then Jack.

Everyone who spends time on the lake has a close call. They can tell you how easy it is to get lost or how a tornado blows up suddenly or how, if you fall overboard without a lifejacket, the boat will float away fast. But everyone is shocked to hear of a death, as if they had monopolies on harrowing experiences. A fog of discomfort settles on them, rubbing against their brains and reminding them they are luckier than they deserve. They resolve to practice boating safety and they warn their teenage children about avoiding foolishness in the water. But they will gradually let go of caution and within a year, an average of six people's lives will end in the lake, and the fog of disbelief and bad memories will roll over the lucky ones again.

I was not surprised when Jimmy called to tell me he was looking for Collin under the water. I know how it can win you over.

The lake can roll gently, inviting you to stand in your boat, feet apart, looking toward the horizon where the land meets the sky in a spectacle of blue and orange light. At night, the water may rock and whisper, a lilting air, the energy of a river captured by a dam; contained, but pulsing—an organ beating stoically to spite its confinement. The stars and the moon can entice you to stand and throw your head back, to feel the pitch and roll of the energy under the hull.

It's a cruel collusion between the lake and vertigo to make you feel as though you are flying, mimicking the suspension of a grand jeté. Leaping into the air and floating, the result of the shift in your center of gravity. Leaping, hanging, then landing, toe-ball-heel, reclaiming energy from the floor to throw you skyward again. The lake is like dance—with its admonitions and hardships.

"Don't give too much energy to the floor, ladies, steal it back by landing light! Steal it back!" The ballet mistress pounded her walking stick against the firm wooden floor and admonished us during my days in crowded rooms framed by straight lines of the exercise barré. Mirrors lined the walls, exposing each movement, each physical imprecision. Those years of practice are removed from me now, succumbing to the insinuation of mediocrity and contributions from changes in life that no one wants to waste time explaining, except to say that former pursuits can be cast aside, without being deemed unworthy or unsuccessful and without aspersions of waste or blame on the years dedicated to them. There are plenty of other occasions for labels of blame and waste.

On the second day of the search, the air outside my window was dusty and warm. The black asphalt intersections shimmered; even for southern California, the February heat was unusual. Two tall palms drooped over the street corner, a dismal effort by the landlord to landscape his apartment building's property. The sun was setting over the lake when Jimmy called, reflecting the difference in our time zones and I knew how blue-black the trees by the lake would look under the settling darkness. Natural trees, growing from well-loamed soil, instead of the rubbery trees squeezing life from the desert.

"Nothing yet," Jimmy yelled above the static of his mobile phone. The terrain around the lake is hills and dense woods, creeks and hollows. No matter how much money the phone companies spend to plant transmission towers on top of the mountains, my family members complain they never get a signal when they need one.

Jimmy told me how they had been out in boats, looking during the day. Rescue divers had been called in by lake patrol. But underwater visibility was poor and even in their drysuits, the water temperature limited the divers' down time to about thirty minutes.

"Thirty minutes isn't enough. What can they cover, a few hundred yards? It isn't enough time." It was three o'clock according to the digital clock on my microwave oven. Too soon to pour a glass of wine, too late to visit a career counselor.

"The deeper the dive, the less time they can spend underwater. The lake's eighty-feet deep in some spots," Jimmy said.

"It's not like they're being asked to raise the goddamn Titanic. It's an eight-foot boat. It's there somewhere."

"Rory," he said, "All I can tell you is what they told us. I'm learning more about the human body and the cold than I ever wanted to know. You on tonight?"

I had not told him, had not told anyone about the combination in an afternoon rehearsal two months earlier, the fantastically difficult jumps, the glasses of wine at lunch, the corner I was supposed to spot to maintain orientation, crashing to the floor, the company director loosening the ribbons of my pointe shoes and carrying me offstage, the barely concealed anticipation of my understudy, lighter by ten pounds and ten years worth of living, the pronouncement of the doctor that I had, perhaps irreparably, injured my anterior cruciate ligament, those words leaving his mouth, suffocating me like clumps of soil filling my nose.

I hesitated. There might be no harm in enlightening him— injury was no shame, perhaps avoiding a greater shame—the weigh-ins, the breath tests, the reduced roles for mature dancers, the dismissal with cause.

Jimmy spoke before I could answer. "I have to go. This connection is shit." I imagined him wearing a heavy brown jumpsuit, with a stocking cap on his light blond head and thick brown work boots on his long, narrow feet. I hoped he was warm enough, was protecting himself.

"Who's taking care of Midnight?" The old dog would have gray hair on his muzzle and paws and would likely limp stiffly, instead of trotting on the shore. The cold wind whipping off the water would be hard on his joints.

"Aunt Helen's got him. He's been going out in her boat." Jimmy sighed, annoyed with my suggestion the family would forget about Collin's dog.

"That can't be right. Midnight's afraid of the water."

"I'm sorry, I can barely hear you," Jimmy shouted. The crescendo of static cut the phone signal.

"Why have a phone you can't use?" I could not hear if he answered me before I placed the receiver into its black cradle and opened the refrigerator, looking at the jug of white wine I had not quite finished the day before.

The lake glistens under Table Rock Mountain, a level-topped protrusion reaching above the heads of fisherman, swimmers and bikini clad sunbathers reclining on boats with cold beers and trashy paperbacks. If you hike to the top of the mountain, avoiding the poison ivy, the thorny brambles and the rattlesnakes, you'll find a round space, clear of trees. You'll find a crumbling rock wall, remnants of the lookout point of southern rebellion. If you can balance on the stacked stones long enough, you will see past the tops of the tree branches to examine the trails up the mountain and satisfy yourself that no one is headed your way. Then you can settle into the thinking you need to do or stare at the water below.

During calm days, the green gray surface of the lake ripples; during rough days, the splash of waves against the shoreline and gray rain sheeting from the sky reminds you of two lovers colliding, biting at each other, tangling together in an embrace so fleeting they will attribute the moment to a scene in a movie, forgetful of their own passions.

And you have the sense that if the water is going to take you—it will—then no amount of care or caution or invocation of God will aid you. The ferocity of the river that was choked by a dam did not disappear; it only pooled and condensed, licking upward with protruding fangs, a freezing embrace, settling over graves of Indians and pioneers, over bodies sacrificed to the divided state's border conflict, the bloodiest fighting of the secessionist struggle. The river that once washed away the detritus of human settlement now hosts the wrecks of consumer culture: car parts, food wrappers, and plastic storage containers. The water harbors waste for future generations, perhaps people for whom the lake will be a fantastically preserved archeological dig. They will drain the basin and unearth treasures that we cast away, careless in our hurry to rid ourselves of objects without value.

Ten years before he went missing, Collin took me out in his father's boat. He had graduated high school the year before and lived in a trailer the shape and color of a silver bullet, befitting the green gray tint of leaves and oval pinecones in the half-acre of land his mobile home occupied.

He had planted a vegetable garden and ate smoked venison from the deer he shot in season. His dog, Midnight, had limped out of the woods, probably a fighting pup that had escaped his chain or his cage. Collin fed him and soon after, Midnight slept beside my cousin and followed him everywhere—except on the boat. When Collin and I pushed off from the bank, we left Midnight a pile of dog biscuits and a deflated basketball. The dog yelped and ran along the shore, ignoring the toy and his treats. I heard Midnight's barks fade as Collin opened the motor, taking us around the bend of the cove, into deeper water.

"Collin, you have got to be the only guy in this state with a dog that can't swim." Our private jokes were plentiful. A disaster, I teased him, a dog that could not swim.

"Rory, you've got to be the only girl in this state who hasn't been kissed." He smiled. Another disaster. A girl who could dance but had never been asked to do so by a boy.

"Shows you what you know." I always alluded to the possibility of mysterious lovers, tall and dark men who walked over the mountains to toss roses on the floor of the barn where I practiced. I wasn't ugly, but had small breasts and thinning hair, the result of required buns during lessons. On stage, though, hair didn't matter and small breasts were advantageous, so no, it wasn't impossible about men and flowers. The existence of adoring men was definitely possible.

"Imaginary boyfriends don't count." Collin cut the engine and opened the lid to the fish live well. Instead of fresh lake water, it was filled with ice and beer. "You want one?" He picked a can out of the ice, popped the tab and pitched it back into the live well. Collin cursed every piece of trash; he was meticulous about keeping the lake clean.

"Nope." I was not a drinker, then, believing ballet required more discipline.

"You leaving next week?" he asked. Collin had brown hair, brown eyes and brown skin, a deep tan that covered him even in the winter. I did not know if he had a girlfriend—we had never spoken of it—but I hoped he did not. He was too much a part of the woods and water. I didn't want to think of him leaving it for a girl.

"Day after graduation." Everyone else in the family knew the day I would board a bus to California, the trip that would ruin my life, get me pregnant, cause me to be homeless, or some variation on those outcomes. But Collin didn't participate in family gossip or pretended, for my benefit, not to listen.

"You need to learn to have a drink," Collin thrust a hand into the compartment full of ice. "Cold beer is the best." He turned the ignition key with his free hand.

"I can't drink this." The can was near my face and I reached for it, hoping Collin would take control of the steering wheel. The boat was moving forward, fast.

"Yes you can, you've got all that balance. I'm not stopping until you drink it all." Collin opened the throttle, flinging my body against the passenger seat. There were no life jackets and I gripped the open beer in one palm and the seat under my legs with the other.

Collin stood up in his seat, squeezing the wheel between his knees. I watched the front of the boat rise. Bass boats are designed so that at high speeds, most of the hull hovers above the water as the speedometer climbs. Thirty-forty-fifty-sixty. That's miles per hour, and that's not as high as the needle can lean.

"We're going to die!" I screamed. The craft began to chine walk, a severe side-to-side roll of the boat. A chine walking boat was unbalanced and required *more*, not *less*, input from the driver. I was afraid to grab at the wheel, afraid it might flip the boat. Collin was still standing, his body jolting. The steering wheel gripped between his knees was his only source of balance, the boat's only source of guidance.

I threw the beer at the water to use both hands to hold my seat. Liquid sprayed against my lips, the fermented beverage tasted like the metal needles I threaded to sew ribbons to pointé shoes.

"Stop it now! This is insane!" The violent rocking motion turned my stomach. I knew I should orient myself, *spotting*, it's called in dance. I fixed my eyes on the visible bald spot on top of the unmoving mountain.

"No. This is like dancing on both feet!" Collin yelled and raised his arms as we sped forward. We bucked from side to side, racing toward the deep middle of the lake, under the mountain's shadow. I sat crouched and still, running my tongue around my lips. I wondered if the tank would run out of gas or if we would be tossed out. Either way, I prepared to swim back to the shore that was at least a mile away in any direction. I kicked off my tennis shoes and breathed deeply to fill my lungs with oxygen, mentally rehearsing the correct way to hitch a person around the chest to keep the nose and mouth above water.

Collin was a terrible swimmer.

"We found him." Jimmy called again on the third day when the sky was dark outside my window, safely past the time to be drinking a guilt-free cocktail. The drink required olives but because there were none in my apartment, I improvised with peeled grapes. At the rate of two grapes per drink, discounting the possibility of spoilage, I had approximately a month before I would be forced to enter a grocery store. Luckily, the nearby liquor store took orders for delivery over the phone.

"Where are you?" I asked. Jimmy's voice came from a clear signal, indicating use of a landline.

"I drove back home. Made record time," Jimmy replied. "Listen, you should know…."

I cut him off. I imagined Jimmy standing in front of a fire his wife of five years would have built for him, the care she would have taken to help him remove his wet and soiled clothes, the hot coffee waiting as he pulled into the driveway of the house I had never seen.

"I've read the news on the internet." This was true. I had been logging in throughout the day, monitoring the regional wire service's website. "Besides, I think I know what happened." This was not true. The news had mentioned nothing about the cause of the accident.

"Did you know he was wearing his tool belt?"

I understood Jimmy's question. Whatever had gone wrong with his homemade boat, Collin had tried to fix it. He would have been heavily weighted, drawn to the bottom of the lake by an assortment of screwdrivers, hammers, pliers, an awl, metal screws, bolts, nuts and nails, a level, a tape measure and a flashlight, to help him find the problem. Implements of independence from banks, contractors, stores, salesmen—and obsolescence—pulling him down past the dead treetops to the rotting tangle of roots of the underwater forest.

"You on tonight?" Jimmy interrupted my thoughts and the salty water slipping past my cheeks.

"Yes," I said. Tasting vodka in the grape, I glanced at the digital clock. It read nine PM "Yes, um, yes." It was fine, I decided, to continue lying. I could blame it on my grief later.

"Must be a really late show." Jimmy voice was even. I heard plates and silverware being set on a hard surface in the background. "I've got some more calls to make. Aunt Helen knows you probably won't make it back here for the funeral and it's ok. She knows what you thought of him."

A bubble of nausea erupted in my stomach, gurgling with acidic pain up to the back of my throat. "Wait, Jimmy, wait. Who found him?"

"Midnight. Started barking like hell over this one spot. We hooked Collin and pulled him in the boat."

My memory was fluid, disbelief mixing into the pool of Jimmy's stated account. It might have been the alcohol. It might have been acceptance flowing easier with the advent of the unthinkable that was easily imagined, the shock that was easily predictable. Maybe I didn't know anything about what had happened in the years I had been gone. So I murmured, "I remember…Midnight being afraid of the water."

"Well, he's fine with it now." Jimmy replied, an edge slipping into his voice. I could imagine him thinking, *the damn dog is fine, really.*

We ended the conversation with Jimmy telling me how the family thought it was such a shame they had not seen me in six years and perhaps they should make more of an effort to get to California to see me dance.

The boat didn't run out of gas that day on the lake and I don't know how long Collin could have maintained his balance. We were brought to a stop by the flashing lights and bullhorn commands of the lake patrol officers who had, they said, been radioed by the retired farmer near the launch ramp. The officers knew Collin—everyone around the lake did—and they let him off with a warning for speeding and a citation for missing life preservers. The younger of the two officers tipped his cap to me and said "Have a good day miss," when he was finished with his business.

"Were you trying to get us killed?" I yelled at Collin after the officers had powered away. My hands trembled, but I reached into the live well and pulled out two beers. I handed one to him and popped one for myself.

Collin did not answer. We motored, slowly, back to shore

where Midnight barked and leaped, dropping his deflated basketball at Collin's feet. Instead of riding in the cab, I lifted myself into the bed of the old pickup truck. Midnight grabbed his toy in his mouth and followed me, jumping easily off the ground. I wrapped both arms around the dog's fuzzy head, gripping him tightly. The truck rolled and bumped over the rough chat road and I fixed my eyes on the bare mountaintop, orienting myself for the ride ahead. I remembered the leaping arc of the boat and the feel of skimming over the lake like a low-flying bird and considered: if I had been tossed to the air, would I have sunk, graciously, through the crest of the waves, opening my eyes underwater to look for my cousin and after satisfying my conscience, have swum to shore?

I turned to peer through the truck's rear windows. In the rear-view mirror, Collin's face was set and calm; he sipped his beer and drove slowly. Or would I have struggled to hold onto the body that could manage anywhere but in the water, promising that we would either swim to shore or enter, together, the forest below us?

As the truck turned onto the main highway the mountain disappeared behind a crest of tall trees and my questions leaped away from me into the air, jealous of their own energies.

The Southernmost Point

T hose were the days we left the beach house at sunrise, full with quiet. The mornings were simple enough, brought to us without hesitation by a broad screen window Henry had never shuttered, not even before I lived with him. It was important for him to turn to the sun and then away from it, always, and when he discovered I had never covered my windows, he invited me to share his home. Or so he told me, that my common appreciation for the morning light and the white noise of the early tide caused him to consider me more closely. As he considered each rock on the slip of beach we tracked in our bare feet in the mornings. Henry had one theory, among his many, that it was a sin to remove a pebble from the tumbling loll of the tide until its time.

"You suppose there's a proper time? Bit overdone as a metaphor, don't you think Henry?" I gripped his hand, more tightly, and felt the mass of him pull me back, one of many times he pulled me.

"A white pebble lifted by chance of a man's fancy before it's ground into sand? Perhaps." Henry stopped walking and I looked at his feet, those singular sources of his motion, caked with wet grit and a tan that did not disguise his veins, or his sunspots, or his wrinkles. "Maybe I've run through the list of clichés and need to start again with the first and the oldest." He pointed at a pink round rock beside my own feet. "That one, it looks ready. Take it back, I'll wash out a jelly jar and you can start a collection."

I leaned and slipped the rock into the pocket of the white pants I had rolled to my knees to keep clean of the wet sand. As I straightened, he stared at my toes, the ten longer than his own, with eggshell polish on the nails. He anticipated me and carried my hand to his chest before I could offer it. Though Henry would not look at me, he raised his eyes to the sea. Then we followed the imprints of our feet back to the house with the open window, the smooth rock pressing my skin through the fabric.

In those days, Henry and I both ate raisin cereal and drank coffee at the round breakfast table that could only accommodate two chairs. Millie was the housekeeper and she had set out his breakfast with me for three years and before that, for twenty-six years with his wife, Carol. Millie was jovial and competent and I imagined Henry fought Carol for the housekeeper more than anything else they had shared during their marriage. Henry was not, at least during my tenure, overly formal with Millie and they joked as she served.

"Millie, did you see the surf this morning? It almost dragged me under. Would you run to save me, Millie?" Henry did not change the inflection of his voice when he teased her. He maintained an even tone, to match the steady arc of coffee Millie poured into his cup. She never missed, never splashed the beige damask tablecloth or saucer with hot liquid.

"Ah, Mister Henry, you gonna make my heart hurt, no surf gonna take you. You want Millie come run after you, you better plan on waiting a while." Millie served Henry first then offered him cream from a thin pitcher that did not match the china because Henry had not been particular about the odds and ends of housekeeping he accumulated after his marriage ended.

But it had to be cream for his coffee, because Henry could taste the difference and had sent Millie to the store the time I spilled the cream and had offered him milk instead. He apologized to me and explained that Millie knew him, and did not mind the trip, that some of his habits were so old he did not want to shed them.

"At least you'd tell someone I was in trouble?" Henry chuckled as I lifted the coffee pot. I did not want Millie to serve me, although she protested before I had insisted I preferred to help myself.

"I'd go tell Miss Loreen, after you get wet. Teach you right for wading out that far." Millie crossed her thick arms, resting them over the bulge in her lightweight blue dress and shook her head. "You got no business by the water alone." I wondered then, as I often did, how much older Millie was than Henry, and how many decades older than me that made her.

"What if Loreen wasn't there to save me from drowning?" Henry laughed again as Millie snorted and walked away from us, into the kitchen with its swinging door and mismatched pots and pans hanging from the ceiling.

Henry sipped his coffee and would not raise his eyes directly to mine. Instead, he stared out the window, the open one we both loved, and his eyelids flickered, slightly, against the sun. I saw a fishing boat, trolling about one hundred yards off our shoreline, motoring under modest power to the dock at the end of Duval Street.

"Looks like the fishing was good today for the crew." Henry rested his empty cup on his saucer. He drank quickly and always took a second cup, which I poured for him. I watched his face smile in profile. My hand slipped under the table.

"Why is that Henry?" I found his left hand, the one he did not use to hold his cup, and squeezed. His palm was hard, like I always had thought a man's should feel.

"Looks to me like they had a reason to keep fishing. They're a bit late into port, but still may set the market with their catch." Henry drank his second cup as quickly as he had the first and stood. He was finished with our breakfast. Although I usually sat at the table to read and watch tourists sprinkle the beach with towels and coolers full of beer and food, he shuffled toward his study, the room adjacent to the kitchen with its streetside view, shaded from the sun. Then, as a woman might retrieve an item from a shelf even as she maintained her place in the checkout line of a supermarket, he turned and kissed my mouth. When that man kissed me it was with a full, crushing pressure, the kind any man should give his wife, or more appropriately, to his lover.

"When you get back today, Loreen, I've got just the jelly jar in mind." Henry shuffled, again, away from me through the kitchen door. I could not make out what he said to Millie, but I heard that laugh of hers, an unashamed bellow. Then he must have passed to his study, because I heard Millie slamming cabinet doors and complaining to the air about her back and her arthritis and her bunions. The boat had veered beyond my plane of sight when I looked for it again, but I decided to walk to the dock to determine if Henry was correct that the fishing had been great for the last crew into port.

Henry spent those days in his study doing what he called his 'retirement reading.' All the subjects he hadn't gotten to in his normal life, or so he told me, waited for him then. I never pegged Henry's taste in reading, not while he was married and not when I lived with him. After Carol gave him a divorce, and after an appropriate amount of time, I was invited to attend his book shopping excursions at the island's one good bookstore. Henry told me Carol had not been much of a reader, except when she had seen the movie and then decided to pick up the book. She was more of a decorator, he said, and used her free time to keep their home comfortable and full of fresh flowers.

Together, we bought collections of poems, short stories, and a truckload of classic fiction he could never hope to finish in his lifetime. We bought books written to compare the religions of the world, the history of the art of calligraphy, mapmaking, and the origins of the modern calendar. We bought books in original language and English translation versions, convincing ourselves we would read both, side by side, line for line and in this way, learn German, Russian, or more exotically, Gaelic from a book of Celtic legends. We drifted through the stacks, slowly, often with my fingers touching his palm or my toes, in their open sandals, curling around his Achilles tendon.

We bought books about sex and sensual massage and during that last fall, we bought the books I would need to finish my thesis in history for the state's university. I had been studying on the island the year I met Henry, desiring the sun and isolation and had been slow finishing my work since we took up together.

That Henry paid for my schoolbooks, as a father might assume a daughter's bill for tuition, was not an irony lost on either of us. But it was all a variation on a very tired theme and I only said, "Thank you Henry." We continued through the store, laughing when the clerk told us to hurry up because he wanted to cross the street to buy a sandwich. Henry offered to watch the store for him and he happily agreed, cautioning us to wait until he returned if we were not sure about an item's price.

The bookstore conducted a lively business in maps of historical points of interest in the islands. The sunburned tourists smiled when I told them the most famous literary house was around the corner, that they need not pay the admission fee, that they should tell the man at the desk that Loreen, the weekend tour guide, said they could pass on for free. In the first minutes the clerk was absent, I sold five plastic foldout maps and three copies of *The Old Man and the Sea*. Henry walked through the store, pulling novels and biographies from shelves, filling five baskets before he lugged them to the top of the counter where I stood. The other shoppers left the store and after half an hour, the clerk had not returned.

"Maybe he's having a liquid lunch?" I motioned to the street lined with seafood restaurants and frozen drink bars. Lunch was a busy time for the island, nearly as busy as sunset in the square, but not even the locals, the people who waited tables and tended bar, hurried to return from their breaks. They called it 'being on island time' as if there, at the southernmost point, everything to be accomplished had time wrapped around it, waiting to be unfolded and stretched and used.

Henry picked through the books in his baskets, piling them as haphazardly on the counter as he had selected them from the shelves.

"Ring these up." Henry thumbed through the yellowing pages of a slim hardcover volume with a green title I was unable to make out. He told me to add eight dollars to the total and asked me for the stack of tissue paper. I punched digits on the oldish style cash register and he smiled at me when he finished wrapping the book. I leaned across the counter, with my elbows propped and blew him a kiss, hoping I looked like something of a proposition to the man.

"I'm surprised you know how to operate that old thing." He slid the book into the rear pocket of the canvas pants that hung lower each year, exposing more of a blue vein above his hipbones.

"You'd be surprised at all the old things I like to operate…" I squeezed my lips and leaned closer to him.

The dust from the inventory in the bookstore caused Henry to sneeze and I put my palm on his forehead then pressed his temple and his scalp. His silver hair was thick, but downy, the sort allocated only to the young and the aging and after the decades of grooming, the hair follicles curved into place under the light pressure from my fingers.

"I should sit Loreen," he said.

I walked from behind the counter, and piled his purchases in a circle, five books high, with one break in the ring, enough space to walk through. Henry watched me and I could not determine, could never determine with that man if anything about me surprised him. I lowered myself to the ground, sat Indian-style and curled my forefinger.

Henry walked to me, through the narrow cleft in the wall of books and stood still, a straight and tall form that seemed even taller than his six-foot frame from my perspective. I curled my finger again, instructed him to turn around and when he rotated his body I reached to pull at his belt loops. He lowered his body to mine and I closed my arms around his torso, closed my legs around his waist, nibbled his earlobes with my teeth.

"You're a beautiful girl Loreen but you know that." Henry leaned his back against my chest, and I unbuttoned his white cotton shirt and slipped both my hands, with their long brown fingers and fingernails with their eggshell polish, underneath.

I had always rubbed his arms and his chest, lightly, with the tips of my fingers. In our bed, we called it giving him 'body tickles' and he would ask for it nearly every night we spent together, huddled in a nest of a thick comforter and pillows stuffed to bursting with goose down. I would build a wall of pillows around us and angle the lamp to point in the middle of the ring, so when we made love, we were in a spotlight's circle. Henry had told me that Carol would only have sex in the dark, that after both of their children were born, she said it was undignified for a woman of her age to carry on like a horny bimbo.

"I know you think so Henry. I'd hope you think so, after all this time."

"I don't say it enough. I'm a lucky man, the luckiest."

"Why's that Henry?" My fingers traced the path of his ribs and his abdomen, still flat and small and I pushed in further, to feel the smooth muscles underneath. When he had been younger, Henry was a runner and I wondered what I had missed, what had left his body before I knew him.

"I've only got age and experience on my side, you've got youth and beauty. It adds up you can have anyone." His hands covered my hands, stopped my fingers. "And soon, you'll have less of me, Loreen." Henry's hand released its pressure.

I thought about Henry's former life as a lawyer and how we had met: he had been vacationing with Carol on the island and I was working as a tour guide, the same job I still held on a part-time basis. Henry had been alone, leaving Carol to sip frozen drinks poolside at the hotel. He had followed me on the tour, rolling his eyes when fellow tourists asked questions with obvious answers. He tipped me with a rolled five-dollar bill with his business card inside. I read his Boston address and threw the card away. Returning the next day, and for the next eight days, he tipped me five dollars and a business card for each tour, which he recited back to me over our first drink at the sunset festival in Mallory Square. The tightrope walkers juggled knives and the fire-eaters walked on their hands against a backdrop of the sinking sun and sailboats, their sails full with the evening breeze. I related the history of the festival, how the natives had summoned green flashes from the sun with dancing supplications. As if all the capering and merry-making could prolong, even a second, the disappearing day. Henry spoke of his Boston practice and his plan for buying a home on the island, a large clapboard house on the beach. I pointed to his wedding band and asked him how his wife liked the island, how she liked the idea of moving from one end of the country to the other. Henry told me Carol would never consider leaving her Boston brownstone.

"There's enough of you." I felt the book in his rear pocket press against my belly, its corners protruding, reminding me. "What's the book Henry?"

Henry's slight figure slumped against my chest. "It's a book about flowers, for my ex-wife."

"Really? You're sending it to her?" This was the woman he had not left in a fit of anger or dislike. They had separated as friends, people who had agreed to stop being lovers. Henry told me when I met him he had nothing but respect for his wife.

"No, I'm going to Boston next week. My son, his wife had the baby. Millie took the call yesterday." Henry always described them as 'my son' or 'my ex-wife' to denote members of his family, as if, after my time with him, I did not know their names.

"Congratulations...boy or girl?" I unfolded my legs, pressed my weight on my wrists and closed my eyes.

"Baby girl. Can't believe we're grandparents now..."

I stood and this time I was tall next to Henry's seated figure. "You and Carol are grandparents. We aren't anything."

He looked at me and smiled, that smile of his I could not describe but could only enjoy for the time I had it. "That's not true Loreen."

I thought of my research about the natives of the island, how they had blended with nearby islanders and their languages, and had survived the Spanish and their religion, and had welcomed the French and adopted their cooking into conch-based recipes. Then the northerners had come, from the newly formed states, with their wrecker boats and militias to protect against coastal threats. Those newcomers, the ones with the pale skins ill-suited to the climate, stayed to build houses and schools. History washed around the last arrivals, absorbing only their money and their bridges that connected the chain of islands. The natives, with their Spanish spirituality and

French aesthetic had already been sanded smooth and their culture was fixed, impenetrable.

"I do love you though." I squatted in front of Henry and touched his chest.

"Let's walk to the square this evening, watch the gang come out to entertain the tourists."

"If you like, Henry." I put my hand over his chest, feeling his heart's rhythm, which was anything but smooth.

The clerk returned eventually and asked, "Is everything under control?" I responded with, "Do you think everything looks under control?" Henry coughed and I told the clerk that I'd be back later to collect the books we had bought.

"Let's go home." Henry turned away from the silhouette of the clerk in the late afternoon sunlight.

The last thing Henry would have seen of the bookstore that afternoon, had he looked, was the clerk shaking his head and forming the words 'gold digger' to himself as we passed through the door. But I was the only one to turn back and the clerk's eyes met mine. We both looked at the circle of books with a gap, like a missing tooth.

That was our final trip to the bookstore, together. I continued to shop there, avoiding the eyes of the clerk, selecting books I needed, or wanted. Henry insisted, after that trip, upon reading the books he already owned before buying new ones. He slept later in the mornings and took his breakfast alone, with Millie to serve him when I left for my shift at work. Then he boarded the tiny plane to the mainland, taking Millie with him, because his family was anxious to see her and to introduce her to the baby.

I read and wrote my papers and walked to the docks in the mornings, early, trailing the boats. The fishermen were locals, hired into the crews for two weeks on, one week off. They shouted to one another from the decks, a mishmash of sailors' jargon, Spanish, and French. Most of them did not look old enough to buy beer, but a few looked as old, or older than Henry. One morning, I waited for the last boat to dock, nearly an hour after the others.

The catch came from the ice beds in the berths smelling of brine and seaweed and most of the gills had stopped pulsing and the fishermen swore as they pulled out their knives to cut the heads. I watched, from a good twenty paces away, and saw the crew unload twice as big a catch as any other boat. I asked the dock master why the last boat in had the biggest haul. He spit out his tobacco and yelled into my face, "The fishing was great, why the hell else would they stay out there?"

I wrote comments for my thesis, noted the dialects I heard amidst the swearing and then walked Main Street ten blocks to my job, where the tourists waited to hear about famous men who had lived on the island.

When he returned from Boston with Millie, Henry was gray and quiet. Baby Erin O'Shea was the spitting image of Carol and he related that everyone had gotten along splendidly. Henry had spent the three nights at Carol's brick home and told me they had shared a bottle of wine and joked about the effeminate lawyer who had represented her during the divorce. Their first grandchild, "was pretty as any picture," according to Millie, and Henry returned with a leather briefcase he said were full of photographs. He did not offer to show them to me and later, when he needed some other papers from the locked case, I asked Millie for the combination and opened it. There were the pictures I expected, those of him holding his granddaughter and group pictures in front of flowerbeds shaded by drooping trees. I also found a photo of Henry with his arm around Carol, both of them smiling, their blue eyes shining, with Carol holding a dozen roses and the book he had wrapped in the bookstore. I laid the pictures on his desk and brought Henry the estate documents he had requested.

Henry's doctor visited us the next week, after Henry complained of pain in his chest. Henry's prognosis, in keeping with everything else I tried to understand about that man, was uncertain. I was not surprised to learn Henry had concealed the extent of his heart failure from me, along with other secrets from his life before we had met. They were his to keep, although I wanted him to make them ours.

After the doctor visited, our time together changed. I brought his unread books to him, to let him choose which ones to skim through so that he could acquaint himself, if only briefly, with their contents. We could not make love, so I built the wall of pillows and angled the light at my hands, stroking across his body. Henry could not walk with me in the mornings.

Millie planned Henry's special menus, based upon the doctor's advice, during three months that followed and she ordered special equipment sent into our clapboard house. I remember signing for the items, the deliverymen tramping past me, listening to Millie shout instructions, listening to her warn them, "Not to bother Mister Henry!"

I moved the jelly jar, only half-full of rocks, to the windowsill by the breakfast table where Millie and I rolled Henry's new, mobile hospital bed. From this position, he could face the sun and the beach in the morning. At the sun's highest point during the day, Millie wheeled him away. When I was not in class, or conducting tours, I sat beside Henry, to read selections from my thesis. I was reading to him about the incorporation of the island into the state when he took my hand.

"Don't go to the funeral with Carol. She's not able…" His hand held my own, close to his heart and his palm was still firm, the only firm part left to that man.

"No Henry, I won't. You know I wouldn't." I squeezed, tightly, until I knew the pressure was hurting him.

"You aren't finished with your thesis, are you Loreen?"

"No, I was waiting…"

"For me to go." Henry interrupted and I nodded.

"Waiting for a lot of things Henry." I sat on the side of the bed with our pillows, that time, stuffed underneath his back and elbows instead of circling him. Each day, he told me, his bones felt more brittle and more porous. He said he felt ready to break. I resumed reading to him until he asked me to go to the sundown festival and describe it to him the next morning. I watched the antics and made notes on the costumes of the people and the color of the sails of the boats in the harbor.

He died that night, as I knew he would. I called in sick to work and everyone clucked kindly, as I knew they would. I spent the next week with the undertaker, Henry's lawyer, and his insurance agent. Henry left me the house and his books and a sum of money. He left Millie a similar sum and the rest he divided between his children. I left my thesis, that long and unfinished history of our island on his desk where I could look over it during the afternoons. The medical center retrieved its equipment and I sold the bed and the pillows Henry and I had used to an elderly weekend couple that had purchased a condo on the northern, quiet side of the island. I slept in Henry's study, on the couch where he had spent his time reading.

Carol attended Henry's memorial service on the mainland, where his daughter and son had arranged for a wake and then a burial. I heard this from Millie who told me Mrs. O'Shea had looked "amazing beautiful," and that Mrs. O'Shea had worn a black silk dress with black stockings and black heels. That Mrs. O'Shea had been "the best, classy lady there," and was going to take a vacation with her children, to spend time with the granddaughter Henry had met once.

I thought about the picture I had seen of Carol, the last one he had made with her. Her brown clipped hair and blue eyes and tiny, size one frame. She held peach roses, the expensive, store-bought kind anyone could order by the dozen. It was difficult to imagine her digging in the earth, using a trowel and cutting flowers for the table. It was easy to imagine Henry pressing her to accept his bouquet.

"What did she talk about, Millie? Did she ask where I was?" I poured my coffee and looked past the beach, at the boats drifting in through the morning, with the decks full of bronzed men who pulled their livelihoods out of the water.

"No, Miss Loreen. Just told me thanks for coming, how much it meant to the whole family." Millie groaned and shifted her weight. "Miss Loreen, I was gonna wait a while but I want to retire. Go back north to my own family. I'll wait until you're on your own feet here."

"It's fine Millie. I figured you would want to go." I scraped butter over the toast Millie had prepared for me and tasted the warm bread. "I'll miss your cooking."

"I'm sure you'll be fine, Miss Loreen, just fine here. You're from here, you're suited to the climate." She stood beside me without moving and I believed that she, like me, was watching the boats, although I had never seen her watch them before.

"I'm not from around here Millie, I spent most of my life in Boston. I thought you knew that." I sipped more coffee and wondered how she could not have known I was from the North; surely Henry had discussed it with her. "That's part of what Henry and I love... loved...about each other. We both came from the same place."

"Didn't know that. Don't guess anybody knew that. The family, we thought you was a local." Millie shifted her weight again and pointed to the fishing boats in front of our open window. "Ah Miss Loreen, look out there."

"Henry loved those boats." The men on the deck worked, moving the nets to clear the decks before they docked, so the island's kitchens might smell of freshly cooked fish in the evening.

"Nah, Miss Loreen, Mister Henry may have loved them boats but I'm telling you it's gonna rain. It's gonna rain."

Through our open window I could see she was right, the clouds were moving over the beach and the sunlight, at least that day, would leave early.

Beulah Land

And every Moment has a Couch of gold for soft repose –
A Moment equals a pulsation of the artery –
And between every two Moments
stands a Daughter of Beulah,
To feed the Sleepers on their
Couches with maternal care.

William Blake

Between coasts, a seventy-foot Jesus statue shadows the Ozark hollow town called Beulah Land. Trees flourish up the mountainside as if positioned on risers by a master gardener, exposing only the crown where an expanse of fertilized grass encircles Christ.

Below statue Jesus, pin oak, green hickory, and black walnut grow amongst scrub cedar not suitable for hope chests or shadow boxes. Quality cedar prospers five miles north in a Missouri state park, but steep sloped Arkansas mountains are private property, yielding to human consumption. The master gardener's plan, its conceit of fragrant needles cushioning mountain travelers' footfalls—yearlong cover for silent pursuits—has given over to deciduous fall crackling and woodsy winter baldness.

You maintain interest in space shorn of original accompaniment, sacrifice of form to proclivity, or determined need.

Part I

The land for statue Jesus was surveyed and logged, dynamited and graded on the mountain west and opposite your home. You watched the white, sectioned monument carried up the switchback dirt road blasted for rigs bearing oversize loads. Escort trucks with banners and yellow flashing lights preceded and followed the statue segments. Processional engine noise bounced between mountains half an hour past dawn until half an hour before dusk. Guns sounded after sunset, although even in season hunting was prohibited at night.

Locals complained the construction company was shooting too many brown bears, ruining the hunting season.

"The quicker the assembly, the quicker we'll get this church built," the lead contractor pointed to raw studs not yet finished out with wallboard. "And the sooner we can put people to work."

The thick man wore an orange hardhat, pressed slacks, shiny black shoes.

"What sort of work you offering?" Granddad's face was long and two wrinkled rivulets isolated his mouth, like a stream encircling a rock island. You squirmed, smoothing an invisible crease in your skirt, wishing he had worn his funeral blazer and tie rather than denim overalls, brown flannel shirt, work boots crusted with chicken manure.

A thin man stood and cleared his throat. Pants creased, belted over a pressed white shirt, he wore a dark blue tie. A jacket hung over his arm. Folding the jacket, he paired the sleeves then sized the tailored fabric by half. A redhead nearly your age, fifteen perhaps, laid the garment in her lap and then, as if remembering proper posture in public, lifted her spine. Seated across from her in the circle of folding chairs, you understood she was the man's daughter, carrying traits of his pointed chin, his twitching nose. Her ears collapsed against her head, rabbit-like.

The thin man spoke. "I'm Reverend Timothy Sykes. I'm going to be the pastor here, at Calvary. To speak to your inquiry, we'll look for volunteers from the congregation for leading tours around Christ."

"You mean the statue of Christ." Granddad indicated east, beyond the unfinished house of worship.

"Yes, yes, the statue."

"What kind of paying work you offering?"

"There will be an office secretary's position and some ticket sellers."

"And what else?" Granddad's tall body straightened, his eyelids raised, revealing large irises the color of spring ice.

"And what else?" The man looked to the crowd, to his daughter. Red hair swept her shoulders, her eyes directed to each corner, scanning attendees' reactions.

"What other work you got planned?"

"The work of the Lord. Spiritual guidance, meals for disabled, elderly, the unemployed. We hope to become a church for the whole community."

"We've got five churches for nine hundred people and most live miles from this mountain. Where do you think you're going to get your congregation?"

"Sir, may I ask your name?"

"Buell. Charlie Buell."

"Mr. Buell, people from the local area and not from the local area are welcome at the new Calvary."

"You mean you're cutting the woods for tourists."

"Pardon, sir?" The preacher's eyes settled on his daughter's face, then on the white fur cuffs edging her pink sweater, seeming to contemplate how to answer with a lesson from the Word.

"You heard me."

"Gentlemen," the contractor's voice broke over the last syllable—eliciting chuckles. "We're here to talk about shooting some dangerous bears, not how the pastor's gonna pack 'em in. Now, who here is thinking we should be ridding ourselves of this bear nuisance?"

"Let's go, Granddad," you whispered. He clasped your hand. You threaded the crowd, weaving in front of the redhead's fixed eyes and quivering lips. You did not return the girl's attempt at expression.

Calendar winter arrived, exposing the bare mountain crown where a crane lifted Jesus' head. Granddad walked downhill from his trailer to the back porch. He offered field glasses. "Amanita Buell, there's too many people coming here that don't belong," he said.

"Where do they belong?" You focused the field glasses: four men dangled in traces, welding the statue's neck. Sparks streaked from their hands; they swung, the frequency of passage across Jesus' face determined by vigorous pulling.

"They belong in their own place."

"They're coming to church Granddad. That's not something anyone can talk against."

"There's nothing in this world you can't talk against. They'll throw Jesus down in front of you and claim that if you speak against them, you're speaking against Jesus. But if it offends you, talk against it."

"You're supposed to speak as a brother to those who offend you," you said.

"They say you get into heaven by scraping and bowing. I say you're more likely to get into heaven by thinking."

"I think they don't give a good goddamn what you think," you said.

"Don't cuss. Your mother and Granny will blame it on me."

"They don't know."

"They know."

Calvary Church and its adjacent office equipped for tour guides was near completion six weeks later. After the asphalt hardened, vehicles filled the new two-lane road curving to the mountaintop. Mother found employment as a ticket taker for the monument. Her father-in-law dropped her off in the mornings, delivered eggs, and then met her when tours ended.

In the pink and red streaked sundown, lightning bugs ushered Granddad's old pickup past platy quartz, limestone, and gypsum composing the exposed mountain elbow. The truck descended, cradled between hanging rock shelves and hollow inclines, black blasting scars and Spanish epithets spray-painted by illegal laborers. The truck descended, passing game corpses, deer without instincts to navigate the new crossing; senescent raccoons, eye patches crusted red; broken cats lacking comprehension of white lines when pawing through fast food wrappers, soiled diapers and empty jars of baby food; a box of six dead black mongrel puppies, dumped by a Wanda Pickett out of Hollywood, Florida, negligent in removing the bill of lading from the cardboard flap.

Granddad took the box and Mother regretted insisting he stop, regretted her suspicion that a human infant had been abandoned to Christian pilgrims' charity. The puppies were dehydrated, Granddad said, indicating swollen tongues distended past ivory spikes of teeth. Teeth so fragile that sliding a forefinger alongside a pup's lips caused the enameled spikes to buckle, like a rotting corner post.

"How long they been dead?" you asked after Mother slammed the back door, declaring she didn't want anything to do with a box of stinking dogs.

"An hour or two. See here, no fly eggs around the eyes. But they probably been suffering up there all day, boiling in that woman's car."

"No one would take puppies off a nursing dog." Local practice either drowned unwanted puppies or released them to forage or be shot for trespassing.

"There's some that would. I should mail them to the newspaper office." His voice funneled around a cigarette clenched in his jaw.

"What would they write?" You wondered how a cigarette would feel perched between your lips, smoke flooding your lungs. You had never tried to smoke, said you never would. Tar would crowd out the oxygen necessary to hurl over a sand pit, earning each eighth-inch. The accumulation of inches would bring the scholarship, everyone said, to carry you out of Beulah Land.

"Oh, they wouldn't write nothing but they'd say I'm pixilated, that I've got hatefulness for other people." He flipped the cigarette butt away.

Your falls conformed to that of inanimate ash: horizontal distance a function of velocity and height. Lungs pushing out, gravity breathing in. Distance—supplicant to alveolate tissue, honeycombs dependent on accurate cellular division.

"Maybe someone who would do this deserves to be hated," you offered. Fireflies sputtered against the barn relief, illuminating wormy and weather raw pine. Crisply segmented, the floating hummocks were improbably constructed vestibules of flight.

"Don't say 'oh, I hate *someone* who would do *something* like this,' making out there isn't a specific person inflicting specific pain on these specific dogs. You should hate this Wanda Pickett from Hollywood, Florida and if you ever find her, then get in front of her ugly face and tell her she's evil, bearing the womb of a whore to cruelty and there should be no worrying about the afterlife because there is plenty of condemnation in this life."

"People won't stand for you judging about dead dogs."

"You bet I'm judging. Human intelligence can parcel out mercy as easy as it allots suffering. People think too much of people, think they can gain reward in heaven for kindnesses to the least among us. The least of us is some boiled dogs."

"They're not ours to take revenge for."

"Making something right isn't revenge, Amanita. But you decide what you want to do."

Faint tree frog skitters, male crickets by thousands scraping front wings, diurnal game rooting, collapsing muzzles over sinews, effluvium from hollow swamp parasite. Evening sounds damped auditory emissions of a short-handled spade scraping limestone, turning up red earth.

The slope behind the collapsing barn served as the animal cemetery. Rotting posts outlined an old corral where you guessed the prior owner, a man who had sold eighty acres to Granddad in '39, had worked stock on a longe line, teaching paces, training trotters for harness races once popular in central Arkansas. Mousy traces had hung from a series of wooden pegs in what might have been a tack room attached to the barn, though you couldn't recall seeing bridles or blinders. You had not pried open the leather strap-hinged doors since you were twelve and had chased a barn kitten, disturbed a pine beam and dislodged copperheads nesting in the rafters. Writhing reptiles dropped, splintered wood scraped your face. Cool flesh painted slick lines across your bare feet then disappeared into the cobwebby row of milking stalls.

Inside the abandoned ring, you relied on the summer half-moon to gauge depth and width of the grave surrounded by streams of clover, fescue, and Johnson grass Granddad said would kill a cow that ate it during winter. Tangled roots, worms, and flint arrowheads left by Indians broke over the shovel. You shredded the address label, folded flaps over matted fur and restored the uprooted ground, watching the agitated arc of Granddad's cigarette.

He accompanied you to return the shovel to the tool shed. He pulled the string for the single bulb. "Look at you. Your mother will pitch a fit."

Your pupils shrank, then the burden retreated. Red dirt stained your bare feet, knees, and elbows; khaki shorts and gray tank top were matted with weed pollen, wet earth. Two moist patches blanched your chest.

Granddad shifted his eyes from the clinging cotton. "Amanita, let's get you washed up. I'll bring you a pair of Granny's overalls. Your mother won't have to know."

"What've I been doing out here?" You could offer no justification for the evening. *Your grandfather is a rigid man*, Mother had said after hearing about the meeting at the new Calvary. *You stay away from his kind of trouble.*

"Jumping."

"For two hours in the dark?" A stopwatch secured by a fabric band reported time. Granny had tatted the watchband, using two wooden shuttles and black silk thread. The spools, protected between sweet smelling varnished cedar shells, knotted and looped thread under direction from her blurred fingers. Testament to use of her time: hexagons and crosses worked into doilies, handkerchiefs, edging for quilts.

"I'll tell them you had dinner with me," he said.

"Granny's going to ask what we've been doing if I go in the trailer."

"Not if I bring you a plate. I'll get the garden hose."

Set on the slope a few yards south of the chain link chicken coop, the trailer had been your grandparents' home since you were a toddler, when Mother insisted a girl needed her own bedroom. "We never resented it," Granddad had said when you asked if he disliked living in a trailer, disliked sharing the hillside with his son's woodworking shop and the decrepit barn. "I can see the sun coming in from my window. When the sun's going out, I can visit with you or check on the chickens. I keep them safe if I listen for foxes and raccoons. I can't do that in the house, can I?"

Granddad had converted an old watering trough for bathing. A blacksmith fashioned a drainage plug and beat out metal from a railcar graveyard into a steel brace. Two sets of posts had been driven into the ground then welded to four horizontal beams. Under the raised platform, space for a pyramid of kindling to heat water carried in buckets or flowing from a hose. The tank accommodated your grandparents' baths and the family's laundry, a task you had been spared because Granny insisted only she could wash bedding and clothing properly.

Granddad turned his back as you stripped and stepped into the tank. Fire remains smoked, extinguished after the water was suitably heated.

"All clear." A lye odor rested in the washcloth fabric, residue of Granny's soap. Her soap reddened skin and crumbled in intimate locales. But in the way families compliment a matriarch's despoiled meatballs or cheerfully consume rubber roasts, the Buells praised Granny's lye soap, replacing the disintegrating messes with inventory she restocked during rendering season.

"Temperature OK?" Granddad stood back from the tank. His hand rose and fell, sparks arcing then disappearing on the ground. Insect illumination popped above his head, circled his shoulders.

"Fine. I should take hotter baths anyway. Good for the leg muscles and everything."

"How was practice?"

"I'm fine on the long jump. Going to work on the triple's second phase this week. Get the right thigh nice and parallel to the ground. And I'll be in the four by four relay. Coach said I'll probably run third leg or anchor."

"Any competition?"

"Since we're technically in summer vacation, a lot of girls weren't there."

The next words, sent evenly across the ground dividing you. "But a new girl was. The redhead from Calvary." Bugs flashed, sprinkling the night with flames. Flaring in front of his eyes and lips. "Her name is Sarah Sykes."

"The preacher's daughter."

"Looks that way."

"She recognize you?"

"I don't know. I didn't talk to her." You wished smoke could filter words in the way it blocked mosquitoes and June bugs, a screen to dissipate the message.

"Why not?"

"I had nothing to say." The warm cloth heated your face, heat poured into nodes below your throat and armpits, vesicles responsible for body chemistry. *I have always encountered luck*, you thought. *Nothing has ever disrupted my balance.* "It's fun to do this sometimes, but I don't know how you take baths outside all the time."

"It was time for a change."

"From a bathroom to no bathroom?"

Granddad laughed, motioning toward the shed where he stored traps: choking snares for coyote or mountain cat, common steel-jawed legholds for rabbit, fox, possum, and skunk; Conibears, two keens, blades of long cutting edges set to crush an abdomen, spine, or skull. "Everything's the same as when I was a kid. That wasn't so bad and this isn't so bad."

"Seems like you might be going backward instead of forward, Granddad."

"I maybe am."

The flesh of your palms shriveled and you inspected your fingers in the dim light. Despite the soaking, dirt guttered in the cuticles and under the short, blunt-cut nails. A burn licked your shoulders, like fatigue after a hard workout. "We did the right thing burying those dogs Granddad. We don't need trouble."

"Could be."

Water swished pleasantly between your knees and around your chest but the temperature chilled. Night air pooled in your throat. "I'm ready to get out."

"I'll be back with some supper." Granddad pushed the words with slow diction, precise intention. "Any chance that new girl met with the jumping coach?"

"Looks that way." You hoped he felt your extended exhale, a tailwind to aid his progress up the slope.

You hung on the spiny tub lip, balanced on flexed, quivering arms. Your legs vaulted over the rim, past the ashy fire then finding firmness, sprinted thirty steps; lips muttered three-count pacing, syncopated to alternating footfalls, every third cycle accelerating, counted rhythm inducing leg turnover. Launching your nakedness with a long left hop, a high right step—rote positioning remanded arms back and parallel to earth not like a hawk rising but like a fish swimming through an airless stone tunnel—the body upwardly buoyant and long. Fingers closed and cupped, toes ballerina-pointed. Technical canniness for hiding from drag.

In forward motion, diaphragm swelled, chest forward, shoulders back, you prolonged the ascent, exhaling through the hang in counterpoint to gravity, posture wrought as partisan to inertia.

Bones hit the ground first, because heel spur indentions should properly determine the measuring marker's placement. On top of the collapsed torso, the rear and thighs—in accomplished landings pointed upward—skull flung forward, breathing and eating sand and sweat, falling forward again to exit, leaving no mark for eyes straining for misplaced, particulate sand.

Up the mountain, spotlights crowned statue Jesus with artificial light. Behind the trailer's screen door, a shadow moved, thin stake of a man who had watched the jump, and the fall.

Two days before twelfth grade began, Granddad's truck disappeared from the mountain road, edging past the incomplete guardrail and whistling downhill, you imagined, like Granddad blew air through his lips in the henhouse, summarizing astonishment at unusual egg production. Mother likely braced her hands against the cracked vinyl dashboard. And despite probable protestations of too many responsibilities and not enough time in which to fulfill them, they died, crushed against colluvium dumped from the blasting. The salvage crew found Granddad's right hand thrust into your mother's eye sockets, likely, one fireman told your father, remnants of the driver's "passenger protective instincts."

The county sheriff, double cousin to the Buells, informed your father in confidence the brake failure had been no accident. Later that week, Charlie Buell, Jr., emptied his checking account of sixteen hundred forty-six dollars and pressed travelers checks into your hand at the bus station. The scrip was pinned to your bra when the bus stopped at Union Station, St. Louis. Your mother's cousin, a childless woman twice divorced, refused the checks as you unpacked luggage in the guest bedroom.

"Honey, you keep it," she said. "You're going to need it."

"For what?" The trip had elicited sullenness, anger coated by iterations of reprisal.

"To finish high school. To go to college. To buy different clothes."

"I never needed different clothes before. Don't know why I'd need them now. And I don't plan on paying for college."

"How do you figure that?"

"I'm the best physical specimen to ever come out of Beulah Land."

"This isn't Beulah Land," she said. "And you can't act like it is."

"I'll decide about that."

"I see you take on after Charlie Buell," she said.

"I never thought I would need to." You unzipped the duffel bag, removing first, a pair of soiled running flats you would not wear again.

"You don't have to be like that here," she replied. "Honey, you need some time—"

"Yes. What I was thinking. I need a lot of time. Alone."

Part II

Your left breast had been smaller than your right one. It pointed inward, slightly, and the irregularity always annoyed you until both breasts were gone and now you are not so bothered to be rid of rebellious lumps harboring malfunctioning P-factors.

Pink ribbons do not decorate your shoulder. You do not cry, wail, and metaphorically beat breasts that no longer exist. You are labeled 'in denial' by a support group you attend as a favor to the diagnosing physician.

You say, "I despise women who cry about their chopped-off breasts. We're talking two lumps of flesh and as long as the cancer doesn't spread, all of you should really get over it."

They say, "It's a part of you that can't be replaced."

You say, "Only the weak and stupid lay up treasures in their chests."

They say, "You are obviously not in touch with your spiritual self. Physical pain can call for spiritual healing."

You say, "Spirituality is not derived from pain of the flesh. If you believe that, you should extend the capacity to animals."

They say, "But you have lost part of your womanhood."

You say, "*Secondary* sex characteristics. And thanks to modern medicine anyone can order up a better rack."

They say, "Women also lose their confidence of beauty, their sense of sensuality. The physical change affects intimacy in a deeply psychological way."

You say, "None of you had sex with your husbands before you went under the saw. Why would it matter now?"

They say, "We must kindly ask you to leave the group."

You say, "Like I couldn't see *that* one coming."

But you pause, never having been possessed of grace to rest silent against popular commiseration. "Do you still get to wear the little ribbons if you go up a cup size? What color does someone with a real problem get?"

The path to the elevator requires you to step past tight-lipped women. Folding chairs creak, you brush legs, mutter apologies, and recognize a woman whose name you cannot remember. Ten years older than you, nearing forty, she wears a tailored linen pantsuit, obvious in its expense. Muscles twitch in her neck and you stare at her high, thin hairline until the closing elevator door blocks the view.

Exiting the apartment the next morning, you carry three newspapers and although caffeine is contraindicated, two cups of fully-charged coffee. Summer sun and dress code permit sandals, exposing pink painted toes. A yellow taxi halts three blocks south of the office, forty-eight floors of a building occupying a block in Times Square. Stock prices and headlines scroll across electric screens mounted on the building's façades—testament to around-the-clock watchfulness, corporate disavowal of sleep and languor.

At six fifteen, the fixed-income trading floor smells of donuts and coffee. Traders accept ledgers from the London desk and hedge short positions by buying futures; prepare swap offers for basis point pickup; trade treasury inventory as overnight collateral in round lots of half a billion, a market driven by opportunity to cheapen the cost of financing assets.

You conduct business with several desks—treasury, mortgage,

high-grade, and high-yield—because you sell derivatives that perform based on credit news. The job requires you to monitor, closely, global corporate earnings and credit related announcements. A position suited for an insomniac, a condition you had boasted about during interviews.

The assistant collates news packets for an institutional sales force composed of eight men and yourself. She had graduated from a better college than your own. The assistant's ambition to learn the business is average, trumped by the skilled pursuit of a high-yield industrials trader eleven years her senior.

The assistant does not look up as she shuffles papers. "Morning Amanita. Eaton needs to see you in the meeting room. Now."

"Why?"

"I'm only the sales assistant slash messenger slash photocopy operator." Her diamond ring is looped around her wrist with three gold chains because, she has announced, "I lose everything." She types magnificently and you have watched her hands flicker over keyboards, chains tangling, blurring when she uses an old adding machine to check, manually, the day's trades against the electronic ledger.

"I'm going now." Once, when the assistant caught you staring at her hands, she smiled.

Eaton does not keep an office. Discussion occurs by his seat in the institutional sales island, a row of desks supporting computers and digital telephone consoles with hundreds of direct lines to customers. Only interviews and firings are conducted in the room with blinds that Eaton shutters as you enter.

"Morning." Eaton indicates that you should close the door.

"Morning."

"Sit." Eaton had hired you three years earlier. His brown hair is wavy, his shoulders square, legs slightly bowed but lean. He had established track records at Princeton and his affinity for recruiting athletes brought him to your resume.

Your jumping titles smoothed over the fact you had majored in history—not finance or economics—and had earned a masters in business administration at night while working as a retail broker, accumulating commissions by cold calling widows and orphans.

Entrance to the white shoe world of finance had seemed like a passage through a barrier composed of tinkling pearls threaded on fragile strings. Although delighted to join the full bench of research analysts, a substantial information technology budget, a generous expense account—you feared, as all good salespeople should, that you were only one trade away from being escorted off the premises by a security guard.

"Am I fired?" The relationship is comfortable. You had once farted on an airplane while seated beside Eaton. He had signaled the flight attendant and asked for a match.

"Probably. I can't guarantee it until the HR chick drags in."

"She blows the CFO during breakfast. Call *his* office." Your slumped image is faint against the window. You cannot decide whether a trick of the light or your metabolism creates depressions under your eyes. Lines appear at right angles to your nose and lips. Above the lines, short hair sprouts, a pile of tangled threads. Underneath the flat image, painted toes remind you of stooped women with flabby arms and sagging tits who apply too much blush and lipstick, a salvage effort akin to rearranging deck chairs on the Titanic.

"This is not a joke. You fucked up." Eaton is your height, at five feet eight inches and during discussions you usually stand, testing the tensile strength of his composure.

"How?"

"Your little cancer sermon."

The woman in the suit. She must have attended customer functions, cocktail parties at which you had once been able to drink martinis and speak about credit markets as though reciting the alphabet. Drinking nights had been transitioned—coincident with diagnoses, examinations, and visits to the surgical unit. Statistics about effective durations and weighted returns had given over to probability ratios and significant samplings.

"It's a free country. Last time I checked I can go to whatever group I want. Say whatever I want."

"Not when our biggest fucking customer can hear you. It's a liability."

"What's the Pru got to do with anything?" The insurance

company executes more trades per week than some accounts log in a year.

"The chief investment officer attended a meeting last night. She recognized you."

"So? I don't cover them."

"Listen, Bill's got an eleven million dollar seat and half of that is from the Pru. I haven't seen this month's numbers. Last time *I* checked, yours was a four, maybe four and a half."

"Does Bill want me fired?"

"Bill doesn't know about this conversation and that's one of the contingencies of keeping the business. If I do my job, he won't find out when he's on the wire."

"You can't fire me for my opinions out of the workplace."

"I'll verify that point as soon as the HR chick finishes blowing her hair out or blowing her boyfriend or whatever. Point is: you represented the firm badly. I'm only giving you a heads-up because I like you. You fucked up. It happens. But we'll give you a nice package and I can probably extend your bennies, considering…"

"I can claim medical discrimination. If someone gets knocked up, you have to give *her* three months. I didn't take mine."

"Get a lawyer. I don't have to give cause. I only have to point to the sales figures. You didn't take a medical leave. You thought yourself capable of reporting for work."

"You're an asshole. I didn't take leave because I wanted to help the desk." The cool register air raises bumps on your bare arms and legs. *But not my nipples.* Jokes on the air-conditioned trading floor—tuning up Tokyo, pencil erasers, headlights—have been extinguished, at least within earshot. You have immunity, a vaccination of politically correct sensibility.

"This conversation is over. You can sit at your desk until Human Resources calls or you can leave now and work out the details tomorrow." The manager braces his fingers against each other, forming a steeple beneath his clean-shaven chin. "You do the right thing by us and we'll do the right thing by you."

You stand, off balance, still unaccustomed to the affected center of gravity. "How did you find out so fast?"

"Your sales assistant called me. She met her aunt for dinner last night."

Walking to the desk, you pass flat screen televisions, flashing digital quote machines, supply bins filled with new keyboards, disk drives, and monitors. Tools of employment are rarely repaired, only replaced with deference to urgency, the mandate that no time should be sacrificed to fallibility. The morning packet is in the chair. Salespeople murmur spreads and transaction sizes. Traders aim words at wireless headsets, bidding and offering, unaware of a middle-ranked salesperson's face. Noise on the floor subsides only for broadcast announcements from hidden speakers, thundering from an invisible preacher.

The assistant watches you pull a tatted handbag from a drawer, the only item you want. She rolls her seat closer to the desk, feet disappearing under the modular furniture.

"I give you credit," you say. "Most people would try to ingratiate themselves if they are related to customers."

"I never wanted to ingratiate myself with you," she says.

"Fuck you."

"You know what Amanita? I'm sorry for you, I really am. You're smarter than I am—"

You point to the decorated finger. "You mean smarter than you'll ever *have* to be."

"Illustrates your problem."

"Enlighten me," you say.

"You don't know how to get along."

Statue Jesus faces east, arms extended, molded face forming a ninety-degree angle with the mountain crown. You have never decided whether Christ gazes below to the people or casts his vision above. At proper distance, the peaked, shingled church resembles the Savior's valise, incarnation of the house to be carried in each faithful heart. You have visited your father and Granny a half-dozen times but the impending trip would be the first by automobile.

"Why are you driving?" Dad asks.

"I want to see some of the country. And driving is relaxing."

"Doesn't sound relaxing." A compressor hums, rising above

the static of your mobile connection to his landline. "When will you be here?"

"In a few days."

"How long you staying?"

"I don't know."

"What about work?"

"Not an issue anymore."

"Really," he says.

You listen for breath intakes in the background. Like many residents, Dad relies on a party landline. Phone companies have leapfrogged the infrastructure for single-family lines because most customers trust the privacy and reliability of transmission towers and mobile service. You hear no clicks, no indication anyone else listens, but you spread discretion across conversations like a layer of desiccated leaves on potting soil.

"You got any plans?"

"I think I'll go into town this time, see what I've been missing."

"Well, you've missed a lot."

"I guessed as much."

"Granny will be curious to see you." The compressor increases in pitch, seeming to warrant his attention. "I have to go."

"Tell Granny I'm curious to see her too."

The twenty-six hours of travel time would not be without worries: tractor trailer rigs tailgating; reckless lane changes by women in fuming urban assault vehicles; forgotten dosages, brown pill bottles shaking and thumping, eventually spilling from an unsealed plastic bag to the floorboard of the leased sedan.

But the cross county route was cleverly planned before you, conceived of a distant decade's ambition to transport arms and soldiers between coasts. Military conveyances might still be necessary and would be accompanied by displays. Pedestrian urbanites bussed to carry signs, protest placards distributed to those whose days were not interrupted by employment. Later, assembled minivans, tan and sandy toddlers with legs dangling across their mothers' chests, flags and names of young men and women knit in sweaters or screened on T-shirts, quotes from the Old and New Testaments demarcating allegiances. Even later, outposts supported by exit ramps, congregated pickups, long cars with manual windows, teenagers playing hooky, women wearing waitress uniforms and balancing cardboard flats with complimentary cups of lidded coffee.

Pageantry for armies might still be convened, hue and cry outposts assembled before approaching forces. Public concerns would be borne across sensible roadways where mountain peaks too steep to be built over had been blasted flat. For you, interstate design would discharge private concerns without pomp or protest permits, massive causeways always connecting to destinations of engagement.

Smith would label bottles with dosages and times; would organize medications by hour and date and would program the stopwatch to beep at intervals; reminders issued first, then shrill warnings for tardiness and lack of attention to detail. He would also research convenient fueling stations and food exits. Smith would skirt the detour on the Pennsylvania turnpike; would avoid the construction-snarled route through industrial West Virginia smoke; would reserve a room at a respectable roadside motel instead of settling for a unit smelling as though truck drivers had used the room as a urinal.

You inform Smith about the trip you will not plan before the sommelier arrives with the wine list, deliberately infusing portent into the mutual association with relation to his choice. Perversely, you anticipate how the announcement will influence the wine selection: inquiry regarding tannic performance of certain chateaus in unseasonably rainy seasons or dismay over excesses of brash vintners.

"I guess this is where I ask why you want to leave?" Smith looks over reading spectacles he carries to examine the fine print of contracts and wine lists.

"What else am I going to do? No one's hiring and even if they were, they'd take one look at me and decide they don't want that insurance liability."

"It's actionable for any firm to ask about your health." Smith is a product liability lawyer, junior partner, but he has researched benefits law, uncovering minutiae of employers' duties toward ailing employees. He obtained a non-compete waiver to act as counsel during severance negotiations, winning benefits for three years, equaling your time of service.

"I don't think they would have to ask to figure it out. Besides, I'm not up for interviews."

"You'd rather go back home?"

"Former home. I haven't lived there since summer before senior year of high school."

"You never told me that."

You had forgotten. Smith did not know about graduation from a suburban St. Louis high school, an institution with more students per grade than the entire Beulah Land enrollment. You had only spoken of moving to New York after college, where the numbers of arrivals were too many and urban concerns too pressing for inquiry into the affairs of one girl from Arkansas.

"I've told you about the accident. I went away after that."

"I thought it was after high school."

"Well it wasn't. I lived with a cousin for a year. Then I went to college."

"Why?"

"Because Mother was dead. Granddad was dead."

"That doesn't explain why you would leave."

"Yes, it does."

Smith pulls on the blue dolphin print tie you had given him for his birthday. His fingers squeeze and roll the fabric, a tic you equate with a former habit of twisting hair around a forefinger.

You reach for the dirty martini. "Cheers," you offer.

"Celebrating?" His own glass of scotch, neat, is untouched. Smith never mingles drink with unpleasant news.

"No, commemorating. Commemorating my culinary adventures with you." Draughts of gin wash across the pulpy flesh of your throat. Alcohol is also contraindicated, but some things are too good to relinquish. The menu is open. Fish appear prominently on the starter and second course. Smith had been amused to learn that any fish you had eaten before arriving in New York had been fried.

Sometimes lake bass and whiskered catfish, sometimes river trout or perch. But always fried.

"When are you leaving?"

"Tomorrow or the next day. After I get my stuff shipped."

"I'll come with you. Or meet you there. I can take a leave."

"Not for this long you can't."

"Why are you doing this? We could finally do things, spend whatever time...." His lips part, reminding you of plump peach halves transforming from fuzz to sweetness. This is it: Smith is rounded, sweet, and despite his thirty-five years of relative health, vulnerable as an old man is vulnerable. Afraid of sudden pronouncements, afraid of rising in the dark without a nightlight, afraid of investments without a guaranteed return.

"Whatever time I have left?" you laugh. "I'm truly tickled. That's the most honest thing you've ever said to me." You laugh until the hiccups start, a peculiarly frequent affliction that spikes after treatments. Reaching for the water, your hand shakes but when the spasm rises again you are prepared, avoiding shaking and spilling.

"I didn't say that and you know I didn't mean that. I meant whatever time you have in between other things."

"Other things. Sitting at home watching my hair grow? Writing thank you notes for flowers like I'm in the Junior League? Catching up on soaps?"

"I was thinking more along the lines of reading, going to galleries, using your extra time for something you enjoy."

"From what I can tell, most people in this city don't feel this way but I like making a living."

"Everyone wants to make a living Amanita. The inconvenient part of the business is working for it."

Smith prefers dark blue suits to set off his blond and wavy hair, loafers—a small shout against wing tipped tyranny—the heavy yuppie watch, double-hulled titanium, water-resistant to two hundred meters, despite the fact the recreational dive limit is one hundred ten feet and the fact Smith has not submerged in the ocean in at least fifteen years. Smith books ocean views, foam and froth nibbling his toes. He always pays up for outsized umbrellas and courteous, English-speaking staff. You had taken five days in the Caribbean with Smith, a pink beach populated with even pinker casinos, the luxury shopping district cruised by Nuh-Yawkers slathered in zinc. Blue and yellow Hawaiian shirts strained over unfortunate protuberances; white socks and sandals represented commitment to whimsy and the spirit of tropical outdoorism; twenty-dollar beach braiding jobs rattled against heads of fritter munching women for whom the season's bikinis proved unfortunately fleshy revelations. "Sartorial Armageddon," Smith had held forth at a beachside bar where a conga line assembled. "It's sar-fucking-torial Armageddon down here."

The memory of that trip's humor has passed, like all good memories pass.

"I enjoyed going to work. I do not enjoy living in this city when I can't be productive." You lean on your elbows, feeling like a girl who spreads her knees in church.

The waiter stands beside the table. Dressed in a tuxedo, he folds his hands, left over right, displaying a gold band. Smith turns, asks, slowly, politely, if the man would mind returning in a few minutes. The waiter nods and the thought squeezes your throat: the man has seen your thin hair and drawn jaw, stared as though he were gazing upon one who had followed him but would now precede him, summoning him with backward glances and open palm waves.

I will not offer encouragement or optimism. The resolution feels dank in the way of basements only partially finished because the responsibility has been forgotten.

"Give me a fucking break Amanita. You bitched about your job when you had it. Now you're bitching that you don't—"

"If you think bitching is the same as talking about assholes at work then you bitch ten times more than I do. The coked-up associates, the closet queens walking the other partners' wives? Give *me* a fucking break Smith."

"Fair enough." Smith's pale green eyes rarely blink, a tactic cultivated by studying rhetoric and oratory at boarding school.

There were men…there were men you might encounter who would clap hands over your mouth. You would not resist or dispute their claims that for some places, you could not belong and that for some places, you would have to become accustomed.

"You're easy enough to back down," you say.

"You think so?"

You watch his hand, wait for a sip of scotch, a loosening from stricture.

"Or maybe I fell for an emotionally stunted hillbilly and that makes me an asshole. That's it, I'm the guy in the movie who adores the ice queen, because underneath it all she's in *so* much pain."

"I don't feel any pain. Really. I don't think I ever did." *That's true.* Then you marvel, bone afraid you are two martinis deep into hubris. Like a blind man unconcerned with optical distortions in a funhouse—but who suffers when the walls move.

"Maybe because you don't allow yourself interiority."

"What?" You hiccup over the interrogative. "That's the kind of shit kids got beat up for at recess."

"Popular psychology has always been a dangerous practice." Smith smiles, veneered teeth exposed. Flagrant in revelation of expense. "But I'm sure you've heard that before."

"Only in bad movies."

"So I'm the spurned suitor. I'm an anti-hero, pining for the wrong girl."

"No. What you are is the man I'm leaving behind. Tending his gin joint and that sort of thing. Is that interior enough for you?" Air hisses past your teeth, deflating your chest and—happily—eliminating peristaltic disruption.

"I'm going to order now. Can we please talk about your plans later? I'd like to start the evening." He reaches for the single malt.

You will not discuss 'plans' again because you slip beyond the inlaid mahogany door when Smith visits the men's room. If Smith calls, angry, you will blame fatigue and trauma from discovering a lack of interiority.

The taxi jolts toward your apartment building, set by the Hudson. The converted parking garage is flanked by newly constructed glass towers, monuments to strenuous excess. Because of the towers' tenants—movies stars, an indicted homemaking maven, and a parade of freakishly tall women—your one-bedroom is worth more than you had paid for it. You had contacted a real estate agent, instructing her the goal was to kill the mortgage and pocket cash.

"You'll take a capital gains hit if you don't roll into a new place," she had protested. "I can show you a sweet six with garden only three blocks from where you are now. I'll shave a point."

Nice salesmanship, the kind you would have offered. *Sure, I'll be happy to work both sides of that trade for double the sales credit.* "I know my tax options. I only want to sell. I'm not looking to buy."

"But—"

"What is it about 'just sell the fucker' you don't understand?"

You had lifted a bottle of mineral water from the restaurant. The carbonated beverage tastes like chalybeate potions Granny had administered for sickness: heated solutions for colds; strained and chilled mineral deposits wrapped in tatted handkerchiefs for fevers. "Here's to not sounding like you were born in the twentieth century," Smith had said, clinking his spoon of cough medicine against yours, a salute conceived when mutual illness obliged you to huddle against him. You wheezed, extracting promises of silence when noises spurted from orifices. "I don't like this century either," you had replied, "But I should get credit for living in it."

The taximeter clicks. Though the air is warm, you could not have walked. Six months earlier, you would have stepped down Fifth from the Plaza to Washington Square Park wearing designer stilettos, dodging women jogging behind baby strollers; dogs with leashes stretched across sidewalks, Europeans scanning the skies, bereft of indicators printed in out-of-date guidebooks. You used to enjoy pacing off the streets, each well-executed step carrying you closer to competence. Freeing you from machines and indulgent care workers propelling patients like tillers, aerating the soil of good works.

Driving south and west, you turn over memories, contemplating how you might have told the story to Smith, how it would have tumbled out incorrectly and how you would have been better served to speak gibberish, relying on inflection in the way people converse with their pets.

Putting memories into spoken order would be like untangling a skein of improperly stored thread. The task requires a sympathetic deference to the logic of knots.

You have never been patient.

It would be cheaper and easier to discard the spoiled sample and buy a fresh skein; thread doubled protectively and concentrically, a center formed by shaped linearity.

A tailor mends a garment by examination, setting to ripped fabric with stitches. To complete the task, he must recover injured originals imprinted with the garment's history—a visible record of function and value.

But a catena of memory is not the province of a Being who can hold all of time in his palm but of the One who can extend his hand over time, circumscribing the unknowable, gripping minutiae of human enterprise never captured or described. Only God exists in timelessness—and this is why He is omniscient and unassailable. God-time is not divided into action, digestion, reaction, hypothesis, trial, and interpretation.

You turn south on a twisting Ozark highway. If you devised a method to fold and twist memories, inuring them against repair to original form; if you coated authentic imprints with false pointillism, tracing patterns so minutely as to prevent anyone from gaining the proper focal distance for examination—then you would own memory. Own order and impetus and consequence and the faculty possessed by inanimate objects to return to original shape after deformation.

And be conceived as an apostate to God.

Under the shadow of the Beulah Land statue, a man stands, hunched, dark head edged by conflagration. A wood stove's squat belly shelters fire stoked by a black poker coated in ash by half; heat-forged metal, thin, doubled against itself at the wider end. The working end is braced against the open trap, energy diffusing through the length and you recognize the bathtub brace, converted from the support of water to fire. Who twisted Granddad's heavy, fine piece of iron, rendered it grotesque, bent to accommodate a man's palm?

The router intones under the man's hand, yellow spiral cord dragging sawdust across the concrete floor. The building is designed with practical understanding, wired for electrical outlets spaced in forty-eight inch intervals. Comfortably high counters fit against aluminum siding braced out with oak. Machines balance on platforms, outfitted with safety switches, anticipating damage when the man loses grip on a board he's guiding through the planer: bone-severing force; foot-long splinters launched as missiles.

Accidents are inevitable. Dad's golden-haired dog suffered concussion from an errant board, sent aloft when the saw failed to chew an oak knot. A hairless indention between the dog's eyes marked the distress for six years until you found the creature bleeding through its golden coat in the new pastor's fence line, its front left paw caught in a pelt trap. The dog was three-quarters your size and veins strained in your thighs as you pulled on the steel stake and carried the body, damaged leg dangling in the trap. You chose the shortest route and ran through miles of brushy, wooded pasture. Stroking the animal's head, you poured water from a shine jug into slack, barely moving jaws while Granddad cut the trap, selected and loaded a pistol.

The dog's blanket, wadded and sprinkled with droppings from itinerant mice, occupies its former spot by the scrap box. The man clears his throat; he does not repeat his words, does not subsidize wool gatherers, particularly those with whom he has relation. Waiting to respond, you enjoy your age, imperatives *honor* and *obey* shunted for denotations of *adulthood* and *self-sufficient*.

"Need help?" the man asks.

"Granddad's stuff. Where's the key?"

"What for?"

"I'll take care of it myself," you say.

"Don't mess with his things. They're fragile."

"Fragile?" You step over odd-sized boards, lumberyard irregulars for drawer handles, crown molding.

"Rats and snakes out there."

"That's not fragile."

"Don't tell Granny."

"What am I not supposed to tell her?"

"That you're messing in places you don't belong."

Part III

Amonth before you began twelfth grade, Granddad shot the afflicted dog. He wrapped the by-catch in blankets from the padlocked cote, a wooden structure he painted and repaired himself.

Dad planed and sized boards and wept—the first time you had seen Charlie Buell, Jr., cry. You picked through the scrap pile, locating cedar remnants. Rounding wood that had once nourished green needles, the lathe chewed out curves to accommodate your grip. Four handles, two for each narrow end of the rectangular pall.

Deep pine shelves organized woodworking hardware and sundries. Compartments were not labeled, the designer trusting to memory and transmutability of logical order. Implements to deconstruct wood filled the recesses: brackets, molly screws, screwdrivers, lacquer brushes, plastic goggles, fine-webbed breathing masks, various length levels, claw hammers, electric drill bits, edging blades, tins of turpentine, wrenches stacked by diameter. Occupying a lower shelf, spout-tipped ewers of collyrium. One ewer, larger with an eye-sized plastic basin, was positioned for blind, feeling access. Granny's loment, ground beans and honeycomb, was situated behind other containers, acknowledging the priority of urgency.

Granddad's whittling clicked against pine two by fours, the long piece a forked and arrowed end; the short piece, arrowed at both ends. Nailed together slightly above long center, the shaped pieces would mark the dog's interment. From his seat on an upturned hickory pickle bucket, he tossed the spiny cross to the floor. The raw wood—without benefit of a prep coat or lacquer—would soon become griseous.

"What do you think, son?" The six teeth remaining in Granddad's lower jaw were spaced unevenly and his lips drizzled spit. You pitied his body's failings, but sorrow leaked from the vein of voyeurism.

"This'll do." Dad's eyes flickered, sending elongated droplets into the planer.

"Not what I meant." The knife slapped a leather strap, striking toward Granddad's chest, then away, repeated rhythmically with his resolute, macular grind around a lump of chew. "Amanita, you relate to your father where his best friend was bleeding to death?" The knife slapped, reflecting spires of western light.

"Inside the new preacher's fence line."

"Why were you running across his pasture?" Dad did not look from the planer, a learned habit from previous injury.

"I jumped the fence because I saw something. You should be happy I was on the lookout—"

Granddad interrupted, "Amanita, how long you been missing that dog?" He tilted the pickle bucket to lean against a counter rigged out with clamps. The curved clamps were like perched scavengers, affirming inevitable change of form.

"Going on two days."

"So son, what do you think?"

"I don't need to think. We'll let it go. No good can come of it." Dad blinked eyes blue as his father's. *But more like his mother*, everyone said. *Born into good temper.* But the eyes were his father's and when Dad and Granddad shuffled ivory dominos or dealt across the folding card table, they aped each other's motions. Both left handed, carrying six-foot frames. One had avoided service by dint of his birth, the other through college deferment. *Gap babies*, they called men before a retail concern had trademarked the name, to describe a generation too young for the First World War and too old to be called for the second. *Rich kids*, they called men when guys attending college were exempt from the draft but guys pumping gas were eligible. But Dad hadn't been a rich kid. Granny's willingness to pull double shifts in a diner had kept him enrolled. When college deferments ended, Dad had predicted the conflict's end, predicted his number would not be selected. "When the Harvard kids get their asses shot off, they'll shut this thing down," he had claimed. When the draft ended, Dad had quit school to work in a sawmill, married Opal and saved to open a woodshop.

You chose a drill bit, eight screws, wooden plugs to cap the holes. Fitting a charged battery pack against the butt of a hand drill, you squatted by the box smelling of sawdust, musky human sweat, remnants of resin.

"Handles are too small." Dad stood in front of you. "And cedar doesn't match."

"I like the way it smells."

"I said the handles are too small."

"I'll carry it." The drill bit pierced the wood easily. You selected a level and pencil to align the second hole.

"It's damn doubled-up oak."

"I'm going to take care of this!" Your voice spiked, an involuntary girly wail you wouldn't have allowed during practice. *I'm the captain here*, you asserted if a girl complained about thirst or cramps, *and I don't captain whiners*.

"There's nothing for you to take care of." Dad fitted palms, each and each against the grips. His fingers, bent in service of shaping boards, scratched the reddish wood.

"I'll pick a nice spot."

Granddad allowed the bucket to tilt downward. The rim sealed, resolute against concrete. "Son, it's about time I drove up top to get Opal. You go tell Granny."

Granddad laid the leather strap across the bucket. He stuck

the blade into a soft pine shank on the sanding table. The handle quivered, tongue-like, as they exited.

The woodshop's screened window looked west over a creek sourced from a mountain cave. That spring dwindled during dry summer months and mountain game wandered beyond natural cover, parched for potable water. Granddad sacrificed well pump hours for deer attracted to Granny's vegetable garden. He tendered platefuls of cornmeal and egg yolks aside watering tins on the perimeter of his storage building.

"We're cutting into their property," Granddad spoke of wood-chucks and rabbits, foxes, raccoons, and in rarity, brown bears that partook, "and people look on that as reason to be rid of them."

Glinting pans littered the ground behind the locked shed and past that, the hill steepened, rising to Calvary. Up mountain, air would be breathable, statue visitors comfortable inside a climate-controlled buildings.

Inside, sweat pooled in the ridge of your chest, in declivities banking your nose. You tilted an opaque plastic bottle. Chew spit spilled past your lips. You pushed the door open and gagged. Briny water curdled on your tongue, burning the esophagus. Palms pressed to the ground, you balanced, cornering heady faintness, spooling heaves into order.

Two tall men watched you straighten. Granddad raised his hand then passed into the house. You turned the spigot of the outside faucet and drank, gulping and spitting water. Despite the lowering light, heat draped your skin when you emerged, dragging the coffin. You tipped the short edge against the ground. Shoulders pressed against the small of your back, arms extended, hands laced through the handles. Blood leaked and when you halted, turning to jump the box over the sill, you saw streaks. Serpentine, like garden snails traveling aligned. In sawdust where the dog had rolled, the traces were gone, absorbed by denatured sieve tubes and conductive vessels.

You staggered against the incline, swearing, sweat stinging into inflating, hooded blisters. The body inside the box thudded, settling into gravity. You selected a spot opposite the most recent burial; an incline that in sunrise would fall under black walnut shadow and in autumn would be covered with inky black nuts. Fragrant, needle shade would have offered yearlong cover, but the cedar had been sold to the lumber company. The loggers had been nervous, working while Granddad sharpened knives on a leather strap. They felled trees downhill, sending nesting birds to flight. Fledglings screamed, then were silent.

Walking uphill backward, you pulled the coffin over cropped stumps springing with mushrooms. Draped, transparent white veils extended from the caps to attach with white stalks. The pink and red setting sun yielded to a flavescent moon. Fireflies, fixed in sporadic arrangement, blinked against dusty gray and white clouds. You struck past roots and red black earth but any sounds given out to the world from creatures huddled against it were less than the pitch of your pulse.

The pile of carelessly displaced soil would not fill the indention, inviting creatures attracted to blood. Removing your white nylon running tank, you walked to the rotting stumps and, careful not to breathe or bring musty spores close to your mouth, severed the fungi, keeping stems long and intact. You wrapped the broken caps inside the shirt. You scattered the bundle's contents over the sunken space, then yanked your running shorts down. Feet spread, your bladder emptied on the grave.

Heat from the skillet diffused into the open space designated as kitchen and dining room. At the dinner table, you stank with body odor, blood, dander and musty fungal fibers. You ignored Dad when he asked, "How did you make out?"

Granny's forehead glistened, perspiration traced her marbled cheeks. Her hands flashed at chest level, tatting, making use of empty moments before consumption.

The white fixture hanging over the table was broken, exposing one side of the bulb. Light spread unevenly, casting darker against your seat. A brown moth flew into the heat then fell to the hardwood floor. Dad pinched the shuddering insect and tossed it into the waste can. Mother emerged, carrying a platter of potato salad and Granny's garden corn, still cleaved to the cobs. Chicken fried in the skillet, likely store-bought, because Granddad only broke a hen's neck when it was poor and wobbling—old flesh that could serve as nothing more than stew flavoring.

"Sorry supper is so behind. But I say, why not work awhile, since we've got the longer light." Mother often stayed late, finding reasons to remain in the cool, white building while Granddad waited in the truck, seeking radio reception unavailable in the hollow.

"Long time to keep Granddad waiting. Considering his day. Our day," you said.

Granny's head shook but the shuttle clicks did not slow and you wondered how many women in the world could double tat to the touch.

"I'm sorry about that Amanita." Mother spooned a large portion of potato salad onto Dad's plate.

"So how long did you keep Granddad waiting?" You watched Granny's eyelids open and close in an indifferent cadence. "Must've been pretty hot in the truck at sundown. I'm burning up now."

"He's always welcome to come inside." Mother lowered into a chair at the foot of the table, sipped from a glass of iced well water.

"He doesn't want to wait inside," you said.

"He's so anti-social. Making hateful faces to everyone that comes out of the office. I say, let him rot in that truck if he wants." Air seeped from Mother's mouth as though her lungs had been punctured, her pulse collapsed.

"Opal." Granny turned her face toward Mother's voice. Granny's hands stopped. A white, knotted band spilled against the table edge, dropped on the floor and curled, piling higher. Disparate perspiration clung to the old woman's chin, clawlike against gravity.

"Maybe you should find your own damn ride," you yelled.

The septum broke the force of the open hand sweep across your right eye socket, the divide giving with a gassy noise, cartilage retreating into an empty interior. Your father acted without deference to muliebrity, a predisposition you had always appreciated.

"Next time you better put me down. Or I'll be coming at you," you said.

"That's enough, Amanita." Dad stood, a drip of mayonnaise pinched in the flesh between nose and upper lip. "That's more than enough."

You carried the corn and saltshaker up the slope, refusing a plastic bag tied off with ice. Granddad reclined against the trailer, tipped his fraying lawn chair past its stress point, bending the inexpensive metal tubing. He whittled the end of an oak plank. Flashlights lay next to the trailer, ordered by size.

"I brought you some supper." You placed the platter with four ears of corn on the ground but then saw his cast off socks and boots. "But maybe I'll hold this in case of toxic contamination."

"You saying my feet might infect that corn?" He sent shavings into your shaggy ponytail and soiled clothes.

You tossed splintered wood at him. "I'm not willing to risk it." Pouring salt, you held a cob out to him then chewed through the other three, stripping sweet pulps from rows of ridged casings.

Granddad offered a burnished thermos, held it steady at your hesitation. "It's only water Amanita. Course, I could produce something stronger."

"No, I'll stick with water. I need to re-hydrate." You had never drunk alcohol, though Granddad's special purchases from across the state line had always been available. Too many uncertainties were associated with imbibing: how your stomach would cope; how blood-alcohol levels might embargo oxygen; how you might enjoy those reactions, enjoy numbing brain cells. "But I could probably use something."

"Any trouble down there?" He switched on the flashlight, examining a bump rising on your nose, shadowy vessels bleeding under the right eye.

"Nothing I'm not happy to handle," you said. "I only feel bad you wasted part of the day up top."

"I can't be there Amanita, watching Opal smile and point to maps. It's like those people were coming here to explore a wilderness instead of walking around a damn flower garden."

Whittling continued, slithers peeled from the main stem until the end was smooth and pointed, as if beveled by a calibrated machine. Granddad had carved hundreds, perhaps thousands of pointed sticks, though you had never seen him put any to use.

"Why all the flashlights, Granddad?"

"I'm checking the batteries."

"Why?"

"Batteries make flashlights work. Don't ask stupid questions."

"Come on."

"You've got to be tired. Go on to bed."

The back porch light was off when you entered the house. Granny sat hunched in the dark at the kitchen table, fingers working, a pile of tatted lace rising above the plank floor.

"Granny, I'll take you up to bed." Yawning, arms raised, your shoulders rotated. Joints cracked, snapping like a chicken's neck broken with a tire iron.

"What was that?" Granny's shuttles stopped clicking. Her eyelids opened and closed, reflexively.

"Me stretching. I'm all stiffened up."

"I've studied some of that."

"I'll walk you to the trailer."

"Pick out two reds from my basket. A dark one and a light one."

"I need to get to bed. Let me walk you up."

"I'm waiting down here."

Heeding Granddad's advice, you harbored no coddling, cloying patience for the old or young. *If an old fart's acting like an asshole, don't excuse him because he's lived long enough to know better. If a young fart's acting like an asshole, don't excuse him because he'll live long enough to make you regret it.*

"Do what you want Granny. Goodnight." You placed the skeins in her lap. "Dark red is on your left. Lighter red on your right."

"I'm waiting here."

"Waiting for what?"

"You cuss like a grown woman Amanita. Maybe you should have the sense of one."

You closed the bedroom door. Granny's shuttles clicked, muted noise penetrated the wall. Dislodging the bedroom window's screen, you forced it upward. Lightning bugs burst over the hillside, firing like mythical, phlogiston marvels. You set the watch to beep in five minute continuous intervals should sleep overtake the view of Granddad's silhouette whittling amidst crepuscular accompaniment.

Sleep found you between shrilling alerts. First heavy-lidded but then more awake, you saw Granddad's empty lawn chair. You had not plummeted through the window in ten years, when you believed a red-tongued devil was raking his pitchfork against the box spring. Granny had heard the distress, and Granddad had guided her past precipitous woodchuck holes and tripping weeds. She had clucked that television broadcasts were only a trick of electricity, not God-given truth. Granddad had offered a pointed stick and made you vow to spear the devil's guts if it returned. "We're counting on you to protect us. And I know you can outrun the devil if it comes to that."

You sprinted, barefoot, up the hill to find the door to Grand-dad's shed open. The shed was off limits. He had promised your mother and father to keep it locked because of its contents. Similarly, you had promised never to try to enter, a covenant with which you had abided.

The interior glowed from separate beams of directed union, bracing back darkness like a revetment and you understood his need to verify battery strengths.

Metal traps were stacked in no discernible order, piled and tangled, stakes dangling, crenulated edges locked against tall spikes, an inanimate consanguinity. Teetering up to the rafters, some traps were rusted and seemingly unused for decades, some were coruscant, burnished like coins rubbed out with nickel polish. Each of the four pine walls, excepting door clearance, were hidden. As though the twisted clash of metal, not vertical posts, supported the roof, like a gnomic cave filled with plundered, haphazardly pitched fortunes. Near your feet, a large flashlight balanced against a cinderblock. You aimed it at caged eyes, unmoving, unblinking, and shining back.

A dirt patch separated tangled pilasters from the shed center. In the square, five pressboard rectangular boxes were raised by rolling wheels. The boxes were simple traps, the single-hinged door fastened by a weighted spring at the back of the cage. The captive raccoon quivered, in a heaped clover and straw mound, expectant.

Two-inch wire diamond bottoms supported nesting straw and water served in ceramic basins. Underneath, plastic pans captured liquid waste. A row of hardboiled eggs lay on the musty, packed earth and shells crunched as you stepped toward the incarcerating box. Kneeling, you took care to keep your face and eyes out of biting or clawing range. Eggshell cracking caused you to stand and a light projected your shadow onto the sundry metal piles, angular layers causing a long and outsized distortion.

"Amanita."

You turned, flashlight forward. Granddad's wrinkles had multiplied, converging into a mask of indentions. His nose was like a weathered, lapidarian epitaph.

"I don't have to tell you to leave. This ain't something you need to know about."

"You said you quit this." Granddad maintained his heart had turned after he married Granny. *The price I got for a pelt*, he had said, *wasn't enough money to explain to her how the skin had to come off.*

"That's not what this is about." Granddad lit a cigarette with a silver butane lighter engraved with his initials. Work he'd done with a wire and tiny diamond Granny had refused as a belated engagement ring, insisting she would not be party to such foolishness. "This is about something else."

Part IV

Three days into your return to Beulah Land, former speech patterns emerge, gurgling over clipped consonants. The lower jaw slackens, vowels flatten and your tongue slows; the tenacious original inclination trumping practiced stylistics. You devote days to exploring. You cut the rusty padlock and throw back the old shed's sagging door, beginning to dislodge pulverulent boxes, taking care to skirt traps teetering underneath rug-thick cobwebs. Creatures scurry from weathered holes when you engage a flashlight powerful enough, the decal advertises, to cut fifty yards of dark. You take down traps, untangling thousands of teeth, metal chains and stakes but run when a precipitously leaning column shudders and explodes in a jangling dust cloud. Engorged spiders and respectably sized rats emerge from the shed, seemingly more aggravated by the disruption than afraid. You drag four boxes outside, leaving one occupied by an agitated rattlesnake you estimate would uncoil to five feet.

Inspection of Granddad's chicken coop produces whittled sticks, wire egg baskets, some fruit bats sheltering in crumbling eaves. You fear to investigate the ramshackle barn, suspecting the roof might plummet along with the snakes. The outhouse leans against the barn, yielding only mice nesting in a rotting angler magazine. Grown high with Queen Anne's lace and dandelions, the corral ruts are indiscernible, grave markers hidden by weeds, old posts fallen and disintegrating around Granddad's remains.

Sleep comes as hard as it did in New York and you wait, open-eyed, for daylight. Granny sleeps on the couch preferring proximity to the bathroom and kitchen table. You appreciate that she wakes early to tat, freeing you to leave the house without disturbing her. Dad has hired a woman to visit each day, to help Granny bathe and to clean the house. The woman is a quick, efficient local and needs no introduction to recognize you. When she sees you, she stops working, as if you must leave the room before she can finish cleaning it.

Though it was not his custom when you were young, Dad prepares breakfast, skillets hot before seven. Granny does not interrupt meals with conversation and she finishes first, pushing the plate away to feel for thread.

"Can I borrow the truck?" you ask Dad early on the fourth morning.

"You got a car."

"I need to haul some things. Please." You motion to Granny. "Maybe I've got a surprise to spruce up the place."

"I need it back by two. Got a delivery."

"Thanks." You push away soggy syrup toast, watery eggs. But you gulp coffee, enjoying the burn.

"You don't like my cooking."

"I don't get much of an appetite, Dad. But thanks for cooking."

"Not fancy like the ones in New York City."

"Honestly, most of the time I skipped and ate an early lunch."

"Not good for you Amanita."

"I'll add that to the list."

Main Street of Beulah Land, formerly host to barber shop, gas station, greengrocer, doctor, dentist, and competing beauty parlors has been converted to Christian curiosities. Retailers list prices for framed and unframed posters of the white Ozark wonder. Visitors from many states, many countries, weave in and out of shops, carrying shopping bags, eating Ozark fudge, funnel cake, and candied apples. Christian rock trickles from speakers mounted under retractable green awnings.

Like children assigned uniforms for gym class, visiting acolytes wear elastic waistband pants and silk-screened T-shirts proclaiming 'Jesus is Lord.' Married couples swathed in matching synthetic windsuits broadside pedestrian walkways, shouting locations and intended destinations into mobile devices. Buses transport touring seniors to curbside. Passengers disembark with preparations akin to rappelling a mountain. "Take cover!" Smith would have yelled in the midst of similar spectacles in Times Square, "They've opened up the Krispy Kreme buffet!" You would have pulled him from the inert cluster. "Those are the people that boost our tax base. So we don't pay so much." "But at what point," Smith might rejoin, "does someone get up in the morning, strap on a fanny pack and decide, 'I'm looking *good?*'"

In one shop, ceramic Jesus figurines occupy eye-level shelving. Miniature painted dogs, kittens, lambs, donkeys, and serene, kiln-fired Marys and Josephs are displayed on lower shelves. Other shoppers, all female, examine prices by upending the merchandise. They groan, bending toward lower objects of interest.

"I'm sorry, did you say something?"

A woman wearing a yellow dress and white shoes—a golden pear speared by Marshmallow tipped toothpicks—taps your right shoulder, near where your breast would have been. She pulls her hand away. The deliberation is clear: has she approached a man or woman? Wide black sunglasses, black tank, close-cropped hair, blue jeans and brown leather work boots; the ensemble could outfit either sex.

You've been muttering aloud. Habit conceived from days interrupted only by a nurse or an orderly checking bedpans.

"I said this town is sartorial Armageddon."

"Sorry?" Her head tilts, cat eyeglasses slide away from the collapsed plane of her forehead.

"Sar-tor-ial Arma-ged-don."

"OK?" The women pushes her tongue into her right cheek, giving the appearance of a hot air balloon listing, doomed by gravity. "Well, you let me know if you need any help. Many of our items are on sale."

You point to the Jesus shelves. All postures are represented. Jesus' white robes are draped by pastel mantles resembling banners assigned to contestants in beauty pageants. "How about the Jesus figurines? What's your offer?"

"Excuse me?"

"Are the Jesus figurines on sale?"

"We never discount the miniatures of Christ."

"Fair enough," your lips twist. "I'm going to take a sitting, standing and kneeling figurine—"

"*Miniatures* of Christ," the woman interjects.

"If you could wrap up one of each, I'd appreciate it."

"Will that be cash or credit?" The woman tilts toward the sales register with the items, exerting to distance herself from perverse ambiguity.

"Cash." Money offered, you watch the woman print the sale amount on a triplicate carbon pad and count out each bill and coin twice—the same exactingness you had employed to program a file alerting you when a trader's ledger did not reflect proper sales credit. "Who owes Amanita money this month?" the head trader would shout when you distributed the report titled *Rears in Arrears*. "You and Junior," you would respond. Son of a former desk head, Junior refused to compute commissions. You had challenged him to wrestle you for it, eliciting cacophony of howls from the floor. Junior complained to human resources, citing amongst his grievances 'sexual harassment, public humiliation and threat of bodily harm by a member of the opposite sex.' A letter was appended to your personnel file but nothing more came of the matter until Junior was blown out. Ten days later, the sales assistant dropped a postcard on your keyboard, a picture of three naked, endowed, women on a beach. *Hey cracker—Nice tits*. You taped the postcard and a large font caption to your desk. The sales assistant had always complained she felt objectified by the image.

The woman coughs, her palm offering money.

"Ma'am," the word is hesitant from your mouth, like walking through a schoolroom in which you had taken naps. "You know of a Sarah Sykes around here? A preacher's daughter?"

"Yes, I know her. But her name's not Sykes anymore."

"What is it?"

"It's Edwards. Bless that poor girl's heart—"

"Thanks," you interrupt. You unclasp your handbag.

"Don't you want a shopping bag?" she asks.

"No thanks. Save a tree, you know."

"Uh-huh." Forehead wrinkling, her mouth drops, lips loose like a kite falling out of the wind. "And one more thing—"

"Yes?" You shift, ashamed of the fatigue, thinking Smith might forgive you if you purchased comfortable, soft shoes.

"She isn't the preacher's daughter, she's the preacher's wife."

"Up at Calvary?"

She nods.

You walk toward the door, toes pressing into the parquet floor. The small appendages are familiarly firm, a sensation for which you were never grateful until other body parts had failed you. "Do you know where I can buy some seed?" You direct the question past patrons in the line, disturbing the pear woman as she squints at price tags.

A female shouts from the Jesus aisle. "Go south on Main Street and when you get to the bottom of the hill, take a left on Church road. You'll pass the First Baptist and Shoemacher's tire dealership. You'll see the supercenter. There's a garden department."

"Ruthie, you should be telling people to buy at Fletcher's," the pear woman yells.

The woman answering to Ruthie straightens. She could be the pear woman's twin. But Ruthie wears a cotton orange dress with a bulging pocket of pencils, a pricing gun and measuring tape. "Vera, the supercenter has got *everything*. You want African violets, nice potted ferns, baby rose bushes?" Ruthie flicks an index finger. "The best selection is there."

"And I'll be sure to let Fletcher know you're referring someone to Wallyworld. That's nice hometown commitment—"

You interrupt Vera, wishing you had thought to purchase online in New York. "I'm indifferent where I shop."

"What're you fixing to buy hon?" Ruthie runs her hands along the orange shift, as though searching for lumps beneath the thin fabric.

"Alfalfa," you fumble the word you had not heard pronounced in over a decade. "And I need someone to tell me how to grow it."

"Well, for service, I'd always send a visitor to Fletcher's," Ruthie announces. "You won't get better service than Fletcher's."

"I'm glad to see you show some common sense," Vera shouts.

"I've had enough of you correcting me. I was asked where to buy something, not where to get farming lessons—"

"Thanks, thanks." The door, swelled by humidity, sticks.

"But do you know how to find Fletcher's?" Ruthie barrels to the front of the store.

"I'll find it." You pull harder, elbowing her as she attempts to assist.

"Easy does it," Ruthie says. "It sticks a little bit…" The woman smells of vapor rub and antiseptic, an odor that lingers with medical offices, hospitals, and hypochondriacs.

You pull again and the door gives, swinging toward Ruthie. She yelps as if you had brandished an automatic weapon or porno magazine. *Somewhere*, you think, *Smith is watching this and laughing his ass off.*

"You have a good day, sir," Vera cries from behind the counter. "Come back and visit us again."

You turn, pushing the sunglasses to the crown of your head. "I'm not a tourist." Summoning your best original accent, "I was Charlie Buell's granddaughter."

Inside the old corral, white, weedy flowers grow amongst a multitude of other weeds. Deer trot downhill, rising from shaded brush piles and cool undersides of mossy trunks to forage in the poor offerings. Fetlocks buried, game search for grass, wary only of humans on the mountain. The brown bear population has increased, along with fox and coyote. But those populations thrive across the state border in the Missouri wildlife refuge. Proximate to the Jesus statue, locals use pesticides to control rodents once thinned by natural predators.

Through Granddad's field glasses, you inspect bald patches splayed on surrounding mountains. Vacation homes in Beulah Land are selling on spec. Developers have obtained zoning permits atop overhanging inclines for timeshare condominiums, view-inspired resorts. Newspaper editorials debate construction of a civic center to accommodate a human circus, the traveling Radio City show, the Southern Baptist Convention. The stock boy at Fletcher's is anxious for the center, says he hopes it will be accompanied by a burger restaurant, a movie theater, and an extreme sports complex.

"That would be something." You count out a cash deposit for rental of a riding lawnmower. The kid has already loaded seed bags and fertilizer into the pickup; the first occasion since childhood you have allowed someone to lift or carry on your behalf.

"Yeah, it would be very cool." Examining the address, he yells toward the office, "I need a delivery." Explaining, "I don't have a commercial driver's license."

"Does that matter?"

"These days it does."

The man emerging wears a tractor logo cap, overalls, brown work shirt. He examines the information on the clipboard. The question is perfunctory. "Where to?"

"Eureka Mountain fire road. The Buell woodshop."

"Something wrong with Charlie's mower?"

"No." You do not wear sunglasses. There can be no mistake by the senior Fletcher. You have applied lipstick, fluffed your hair. "It's for me."

"Who are you?"

"I'm Amanita Buell."

The senior Fletcher folds the sheet of paper, stuffs it into a back pocket. "That's something, you coming back here."

Dad returns from delivering a custom oak cabinet job in the late afternoon. He refolds the furniture blankets, stores the dollies.

"Can you make me some things?" you ask.

Dad's face contorts, lines compartmentalize his eyes. Chipped fingers wipe canvas work trousers. He grasps an air blower coiled around a wall hook, grips the nozzle, and releases the valve. Pressurized air hisses through the plastic cord. He directs sawdust toward your feet. Wood chips, nail heads, lacquer residue scrapes your bare toes, flicks your shins, a stinging shower.

"What some things do you need?"

"I want to close in the corral."

"No."

"What's your problem?"

"I'm not wasting my time. Fence posts rot and I'd like to know who's going to repair that."

You do not append the obvious: *Looks like I won't be here to do it.* "Not fence posts, Dad. That's not what I need." Pausing, then breathing. "I need for you to listen to me."

The Fletchers—senior and junior—deliver the riding mower in the evening. High summer offers longer light. You circle the machine carefully on the incline, avoiding the stone markers—one for Dad's dog, another for Granddad's ashes—and pull weeds and grass from the graves by hand, scraping and staining your knees. When finished, you open a bottle chilling in the spring. Because of Protestant influence, the closest package store operates across the state line. You had wasted two hours hunting a business you had never frequented as a teenager, driving the sedan on routes paved and diverted since you left Beulah Land. White Zinfandel was cheapest and you purchased four cases, relishing the potential of Smith's consternation should he learn of the purchase.

You salt and eat raw tomatoes and green beans from Granny's garden, appreciating her vigor in supervising planting, watering, and growth. When the bottle is finished, you strain uphill to the reduced summer stream. Weight on your flattened chest, face dangling, you lap the light flow of sweet water. You thrust the posthole digger, groaning, grateful for alcohol and solitude, both functional salves for soreness. "Ghost pains," the surgeon had warned, "you'll feel ghost pains for a while, even though the nerves are dead."

A hand trowel works in your left palm, turns the earth. The quarter-acre is loamy—split roundworms undulate, toads leap, insects too tiny to identify drift across your skin, comforting ambassadors of evening.

Lights directed at statue Jesus are timed for the period between sunset and dawn. Should fog or cloud cover settle disproportionately on the east or west side, triggers are in place to guarantee noctilucent precision. Tonight, clouds blot the firmament, summoning light for statue Jesus, pitting artificial illumination against the wrinkled, teary face of the moon.

Part V

Y
ou retrieved a pair of running shoes and socks then helped Granddad roll the truck past the house. The box with the raccoon rested in the bed, prevented from sliding by cinderblocks. You waited to speak until Granddad switched on the headlights. "I'm not sure it won't get dug up."

"I never consulted a manual, Amanita. But where I do it, animals stay away."

Lights outlined the highway, a route north toward the state line.

"Well, I pissed all over but I don't know what the hell good it will do."

"Girls don't get along with that kind of mouth."

"That's not the point. The point is, I did what I thought might work."

The early morning moon was wispy and lingered against imminent sunlight. Fatigue had relented to excitement when sliding the raccoon box into the truck. Energy burst from pits, hidden lymph nodes and glands.

Granddad packed his cigarettes. He replaced them in his pocket then alternated fingers against the steering wheel. "Main things you need to know. You always, *always*, identify yourself as lost. Anybody, game warden or anybody else comes up, tell him you're sixteen going on seventeen. That's a minor in both states. Second thing you tell him is that you were sleeping when I took off. Don't let on you knew were we were headed. That's acting as an accessory and this is interstate."

A brown, white-lettered sign delineated border agreement. Granddad slowed in conjunction with the advertisement for governor, lieutenant governor, county sheriff.

"Where are we going?"

"If you don't know, you can't commit a crime."

A skinny dirt road wound through hills bordering the Missouri plateau, a great expanse flattened by prehistoric glaciers and millennia later, defended by the divided state's rebels. There were limestone caves, old-timers claimed, where anyone could find artillery, uniforms and Confederate scrip. Guerrilla regiments had once controlled the terrain, killing Union partisans even after General Lee surrendered, a unilateral obeisance Confederate descendants continued to denounce as treasonous. The cave-riddled territory had been designated a state park, abutted by junkyards and unlicensed liquor joints. An area you had never visited in which lived the kind of people you had never encountered.

At the end of a double-rut path, Granddad cut the headlights. The truck advanced through weedy undergrowth until the concentration of cedar, pine, and oak blocked further progress.

"I'm coming with you."

"Leave your shoes in the cab," Granddad said. "Socks too."

You each grasped a handle and brought the entrapped creature to the ground. Granddad offered you a flashlight. "Don't turn it on unless I tell you." He indicated you should take one end of the box. A six-foot whittled stick was pinched under his elbow.

Flickering moonlight caused foliage to appear variegated, silver and black. Insects hummed, secreted by tall scraping brush. Burrs and thorn weeds pierced your feet, your hands, and forehead. If

Granddad felt his flesh being torn, he gave no indication. Humid air settled under the leaf and needle canopy as if a constricting blanket. Noises were muted, except for crickets and the methodical, paced advance. By sweeping toes and free hand ahead, you found passage and climbed, goat-like, up a rock ledge into the greater forest. With the sound of purling water, Granddad lowered his burden.

"Get behind me." Granddad's face was striped silver and black, like columns that stand long after the original structure has crumbled. He switched on the flashlight. The beacon collapsed his flesh into canyons; beyond him, a rushing creek. Granddad pushed the stick through the box wire, levering the door downward. Driving the forward point into the muddy bank, he found the tension level to counterbalance the spring. He whispered, smile crooked and pursed, "He won't come out if we're here."

You aimed the flashlight to pick out splinters, burrs and seed ticks. "Let me see your feet, Granddad." He held the door handle, balancing while you searched. Ticks crawled over his ankles but nothing had penetrated ligneous footpads. "What are you going to do about the box?"

"Pick it up next time. Get in Amanita. We have another stop."

The tires groaned as Granddad sought traction in the clearing. The truck turned, continued down the hill. You crawled halfway out the window, wondering if blinks were satellites, aircraft, or shooting stars. The fading night swelled with kicking breezes and shimmering tree leaves seemingly displaced from the western to eastern horizon as the truck advanced along the winding route. Engine noise sent into the woods would foment a disquieted predawn, disturbing preparations for nesting.

"Where'd you get the raccoon?"

"Found it in a leghold except its tail was caught, not a leg. Of course, the tail was about chewed off."

"You go out looking?"

"Sure. Some I find dead or near dead. I shoot those and cut off a paw, all jagged. Try to make it look like the animal chewed its way out. Makes them move along if they think animals have gotten trap smart. Anytime I find where a guy's set up, I spread my own scent. Ruins that spot for a while. I try to help the live ones."

"You use sedatives or something?"

"No. I use tarpaulin bags and tie up their muzzles and paws while I'm doctoring."

"What kind of doctoring?" The revelation was like mounting a castle wall to discover the lookout posts were vanished. "Why didn't you tell me?"

"If they got a paw chewed off or lacerations, I do what I can, feed them and watch. For broken legs, I make splints. About your second question: it's your folks. I never made out much of what I do, but your Dad knows. Opal knows. I figured you might know."

"Why the big secret?"

"Transportation of wildlife across the state line's illegal. Then there's what they call theft."

"You ever been caught?"

"Came close. Been approached by wardens. But there's nothing illegal about having a coon in a trap. It's only illegal to let it go." The cigarette burned lower and he stubbed it out. "That property was posted a long time before the preacher moved in. I want to make sure Potter ain't taking advantage."

"Potter?"

"Guy who's running that line."

"How do you know?"

"Like I can tell deer shit from chicken shit."

Your head bobbed. Light streaks reminded you of early practice, the shower you needed, the training sleep you had missed.

"You rest. It'll be a while till we get up to Potter's."

The engine was silent when Granddad shook you awake. He had engaged the emergency brake and the pickup inclined below a massive rock overhang. A drive too precipitous, you thought, to have been attempted. Denuded of foliage, friable wood shoots jutted above the rock-strewn earth, as though a bomb had detonated over the steep tract. Some dying, most already dead, trees had been stripped of branches, exposing miles of neighboring mountain purlieu. Layered sediment outcroppings were visible from hillside erosion. Under the cliff: ricks of strewn wood, junked cars, piled traps and though you could not imagine children inhabiting the stricken slope, a swing set and rusty slide. Glass jugs, numbering in the hundreds, lay half-buried in the red dirt.

Potter's shanty was a lean-to, three walls clapped against the cliff. Skulls lined the shack's edges in the same way Mother decorated the exposed house foundation with halved, sparkling geodes. Skeletons were nailed around decaying trees. Ribcages had been parted and linked to form corsets binding the height of stripped trunks. Skeletal fastenings extended beyond reach, as though a giant had played ring toss in fastigium, crazed and piling bones, cutting branches, debarking trees, continuing the game.

To the west, orienting you, statue Jesus was illuminated by natural sunlight. Surrounded by its own defoliated expanse.

"We're on Silver Mountain?" Named because of the multitude of caves, the lives lost by miners and highwaymen looking to find or steal a strike. A mountain you had never explored, warned away because of sinkholes, rockslides, liquor, and marijuana operations.

"Yep." Granddad extinguished the cigarette, flipped the glove compartment and pulled out a .22 pistol. He switched off the safety. "Take it."

"What for?"

"In case Potter shows too much interest in you."

"OK. But I'm a bad shot."

"Try."

Sunlight spread. Granny would be tatting at the kitchen table, impervious to fresh light. Had your grandparents chosen each other or had they been paired by social order? She, the daughter of a school board member and he, though only having finished eighth grade, owning a Model A, the single local example and the last new automobile Charlie Buell could ever afford. Larger egg operations crowded a chicken into space less than a sheet of paper, producing a dozen eggs for the cost of his one. Factory birds would be molted, debeaked and killed, having never opened their wings. Granddad fed his chickens by hand, allowing free run of three acres of fenced property and a shelter of fresh hay roosts. *Had Granny ever wanted Granddad's ideas?* you wondered.

"Is Potter a moonshiner?" You imagined corn liquor, midnight deliveries, money buried where the government couldn't find it.

Granddad laughed. "Not in the years I've known him. He's too stupid to tend a still."

"Why all the jugs?"

"Catechu. Forty years of taking game and being too lazy to haul it off."

"That runoff's got to be seeping into the aquifer."

"The things you think about." He opened the driver side door.

"I'm right behind you."

"Don't come in unless I call you. Potter!"

The salutation echoed against the cliff, repeating like a chanted incantation. You expected half-flesh, half-fur men crawling from the caves, albino skin and pink eyes blinking against the apparition of automotive locomotion, upright humans clothed in woven fabric.

"Potter, I'm coming in!" Granddad pulled the flap of leather hanging in place of a door.

You slid past a heaped pile of skulls. The pile shifted, settling, and then you were hidden between the shanty wall and the bleached, stitched cranial gourds.

"What in hell you want?" A twangy patois of dropped articles, conjunctions. A banjo giving out sour notes.

"I got a dog dead in the new preacher's fence."

"I get rid of varmints. Make that girl nice muff or coat."

"Land's posted."

"Not now." The taut-stringed voice moved. Metal scraped metal.

"There's people that travel that mountain. Ain't a place for traps," Granddad said.

"Not my lookout."

"What if someone loses a foot, a leg out there? Course, I don't expect you to feel remorse."

"Got permission for private property. Got no remorse talking to God," the voice reverberated.

"Criminals talk to God more than anyone."

"No criminal. Springing traps makes *you* one."

"You think so?" Granddad asked.

Flesh struck flesh, then the redoubtable noise of a body falling against the ragged shanty wall opposite you. Then the noise of straw-laced plaster crumbling, setting the men to coughing, both equal in repercussion of unease. On the distant mountain, the Jesus statue glowed white, more visible from the defoliated height than from lower perspectives.

"No compassion for people feeding theyselves," the trapper wheezed.

"Looks like you eat alright."

"Some sin, putting animal flesh before people," the big man said.

"Why should I worry over the powers of human intelligence? Present company excluded."

"You ain't God-fearing. Be afeared of me," the trapper said. "Afeard of altercating with private property."

Squeezing past the bone pile, you lifted the leather flap. The trapper's girth swayed. A dust cloud swarmed the faces of two men set in opposition, feet spread, anchored to the earthen floor. Behind Granddad, the cave entrance and a fire smoking through a hole in the cave ceiling.

"Nothing's been done to your property," Granddad said. He coughed, lungs given out from taking one punch.

"Law says so." Potter slid a tire iron from under a stack of hubcaps.

"You don't want to take it up like this—"

The pendulating iron cut Granddad at the knees. The trapper kicked twice, heavy-booted, at Granddad's head, then dropped the weapon.

The pistol felt heavy in your palm. "You talk to God for me?" The fight did not feel like a place for a girl. The trapper stepped back. "Maybe you should pray for yourself. Pray that you die before you get any more stupid and ugly."

A girl, you hoped he thought, *I'm being insulted by a girl.*

"Other things than praying. Maybe you find out."

"I don't expect any trouble. We're leaving this shithole." An impulse, not to let Potter know you were a Buell. Self-protective or a betrayal.

"Some places you don't belong. Some places you get accustomed," he said.

Potter lunged, knocked the handgun away. The pistol slid across the floor and you leaped after it, tearing your shins against a toothy metal rack stretching hides, twisting your left ankle.

Granddad dragged himself on his forearms, coughed, convulsed again.

A hand reached your mouth, a body pressed your back. The hand stank of tobacco, food, the latrine. The hand covered your nostrils and when you breathed, only slight air sucked inward, creating pressure, straining your eardrums. The hand tightened with its inhale, loosened in exhale, bringing you into that foreign body's rhythm. Another arm circled both wrists. Too firm to maneuver a hand to the gut, the groin.

You waited for instructions or demands. The right arm snaking across your face was hairy, mottled with dirt and red and white welt scars. Ten breathing revolutions passed. You anticipated the pitch and roll like a boater taking waves. Counting five more revolutions and then sucking air, you bent your knees and jumped.

Feet springing, head flung back—the stranger's nose popped and one wrist was wrung free. You jumped again, feet landing on the man's instep, freeing the other wrist. Turning, then tightening the right hand into a ridge, within the small fold of fabric you drove that hand upward, gripped, pulled flesh down.

Potter swung, impacting your left temple. He regained his posture and you leaned closer, maintaining your grip but spreading your left hand. Thumb and forefinger spanned his nose, pressing the eyeballs, thumbnail peeling at what felt like a grape skin. Potter bent your left wrist backward, cracking, causing you to drop both patella against the ground. You squeezed and twisted that hidden lower flesh with conclusive exertion. Potter's grip released and his bulk folded, landing on his shins, then his chin. You stumbled, dizzy from the injured inner ear. In rhythm with three long, restorative breaths, you kicked his head, his throat, his side.

"Stop, Amanita," Granddad panted. The slatted wall's shadows streaked his face.

"I'm only hurting your body," you whispered, not caring whether the prone figure could hear. "The next time, I'll hurt you worse." Potter moaned, blood leaching from his damaged orb.

"Get your pistol. I don't want him coming alive." Granddad's right leg angled oddly at the knee.

You hopped inside the smoky cave. The pistol had slid beneath a wooden truss from which hung a brace of fox tails. You wadded the fur, feeling like a burglar who wastes time smashing picture frames. "Your leg's hurt bad, Granddad."

"Sprained, I guess."

"More like shattered. I'll have to drag you." You clipped his underarms and pulled. Blood from his broken nose leaked through your shirt, first warm but then cooling and bringing a chill to your chest. As you passed, Potter rolled, groaning. You kicked, feeling the large man's genitals give.

"You need to learn when the fight's over," Granddad said.

The tree graveyard occupied the rearview mirror. You blinked, adjusting to the brightness. "I'll kill that bastard."

"You won't get close the next time. You dodge a bullet once and your odds go down."

"Too many stories end with the girl getting the worst of it." The steering wheel was large, strange. You had rarely driven, preferring to run or walk. The gears ground as you tried to follow the stick's faint schematic. Pressing the clutch, your left foot ached, pain extending from the small toe to the ankle. The truck jerked, hard, when you shifted, causing Granddad to grit his teeth, clasp his knee. "What're you going to say to the preacher?"

"Nothing. That's not the kind of man we can speak to," Granddad said.

"And Potter is?"

"We made our point with Potter."

"It's not only a dog, it's everything," you wailed. A keen you swallowed though Granddad had already noticed.

"I don't like to repeat myself. Potter will let off a little."

"I'll do something. After I drive you to the hospital," you said.

"What about speaking as a brother to those who offend you?"

"Everyone knows that doesn't work."

You missed practice for three days, telling Coach that Granddad was injured and needed help gathering eggs, omitting information about your own icing, wrapping and elevating. On the fourth day, a Friday, you asked Dad for a lift, not wanting to aggravate the injury. He had shrugged and laid an index finger across his watch, convention for the notion time cost money.

In his truck, Dad lit a cigarette. If he or Mother had noticed your limp, they had not insinuated. Granny had answered questions about why you had been missing that morning, claiming her fool of a husband had followed you on a long run and during the "attempt of something ridiculous" had broken his knee. Despite the emergency room doctor's recommendation, Granddad had demanded to be driven home, albeit laced with painkillers. You had accepted, wordlessly, Dad's contribution toward situating the older man in his trailer.

Electric guitars squeaked from the speakers and you ejected the cassette. Ignoring your father's drumming fingers, you inserted Granddad's favorite Hank Williams compilation.

"What time you need picked up?" Dad asked.

"I'll either walk home or catch a ride."

"From who?" Dad did not open his window, preferring the air-conditioning.

Smoke caused you to lower the passenger window to breathe. Morning fog had not burned off. Fluffy integument damped the view of statue Jesus. "Don't know. Someone." The power window rolled upward, pinching your neck. Trees and road signs careened past your face. "Stop!" The scream was pinched, your larynx pressured.

"Stay out of trouble. You hear me? Your mother and me have something started. Don't screw it up for us."

You fumbled for the slender ridge that could give relief.

"You hear me?" Dad asked.

Fingers found the ridge but it was unmoving, locked by the driver.

Anoxia transformed into obstinate triumph. Dad released the window, finally, and you were grateful to have been prevented from relenting. Turning up the volume, you gulped back throaty soreness and whistled harmony to Hank's mourning, as always, enjoying Dad's conviction that you could not discern the proper key.

You claimed to have tumbled from a hen roost when Coach inquired about the wrap. "It's no big deal," you said.

"You hurt that bad from falling four feet?" he said.

Coach's feet were enormous, too large even, for a man his height. Perhaps the size of his feet had, literally, tripped him during the handoff in the four by four conference finals twelve years earlier, the last time the men of Beulah Land had the chance to medal. The women of Beulah Land, however, were defending champions and had not yielded a conference title in the last decade by maintaining a deep bench.

"You need to see a doctor," he said.

"I'm fine."

"Sit out this practice. I'll set up an exam through the school."

"You can't physically make me sit out."

"I can physically kick you off the team for mouthing off."

Ankle twitching, you nodded. But you sprinted off the field

and hurdled through a hundred yard series—perfectly—knowing Coach monitored signs of weakness.

From the bleachers, you watched the two mile warm-up, forty yard sprints, one-legged hops. Sprinters were separated from distance runners for quad strengthening duck walks. Sarah Sykes' thick red hair differentiated her, clouding her face when she waddled, in the female lead, up the bleacher steps; cloaked her pink, bare shoulders and twitching nose. Orange cones marked the jumpers' paces toward the pit. After her practice jumps, you estimated the preacher's daughter landed six to eight inches short of your long jump record denoted by gold hatch marks. A respectable distance, yet a consistently reliable shortfall.

August sun had traveled from your face to shoulders when Coach blew the whistle. Skipping two, then three steps, you descended, cornering the redhead. Her limber, white legs were crossed; her spine leaned against the field-house.

"Nice work." Extending your right hand. "I didn't get a chance to speak to you last week. I'm—"

"Amanita Buell." Her tongue clipped letters, accent from television news. "Coach told me. I'm a jumper too."

Smooth fingertips tickled your palm, then resumed torquing a wrist out of proportion to her large palm and elongated digits. "You wear quarter-inch spikes?" you asked.

"We had a rubber track at my old school. There's no worry about the track here."

"If you practice on dirt you'll kick ass on a faster track."

"Maybe." The redhead's curls covered her eyes as she selected half-inch spikes from the supply box. Her ankles were spindly, skeletal junctions like fetlocks. She dropped the used spikes into the grass.

You bent, crowding her access to the box as you restored the discarded metal points. "What year are you?"

"I'll be a sophomore." She gathered her hair into a bun, creating a pale line to divide her skull. "I placed past the freshman curriculum here."

"Good deal," you said. "Listen, I live near your place. I wondered if I could get a ride."

"I know where you live. I saw you running home last week."

"I don't do that all the time."

"Because you're injured?" Her eyes swept the wraps, the unlaundered tank, scraped and dirty knees, shoes in need of bleach.

Warmth percolated under your cheeks. Breath increased, pulse vibrated inner ear bones. "I'm not injured. I don't want to peak too early. March is a long way off."

"Not so long." The redhead flicked a final spike into weedy white flowers. "You can never train too much."

"I completely agree," you said.

Timothy Sykes' minivan idled in the parking lot. He dropped his pen and legal pad when he saw his daughter and held the passenger side door open for her. You shifted weight to the good ankle as he spoke.

"I'm Reverend Timothy Sykes. It's a pleasure to meet you."

"Amanita." You extended a hand, noting his palms were smooth, his shirt, despite midday heat, was unsoiled. "Your daughter said it was alright if I hitched a ride." In the front bucket seat, the redhead adjusted the cooling system.

"You have an unusual name," the preacher said, turning over the key.

"Yep." You watch him draw the belt across his chest.

"Seatbelts, please." The pastor watched in the rear-view mirror as you continued, unbelted. "Well. Where to Amanita?"

"I can walk from your house." You loosened the ankle wrap, feeling blood return to the extremity.

"You live on Eureka mountain?"

"Down mountain. The new church hired you, right?"

"Yes. I was called to Calvary a few months ago. It's a beautiful site."

Behind the pastor, you swiveled the bucket seat in methodical meter, affording purview of the automobile's interior: television mounted behind the driver; box of bulletins dated for the forthcoming Sunday service; plastic-sealed package of youth New Testaments in the rear bench seat; thick King James Bible sprouting with bookmarks on the console; a magazine from the Society of Athletes for Christ, its cover depicting teens bowed in prayer. "You interested in some extra practice?" you ask.

"Maybe," the girl said.

"How about next Sunday? I'll show you some good routes."

"I have church. Morning and evening. Don't you?"

"No," you said.

The preacher's eyes flickered in the rearview mirror. "Does your family belong to a church?"

"Parents go to Antioch."

"And yourself?"

"I don't go," you said to his reversed image.

"Why is that?"

"My Granddad told me about a fight when he was young. Granddad's friend had been courting a girl and the preacher's son didn't like it. The son challenged Granddad's friend to fight."

"What happened?"

"Everyone—the preacher, the girl, the choir—came outside to watch while Granddad and his friend beat the shit out of the guy."

"Please," the preacher said, "no foul language."

"Have you been saved?" The daughter's red hair spilled against the leather seat as though it could conduct oxygen or water, conduits with functional reach.

"Saved from what?"

"Do you believe in Jesus?"

"It's not about what I believe. It's about what I do." The ankle throbbed and you began to rewrap it, frustrated with the appendage.

The preacher sheltered his words until the van completed a full stop. "Life requires faith in Christ. For anything you attempt."

"Maybe I could come between services," you said. "Not this Sunday, but the next."

"That sounds like a very nice offer, Sarah."

Pressuring the steering wheel, the preacher executed the right turn without jarring his passengers.

"I guess so." The redhead rested her long, jointed elbow on the console, piled curls on the crown of her head then yawned. "But I get plenty of regular practice."

"It will be good," you asserted. "For both of us."

When the wind advanced at dusk, statue Jesus appeared uncloaked, frail and assailable. Tornado season effected a streaked, green skyline. Puissant funnels descended, beckoning slender fingers. Whistling air masses breached the hollow, detaching laundry from the clothesline, carrying away feeding porringers and chicks nesting at the coop's edge. Tensed for motion, you leaped from the trailer's steps.

Drugged, Granddad slept when the sirens opened, the sound of hobos wailing from a moving boxcar. Landing hard on your ankle, you sprinted uphill to disentangle two birds choking, wings beating against the wire fence. You threw the birds on an interior roost, then pulled the door shut. Muted lights flickered then extinguished. Ventilating fan blades slowed, noise of invisible motion crept to stalled quiet. Dark heat settled, fulsome ordure swelled, constricting and separate from the outer pounding atmosphere. You moved toward the exit, favoring the wrapped ankle, excrement squishing under bare feet. Opening the door required a running start. You were thrown against the exterior by the migrating vacuum. The door slammed shut, crushing a hen caught in the opening.

A cord-activated generator operated on the steep side of the henhouse and you dropped as you had been taught, crawling, eyeballs punished by eluvium. The old generator roared, reliable and impervious to barometric fluctuation, tree branches and loose nails. Green haze diffused through trees, licking over the barn, enveloping and obscuring the house.

Ionic discharge stung the intersection of earth and sky but no thunder followed, the worst indication. Granddad lay toppled, immobile. You crawled, flinching when an eddy swept one of his crutches. The crutch slammed your locked elbow then lodged beneath the trailer.

"Power's out!" you yelled.

"You get the generator on?"

"Yes!" The shout flew away, detritus cast into an abyss. "Won't matter if the roof comes off."

"Get away from the trailer," Granddad yelled.

"On my back!" The words spilling, pulse pounding, each new beat evoking fortuity of the last. "Lay across my back!"

Palms pressured your shoulders; his weight squeezed your lungs, shifted vertebrae. He lay draped as you crawled under vortices dropping and ascending like erratic, misfiring pistons.

Wailing swirls distressed bound objects with force systems and shear. Masses rose through electrified layers as if a hand had pierced each fiery stratum and cast a line, jigging objects of interest and scorn; animate and inanimate, crushed or released between unpredictable moments, an indeclinable liturgy.

Had not a living burden pressed you to earth, you would have run with the storm. Anticipating distance and the call of a fickle, spooling wind.

The twisters took roof tiles, the garden and all your clothes-pinned underwear. The generator had held. Most chickens survived, though Granddad's favorite layer, a hen with markings forming a profile of young Elvis, was among the dead. Granddad insisted that you inspect the entire chicken house. You carried out twenty-nine females and two roosters—choked to death from being thrown against the fence.

Dad emerged from the root cellar when the clouds had passed. His flashlight swung over the trailer roof, across the outhouse. You limped while he inspected the woodshop, leaving Granddad on the trailer steps.

"What happened?" Dad asked.

"We made it uphill. Laid under the overhang."

"I mean what's his problem?"

"Little Sister died. And some others."

"Crying over chickens."

Dad's flashlight burned your eyes.

"He feels a responsibility," you said.

"You feel his kind of responsibility?"

"Maybe there's room for that."

Familiar night did not return after the blow. No insect chants or creaking frogs issued beyond the sickish, intransigent humidity. Young evergreen trees cushioned the earth abscised of shallow-anchored growth.

"Can you walk?" You had brought out two black flashlights, two tarpaulin sacks.

"Depends where you want to go," Granddad said.

"I want to go out with you. Tonight."

"Wind could come up again."

"Even better reason. We'll be the only ones about." You extracted the cigarette from his mouth. Hesitating to use a bare heel, you extinguished the butt with a flashlight.

"You can't wear shoes out there," Granddad said. These guys know tracks better than English."

Any sentinels assigned to statue Jesus would have a clear view of wanderers shambling between cover of restless, shaking treetops and open pasture. Two shepherds of a retreating disturbance.

A hunched traveler, pouch slung over a shoulder, would sweep a long, pointed stick—the blind seeking safe passage. Another traveler, gimped and clutching a bundle of sticks, would direct the smaller wayfarer to leaf strewn mounds, mossy, protruding root systems. The processional of strange-gaited creatures would be seen burrowing beneath hillocks and bowers of fallen, molding cedar. Under the height of scarred moonlight, the two figures would divide: the taller—wooden support jerking—advancing into thicker forest; the smaller form diverting to open fields, sweeping a staff as if testing for sudden precipices or spitting coal.

At a drooping fence line, the smaller figure would halt, lift the unwrapped foot, direct a flashlight to fleshy pulp. With greater enraged motion a staff would be launched—a sharp-edged harpoon— and splintered by springing, coiled energy. In foray toward collapsed barbed wire the thrower would halt, holding another wooden spear poised. Steps punctuated with crippled rhythm, the figure would pace between boundary of road and field; verifying the action, repeating toe to heel, toe to heel. After squatting, buttocks bare, the lesser would wave a long staff, flashlight tied to its thicker, rounded end. Any sentinels would drop, caution against potential for sighting scopes and communication between collaborators.

From amidst the woods, sentries would see strong light rising, joining with another beacon to arc over land littered with tiles clipped from roofs, children's plastic toys cut from sandboxes, antennae severed from automobile hoods—detritus ferried then dumped by the first passing force.

Granny tatted in the kitchen. The skin of your right footpad puckered; the sharp sensation overpowering thuds from the opposite, damaged ankle. You passed her without speaking, the products of transpiration dripping from your arms, neck, and forehead.

"I can hear you walking strange," she whispered. Her fingers shaped a black cord. Piled high on the floor, it seemed long enough to circle house, trailer, and barn.

"Something in the frog of my foot." Whispered to avoid alerting Dad, undoubtedly lying awake, attentive to the wind. "Nail, maybe."

"You get it out?"

"Not yet." You took the chair beside her, bent the right foot to rest on the left quadriceps. A half-crescent light revealed Granny's long, indented face turned to the darkest corner, eyes without focus, hands dropping thread and shuttles on the tabletop.

"Let me feel." Her fingers trickled across the dirty skin, lifting the flap of flesh. She held the foot firmly, as though it were a young child's wrist. "Smells like metal," she said then leeched with her tongue. "Tastes like metal too." She stepped unerringly to a kitchen cabinet.

You held the afflicted foot extended, shivering as though any warm blood had spilled out when you had followed Granddad to the trailer, dismissing his claim that you should have waited for him.

Red black drops slithered to the floorboards in constant intervals, pooling in sinuous moonlight.

Granny brought out a jar of Granddad's corn liquor and a preserve jar filled with loment. She grasped the foot again, fingers exploring puncture contours. Sweat ran under your arms and knees. Salt slid into slits of scratched skin. Granny pulled the tatting cord tight around the wound. "You don't have any near plans for this foot?" she asked, emptying a fire bath from the bottle.

Nausea swelled and you vomited, silently, on the wooden floor, spattering the thread basket, her face and body.

Granny pulled again, tying off a knot. Functional and neat, the black cord siphoned the oozing spot, aided by pressure from Granny's squeezing fingers and the vacuum created from her mouth. Eyes—open and unblinking—as she expectorated, sounding like a horse trying to spit a choke bit.

"This hurts really bad."

"There's things will hurt you worse than this," she said.

You no longer felt a pulse in the foot, only tortuous sting as she disturbed the belly of musculature. Bile burned your sinuses but you breathed with intent, dropping your head, bracing back a disintegrating orbit into unconsciousness.

"I got it," she said. "This shouldn't slow up your plans."

She dropped the trap spike into the humor where it spun, frictionless until you stopped it with an undamaged toe. Granny's face aimed at the darkened corner beyond your head, fixing a point on the sightless horizon. Her hands moved in greater circles to work medicine into flesh, diluting pain with irenic, massaging pressure. You blinked through red and white flashes, temples palpitating. Moonlight twisted inside the room, pummeled by traveling greenish clouds.

"It's a good thing I doctor up paws better than I make soap." Granny's palms pressed your face, traveled your neck and chest, imprinting the shape. "Sit here. You can tell me where to mop."

You had agreed to meet the preacher's daughter at Calvary but you sat in the lobby to wait until testimonials were finished, final prayers concluded. Through the swinging glass doors, statue Jesus' bare feet were visible, projecting beyond folds of his robe. A long gray crack separated molded toes from the pedestal, an accident, the newspaper reported, from a lamppost crashing during the storm.

Wearing a fur-edged white summer sweater, Sarah Sykes

emerged beside the pastor, draping his black suit jacket over her arm while he spoke to departing churchgoers. You were the last person he greeted in the receding crowd.

"Did you enjoy the service, Amanita?" Pastor Sykes' white shirt contained sharp creases inflicted on the fabric by an intent, steady hand.

"I was here in the lobby."

"Anything that brings you closer to God is a good start," he said.

"You ready?" You shifted, alternating pressure between feet.

"I'm ready," the redhead replied. "We can change in the bathroom."

"Where did Coach say you might work out?" You untied the white ribbon circling the dress waist. You had taken the dress from Mother's closet, liking the dark tan fabric that matched the color of your summer flesh. Unzipped, the dress pooled around your feet, revealing nakedness except for the bandaged foot and wrapped ankle. From a duffel, you pulled out black shorts and running bra.

"Some relays. The long and triple." The preacher's daughter flattened her hand, blocking peripheral vision.

Prolonging the nudity, you relished her discomfort.

"You come to church without underwear?" she asked.

"You come to church with slaughtered animals?" You indicate the sweater and matching white fur band tying back her thick, hide-like hair.

"God gave us dominion on the earth." Her tongue clicked through the consonants. "And animals are only flesh. They don't have souls."

"What if someone's got a bad soul?"

"Then you have to work on improving it. You have to pray for divinity." The preacher's daughter bent, double-knotting her laces.

You tied the laces on your running flats loosely because you liked an air cushion. Coach had told you it was only psychological, that you should brace up the ankle. But you resisted, enjoying the sensation that your feet floated free of earth's pull. Tying Granny's new band around your wrist, cut from the same tatted cord that had bound your foot, you programmed the watch to beep in intervals. "Can you keep up?"

"I can keep up with you," she said.

"I guess we'll find out."

You chose a course over the top of the mountain, descending on asphalt then switching back uphill on dirt fire roads. The pace started with eight-minute miles then quickened. The preacher's daughter shed the fur hair band; your dark hair also escaped its tatted tie. Wisps drifted along your necks—reminding onlookers that they watched two females in competitive exertion.

The preacher's daughter matched you, leaning into the rise. You lengthened stride. The distance between footfalls lessened shock but charged the expense to your lungs. She answered with hare-like bounding.

Statue Jesus and Calvary receded as if pulled offstage by crew-members packing away final symbols of that great, enacted Passion.

Down the mountain, asphalt heat hazed and when a car passed, forcing a processional, you fell behind, allowing her to establish the pace. The preacher's daughter breathed synchronous with her pace, inhale and exhale equal in fullness.

You turned onto a fire road, positioning footfalls to cushion broken skin; purposely pronating to relieve pressure. Twisted posture jarred the spine, revived pain in your wrist. Beside you, the redhead's breath devolved from consistent amplitude to choppy emissions—the breath of a hoary old man. She clipped your heel, causing you to stumble. Her nostrils opened, doe-like. Her hair draped her neck and shoulders, a thick decorative down.

The preacher's three-story home rose against the Jesus mountain, high on the crest. His ambit stretched to the fire road where a segment of fence drooped. You aimed toward the sagging wire fence, expelling hard-earned oxygen to funnel the words. "You'll have to jump!"

Pulling ahead, your lungs bellowed against the burn but gave you priority over the terrain. Moisture pooled in the right shoe, the left ankle cracked at each meeting with earth.

Confident in the launch, your legs pumped as though firing artillery. Limbs extended, you swept across the ground in ugly posture—with grunts of ancient stalking, rigors of ripping flesh from flesh—and arrived over the divide, legs and feet intact.

Sarah Sykes fell in predictable distance behind you, skull flung forward in faithful mimicry. Snapping steel keens evoked an attenuating bleat. The young girl's body had collapsed in perfect, fetal landing. She lay contorted, entrapped, long hair pinched by the same jaws that had split her right foot open.

"I can't carry you out of here," you said. Your left talus was nearly useless; the right sock saturated, blood spreading from sole to laces. "I'll go up to your house."

"They're all at church," she panted.

"So I'll call the police." White weedy flowers concealed tensed, metal coils. "I'll spring these other traps, so you can't get more hurt." With loose storm branches, you engaged, and then handled each trap, imprinting fingerprints on iron teeth, footprints into earth, crushing any record of prior traffic.

"Can you get my hair out? I can't move." The puerile body twisted against itself, each shudder tearing her scalp.

"Sure." You cradled her head and pulled. The strands relented as though you had peeled the fuzzy belly from a centipede.

Screams sounded against the hillside as you flicked bloody roots from your fingers.

Oh, fragile body of life.

"Hurry. Please."

"You bet." You trotted for twenty yards—an ankle-favoring, thrifty gait. Then you slowed, sitting and resting before you continued. A solitary platoon, the processional crept upward as though a storm had set upon you.

Granddad retrieved you from the police station where you sat, legs elevated, staring at laminated posters daring juveniles to reject narcotics. Late sunset formed reticular intersections of orange and pink streaked light.

"You drive," he said. "I barely made it here."

Working the accelerator caused the wound to flow again, filling the sole of the shoe. The pickup stalled at intersections because your left ankle had lost motor control. You drove west into lingering light, as if the night were reluctant to call on the hollow.

"It's going to be out real quick." Granddad flicked a new cigarette into the ashtray. He lit another and after one inhalation cast it out the window.

"It's a shame," you said. "Two girls out for a run, both injured because of traps on one of the girl's property. Unfortunate accident."

"People won't settle for that." His hand dangled out the window, twisting. "This isn't messing with some guy's line."

Energy ebbed, glands tapped, finally exhausted. Collaborative, you continued in silence as the truck bumped and lurched over the road.

"You're out for fall," Coach told you three days before school started. "Maybe out for spring recruiting, too."

"I heal up better than anyone," you said.

"We'll see." Coach turned his back, blowing the whistle to convene practice.

You limped up the bleachers. The alternate captain called out drills and Coach clocked relay splits. Mentally rehearsing the approach with shuttered eyes, you counted the three-beat repetition, bounding of imagined footfalls as reliable and palpable as opposing friction and gravity.

Stilt-like scraping split concentration, pulled your lids open. The preacher's daughter ascended, braced by two crutches identical to those issued Granddad. Her half-shaved skull was sheltered by a policeman's cap. A souvenir. Like a lollipop given a lost toddler.

"Looks like Dr. Jordan's been busy." You looked away from the redhead, fixed on girls trying for the anchor position.

"I didn't get treated *here*," she said. "He had me helicoptered to Little Rock."

"Congratulations."

"I'm telling everyone what you did," she said.

"It's your pasture."

"I've heard what the Buells are up to."

"Is it too tough for you here?" Your voice whined in mimicry of her crisp accent.

The preacher's daughter slammed a crutch across your chest. The ambulatory aid lay like a strange object to be contemplated—a snake or stick of dynamite.

The cavity hosting your lungs and heart throbbed. "You'll go to hell if you don't repent your sins."

The stitches were stiff and unyielding above the girl's moving mouth and twitching nose. "That's what they tell me."

Part VI

Two weeks after returning to Beulah Land, your body rests through an entire night, unconscious. You wake when the cleaning woman enters. She swears softly and retreats. The oven door creaks, sign she intends to fill her hours scrubbing the kitchen.

The bedroom is as you left it as a teenager. Faded posters, edges curled, still hang unevenly on three walls: pullouts from National Geographic magazine; diagrams of human musculature from a biology textbook; photographs of Olympians whose names you can no longer remember. Medals spiral around the window wall, continuing the pattern established in second grade when you had beaten all girls—and boys—in the standing jump. Any medal representing a record holds a place close to the spiral's center; lesser awards are pinned in the extremities. A constantly shifting design that you had once tended, religiously.

Empty wine bottles, pills, pamphlets, and printouts from medical facility websites litter the top of a dresser that had belonged to Granny's grandmother. Drawers are cut with keyholes although the locking hardware had been removed before the piece came into your possession. The ansate cross shapes had convinced you of prior, secret usefulness. When you had learned to read, you peeled the cardboard backing away from the dresser mirror. Hunting maps for lost Ozark silver mines or scrawled directions to Frank and Jesse James' hideouts. Hunting secrets left by women responsible for your composition.

Watch time validates strong light. The sun casts no shadow. You have missed the morning's dosages and do not remember if you should double later cycles or ingest prescribed quantities. You resolve the predicament by dumping all the pills into bathwater, enjoying a long soak in dissipating capsules, red and blue dyes absorbed by clear mountain water.

You had cancelled mobile service but were not surprised when the house phone rang. Smith's assistant asked if you could 'please hold for Mr. Whalen.' She must have spent hours finding the correct number. One of every twenty residents in the prefix shares your last name.

"Why the fuck do I have Jesus figurines in my office?" Smith paces, speaking into hidden microphones as if he is a rock star who needs to be heard from any point onstage.

"Miniatures of Christ," you say.

"You need to help me out here, Amanita, because I'm confused. Did you or did you not dump me to reunite with the flyover people?"

"I thought you would get a kick out of it. A mascot for tobacco command and control. Like a pet you don't have to remember to feed."

"I'm billing my client six an hour for this?"

"It gets better." You laugh. The best consequence of speaking to Smith.

"I'm in no fucking mood," he says.

"Look, I'm not going for the next round." Your voice lowers. Granny's fingers do not hesitate; lace spills from the shuttles. "I'm letting my hair grow back."

"Do you want me to come out there? Is this one of those cries for help?" Smith stomps and you hear furniture slide across the floor. He hides his collection of stress balls behind the couch.

"I don't know," you say.

"I can settle things here in a week. Two weeks tops. Then I'll catch whatever plane or mule wagon can get me out there."

Granny's hands rest. Her face turns from the gray empty corner. Unblinking eyes directed at you.

"No. I don't want you here," you say.

"I can't believe you're doing this on the phone!"

You hear friction against the plank floor. Smith rolls rubber balls under his back like a goat scratches against saplings. "Is there a better way?" you ask.

When the rattlesnake vacates Granddad's old shed you enter, circumspect, to avoid disturbing entrenched, rusting contents.

During evenings, you set out pans of cornmeal mash and basins of well water. You open bottles of wine and between gulps, deposit salt and mineral blocks uphill from the new planting. You wipe the headstones clean of bird waste and deposit dandelions. Crickets animate the audible landscape but are so familiar you rarely remember to listen.

Sleeping on the hill, you rely on the sun to wake you. For bedding you purchase two bales of straw from Fletcher and borrow a quilt of tatted squares, promising the cleaning woman you would have the blanket dry-cleaned. Granny's soap crumbles when you bathe in the shallow stream, splashing water because the water is too shallow to submerge.

Rising in hard-edged mornings, you drop boiled eggs and fresh fruit into boxes housing scavenging, nocturnal visitors. You remove plastic pans beneath the traps and carry the basins to Granddad's shed, closing the door to any view from Dad's shop. Inside, you funnel briny yellow liquid into a preserve jar. Two jars wait in the freezer, hidden behind an ancient box of grape Popsicles Granddad had enjoyed.

When you return, the animals have eaten and wait to be released. Sliding pointed sticks through the wire, you enjoy calling out affectionate names for plump recidivists growing winter coats.

You walk downhill, carrying the jar. Dad's shop door opens and he follows, steps falling in counterpoint to yours. Inside the house, you open the freezer, pupils adjusting to different light.

Granny tats at the table, edging a quilt containing one block for each local killed in recent conflicts. Dual shuttles link white stars. Another woman will sew the trim to the blanket before the VFW puts it on display. Granny had given up sewing in favor of tatting, declaring she would only work with what she could feel.

After Dad enters, the door swings shut slowly, as though he holds the spring's pressure for an extra, deliberate moment. "Your stuff's finished, Amanita. It's stacked outside the shop."

"How much do I owe you?" You reach for a wine bottle in the refrigerator and twist off the cap, appreciating the small luxury afforded those without overly sensitive palates.

"What do you think it's worth?" Dad slides his forefinger under his nose, wiping at sawdust hidden in the fold.

"You tell me." You stumble toward the table, contents spilling from the bottle.

"You're drunk," Dad says. "In the goddamn morning."

"Not drunk," you say.

"Get out of the house," he says.

"Son." Granny's shuttles do not stop. She pushes and pulls thread through wood worn so thin it looks like shavings fallen from a planer.

"No more trouble in this house," Dad says.

"I'm giving up." You place your head between your knees.

"It's not her trouble, son," Granny says and cuts the clicking shuttle noise off.

You doze by the alfalfa patch when Dad shakes you awake. In the disintegrating sunlight his shadow is elongated, falling across yards of fertilized earth.

"Fletcher's here for his mower."

"I forgot," you say.

The mower is parked on the incline alongside the prior days' labors: a vertically uneven and irregularly spaced enclosure of gleaming, precisely shaped pine crosses. Unburied, the crosses stand five feet. As posts, heights range between four and one-half to nearly five feet—a function of fatigue during the setting. But you had been careful around the alfalfa shoots, ferrying any turned-up earthworms into the center of the planting.

"*That* is not a fence," Fletcher says, removing his hat and rubbing his slicked hair. Smith would have referred to Fletcher as 'overly-anointed,' his most polite expression for gentlemen partial to greasy ablutions.

"It was a scratch job. I didn't measure it out."

"I can see," he says. "Deer will eat you alive."

"Well, then," you say.

"I assume you know it's illegal to spotlight." Fletcher leans over the toes of his work boots, giving the impression he is prepared to assist in uprooting the crosses.

"I don't worry about the law." Behind Fletcher, a green haze seems to float above the soil, as if clustering leaflets originate from air and only later take root. "Did you ever know my Granddad?" you ask.

"My mother bought his eggs. Like every other woman who was sweet on him."

"Really," you say. Lightning bugs flash over the old corral, circling the gravestones like sand sucked into a drain.

"No disrespect to your grandmother's affliction."

"None taken."

"Miss Buell, I'm heading out. Pleasure getting to know you."

"Call me Amanita."

"I'm sorry Miss, but I never took to that as a Christian name."

"Granny picked it out."

"Well, then."

At Calvary Baptist Church, testimonial singing erupts, waves ascend to reverberate amid beams that were locally felled, sanded and transported up mountain. Red, velvet-padded cedar pews are bolted firmly; unmoving when worshippers turn to kneel, elbows pressed into the fabric. Achromatic paint hides seams in the wallboard.

The preacher's hobble-footed wife sings in the soprano section, pale wrist bending over a cane. Her purple robe contrasts with rusty, spiraling hair. Hair surrounds her shoulders, falls across her mouth, shutters faces of women positioned next to her. The strands are dense and long—as if her cells cannot stop dying.

You join the end of the receiving line after the service. The pastor at Calvary is your age, balding, wearing a starched white shirt and black suit. He removes his jacket, pairs the sleeves by half and lays the garment across his wife's cane-dependent arm. As do most women in the church, the preacher's wife wears a printed silk dress. But her hemline drops below mid-calf to brush the floor. Draped steel flashes when she stoops to greet a child in front of you.

"I saw you come in. I knew right away. Welcome in Christ." The hobble-footed woman cups your torso under the loose tan dress. She steps away, as if the fabric's palp might invalidate her sentiment. "My husband, Reverend Matthew Edwards. Matt," she continues, repositioning her cane, "Amanita Buell."

The preacher clasps both your hands, pulling you into him. "Welcome in Christ."

The redhead speaks. "You need to know I've forgiven you. I've thought about it for years, about writing a letter. A stronghold kept me from it. You were so young."

"I don't remember apologizing for anything," you say. "Does forgiveness extend to a favor?"

"If it's the Lord's will."

"Can I have some of your hair?" You pull pinking shears from the handbag.

The preacher's wife looks to the husband, shield and shepherd of the Word. In interse communication, their heads bow, his lips vibrating against her ear. Like a recondite poem—motive and consequence is encrypted, foiling the layman.

The preacher speaks. "I believe the Lord's will is for you to accept forgiveness in prayer."

"No." You leave the church, spinning the scissors by the eyehole handles. Bright light reflects from the face of statue Jesus, causing you to look down mountain. Dots of crosses look like a giant's discarded incisors.

Behind you, a metallic ring and shuffle. Gait indebted to mechanical encumbrance.

"I'm really not interested in praying," you say.

"I understand." She breathes in healthy aerobic fullness. "I want you to have it."

Your fingers and palms investigate ridges under the roots, slide into the indention where cervical vertebrae articulate with the skull. You separate a hidden section and bind it with tatted thread before you cut, preserving integrity of follicular memory. "Sarah, you make a fine preacher's wife," you say.

"I'm not so sure." She opens the sedan door, motioning that you should leave.

Under the mountain supporting Christ's image, a hunched woman's fingers work with memory of repeated action stronger than ability of any eye, save one, to detect. Lace falls. Her dual shuttles sweetly entangle threads, each looped around the other, each knotted against the other. She tats in two whites: one bright and delicate, of thin construction; the other no less white but thicker, woven from many threads to form thread. The greater thread cuts blood from her forefinger; the lesser is guided, shaped with hinting motion. When her work is finished, she releases the binding and feels the warm blush spill through conduits, circulating oxygen to living flesh.

Early fall air crisps off fresh ordure in morning; in evening, wind travels in light, innocent pockets, a graceful exhale from twister season.

In twilight preceding a darkened, waning moon, you walk around widely spaced crosses encircling tall, late season alfalfa. Purple flowers will bloom until the first frost.

You close the door of the old shed and lock it from inside, unwilling, in this moment, to be observed. Positioning flashlights, you ignore indignant squeaks from mice nesting in recesses.

Three jars of thawed liquid rest on the ground. You unscrew each of the lids. Stripping, you toss jeans, shirt, and sneakers on a rusting metal pile. Dust unspools from the tremor but the stacked jaws hold, settling into acquired formation.

Dipping a red hair-bristled brush into a jar, you begin with the skull. Then neck, eyes and shoulders. Drops of liquid roll down the arms and pelvis. You paint knees and calves and linger over unflinching ankles and toes.

You wait until the end to outline dual chest inversions. Liquid dries over shapes resembling eyes that have been punctured and drained. Lids sewn shut to form slack, valueless pouches.

Lace falls, covering the table sanded by a man who smoothes cellulose with his hands, eyes coordinating the task. More lace fills the table, unwinding from dual shuttles. Manipulative fingers shape accumulating thread, crowding other pursuits. A dark-haired man moves around the swelling intrusion, reluctant to disturb the work.

In the enclosure of crosses, you lie silent, buried by growth.

Deer trot down the mountain, approaching the barrier. The first pair arrive, then two more, then a late spring nursling, dotted, muzzle buried in the nap of a doe's flank. White-tailed game do not leap to graze; passages between posts are wide.

Beside tremulous hooves, salty residue crumbles in the canyons of perfect toes but you cannot move these lesser appendages. Spare breath inflates your ribs, proximal ridges that will endure after necrosis.

Artificial light above statue Jesus prevents the view of constellations until dawn triggers the timer. Night and day articulate—then a pulse shutters stars long dead or dying. Game retreat up the mountain, seeking shadowed nests.

You drift like a turtle in warming equatorial waters, relenting to tangled, floating grass.

Moments of indifference and loss will follow. The wide great arch to span the journey can be built from only one side. Pursuers will labor for passage and then issue from fortifications, descending from shining white escarpments, the face of their Savior plated on shields, inked on their fleshy, indeterminate hearts, engraved on golden pennies weighting eyes to be borne across. With assailing, burdened shoulders they will sing and sound trumpets. When the walls crumble then these, too, will multiply in remonstrance as they enter Beulah Land.

Acknowledgments

With thanks to the following publications, where these stories first appeared: *StorySouth*, Winter 2003 for Divination; *The Best of Carve Magazine, Volume III*, for The Bereavement of Eugene Wheeler; *SmallSpiralNotebook*, Fall 2002 for Dirty Laundry; *StorySouth*, Winter 2002 for A View from Eagle Rock Mountain; *FictionWarehouse*, May 2002 for Clan of Marsupials; *WebDelSol* in September 2002 for Like Dancing On Both Feet; *Carve Magazine*, May 2002 for The Southernmost Point.

The author's thanks are due to Ken Foster, Darcey Steinke, David Gates, and Tiger John Miller.

About the Author

Krista McGruder

Krista McGruder was raised in Neosho, Missouri. She obtained a Bachelor of Arts degree from Yale, achieving distinction in the major of political science and winning the Katherine K. Walker essay prize. Her fiction has appeared in *The North American Review* and *The Best of Carve Magazine* and has been nominated for a Pushcart Prize. She attends The New School University's fiction MFA program. *Beulah Land* is her first book.

The fonts used in this book are from the Garamond family